FIELD OF REDEMPTION
Copyright 2019 © by Lori Ba
www.loribateswright.com

ISBN 978-1-7326738-2-3 (print)
ISBN 978-1-7326738-1-6 (ebook)
Print Edition

Scripture quotations and references are taken from the King James Version of the Bible (The King James Bible), the rights in which are vested in the Crown, reproduced with permission of the Crown's Patentee, Cambridge University Press.

Library of Congress Cataloging-in-Publication Data

Cover design by Roseanna White Designs

Author is represented by Tamela Hancock Murray, The Steve Laube Agency

SierraVista Books
113 Traveller Street
Waxahachie, TX 75165

SierraVista
BOOKS

To my son, Jarod.
Whose heart like HIS,
and unflinching faith,
reflect the passion
and loyalty
of King David.
Your life is a gift to me.

# FIELD
## OF
# REDEMPTION

# Prologue

Mansfield, Ohio
3 April, 1862

*A*gonizing wails of a distraught mother shuddered the walls from somewhere above. Leaden clouds hung low outside the windows where the first rays of dawn fought to shed light on the mournful hills surrounding the sprawling estate.

An oppressive air of sorrow settled over the dim foyer.

Though she'd spent the better part of four years caring for the youngest resident of this now bleak mansion, her services were no longer needed. Her presence here, no longer welcome.

Casting a final glance around the lofty foyer, ensconced in murky shades of first light, she came to the realization that no one was going to come bid her farewell. None would likely be sad to see her go.

In a simple gray skirt and white ruffled blouse, she grasped the worn handles of her valise and crossed under the imposing transom. With an unsteady hand, she closed the door on all that had been familiar.

Staring blindly into the fog, she sank down onto a white-washed step at the top of the wide portico. Grief reminded her she had nowhere to go. No home to return to. Struggling to maintain her composure, she searched for a well-worn piece of paper kept in a pouch hung at her waist. The hurried cursive was committed to memory, searing her conscience with every blot of ink.

> *Now that I am fourteen,*
> *I must take my place as a man*
> *to fight for my country and*
> *bring honor to my family.*
> *I will forever remember all*
> *that you have taught me.*
> *Be brave. Be strong. Be true.*
> *Yours, Malcolm V. Pearce*

Unshed tears stung the back of her eyes, as she tucked the note back into place.

Strands of sunrise angled through heavy clouds illuminating the eastern horizon. As the fog slowly began to dissipate, the task set before her became ever more clear.

She must go after her smooth-faced charge and bring him back home to his mother.

*"People destined to meet will do so, apparently
by chance,
at precisely the right time."*
~ Ralph Waldo Emerson

# One

Macon, Georgia
1 August, 1864

The war had finally come knocking on Georgia's backdoor.

Three years had gone by since Colonel Ian Saberton was this close to home. For the most part, it felt much longer. All he'd been through since leaving Georgia, he'd just as soon forget.

Defending her in this infernal war of the states had taken an exhausting toll. Keeping the Federals at bay was becoming more difficult by the day. The last thing he needed was to sit and think too hard about things. There'd be plenty of time for that after the last soldier went home. Until then, it was his assignment to get them there alive.

As soon as they turned down Main Street, excited cheers greeted Saberton's bedraggled cavalrymen. Civilians lined either side of the road clapping and waving Confederate hand flags, reveling like they had something worth celebrating.

The war hadn't invaded this far south, but it was coming. These good Maconites were in for a shock, and Ian had been sent to prepare them. Unless Bragg could miraculously take back Atlanta, the Yankees were about to bring devastation worse than this state had ever seen.

Grant's forces had broken through the Rebel lines in Tennessee, and Sherman's men were already surrounding Atlanta to the north.

Pulling up on the reins, Ian slowed his haggard mount and halted the special unit by lifting a dingy-yellow gloved hand. One hundred and fifty of his best men, sent ahead to help prepare the lower western theater for inevitable invasion of blue coats.

News of Saberton's Cavalry had been a celebrated topic in every newspaper south of the Mason Dixon and a reluctant concession in those serving the North. Southerners, starved for a reason to claim victory, had deemed him heroic for having aided General Lee in taking Saunders's Field at Fredericksburg a month back.

A generous commendation at best. Nothing was heroic about this wretched war. Thousands of casualties from both sides littered fields from Virginia to Tennessee.

"The men are hungry and exhausted, Rev." Lieutenant George Fitzpatrick, Ian's gray-headed assistant, urged his weary horse forward. He rubbed a dirty hand over the scruff on his jaw. "Maybe you can sweet talk some of them women-folk into providing a little coffee for the troops. Anything's better than another night of boilt bark water."

Ian wouldn't pretend the thought hadn't occurred to him.

Fitz waggled his fingers at a white-haired lady as they

passed which prompted a playful scoff from the blushing woman. It was evident Fitz had been quite a lady's man in his day and still used his charm when the situation called for it.

"First, we set up tents." Ian gave the signal to move forward, nodding formally at the admiring crowd. "After I meet with Farris, we'll know better what to expect."

A work wagon in the intersection up ahead swerved precariously, causing the driver to shake his fist at something on the other side.

Ian's senses were on instant alert. He'd survived too many predawn ambushes to dismiss the feeling.

He tilted his head to see what caused the commotion, but saw nothing out of the ordinary other than a brown dog making a racket as he ran beside the wagon.

"Ain't nothin' but a mangy little mutt, Rev. Trying to get hisself run over," Fitz offered. As usual the Tennessee mountain man was quick to anticipate his commander's thoughts.

Then she appeared.

A young woman in a simple gray dress with starched white collar darted from behind the wagon to take the boardwalk up ahead. With two handfuls of her skirt, she weaved in and out of the throng of spectators who stood along the street to get a better look at the cavalry procession.

Ian watched her intently as his horse caught up.

Where was she going in such a hurry?

His thoughts were suddenly absorbed by the girl with long, golden-red curls. She moved too freely to be encumbered by an enormous hoop skirt or impossibly tight corset. That all but ruled out a proper southern upbringing. Still, he couldn't help but admire the natural, slender curve of her waist.

When her gaze lifted, Ian's mouth became dry and he was suddenly incapable of forming intelligible thought at all. He was openly staring, but heaven help him, he couldn't look away. Beneath a rim of black lashes, eyes as green as spring clover met his.

Fitz let out a low whistle. "Now there's a fine little filly right there."

Quickening her pace, she left the boardwalk to cross an alleyway and up again onto the other side.

"Had me an ol' foxhound with ears that color once. Sure was a good chaser."

Ian shifted in his saddle, looking back to see where she was going. He lost her in the crowd. Scanning the top of each head, he finally spotted her scurrying down a dark alleyway in what Ian knew to be Macon's infamous red-light district.

Without hesitation, she pushed open a side door and marched inside like she belonged there.

Falling back into his saddle, Ian frowned, oddly disappointed. He wouldn't have taken her for the type of woman to service a brothel.

"Looks kin be deceiving, Rev." As usual, Fitz followed Ian's line of thinking.

"No matter. She's the least of our concern." Ian's focus returned to his troops. It had been days since the men had eaten anything besides hardtack and stale jerky. More than a few had no soles left on their boots and had taken to wrapping their bare feet in burlap. Every last one of them could use a good bath and shave.

The winter had been hard. Army rations were scarce. The mountains of Southern Tennessee had been brutally cold with little more than a thin tent to protect from the biting wind.

Come Spring, Ian got orders take his select unit of Georgia horsemen south to Atlanta. The cold eventually eased, but April brought torrents of rain and with it more Yanks.

Ian had seen enough to know the Confederate defenses were out-numbered and outflanked. His mission now was to report his findings to General Buford Farris here in Macon. And to prepare the rest of Georgia for a fight.

Past the curious crowds, Ian nudged his horse into an easy canter, leading his men to the end of town where he was to set up his makeshift Confederate headquarters down by the old Macon railroad sheds.

"Halt." The voice of the sergeant bellowed behind him when Ian lifted a hand.

Swinging from his mount, Ian saluted a soldier standing at attention before handing the man his reins. "General Farris is expecting us."

"Yes, Sir," came the answer. "He's having lunch in town and sent word for you to wait here until he's ready to see you."

Ian squinted against the midday sun, already hot as blazes. Folks slowed on the platform of the train depot across the road as if it were the first time they'd ever seen soldiers.

To be fair, most in Macon were not used to seeing active troops. Multitudes of wounded arrived by train daily, but few working troops had set camp this far south. Certainly not as motley a crew as his men presented today.

This city, along with his hometown of Savannah and every small town in between, had remained fairly untouched by the war. Seeing the proud sons of Georgia riding in with shaggy beards, borrowed britches hanging much too loose, and somber expressions on weary faces was causing quite a stir.

Hard to believe this mixed bag of men was the best the Confederate Cavalry had to offer.

General Lee commissioned Ian to take his pick of cavalry-men and ride out ahead of Sherman's army to secure the state capital at Milledgeville against possible attack.

"Don't that beat all? Nary hide nor hair of Farris." With an agitated tug, Fitz took a kerchief from around his neck and wiped his brow. "Orders said he and the mayor were to meet us here at two-thirty sharp."

Ian removed a timepiece from his pocket. "Actually, we're a good twenty minutes early."

"Is that so, now?" With a shake of his grayed head, Fitz gave a stern look at the younger soldier holding the reins of Ian's horse. "You mean to tell me, we risked life and limb to arrive a full twenty minutes early, and ain't no one here to say howdy do 'cept you?"

The young corporal gave Ian an apologetic look and saluted the surly lieutenant for lack of any better response.

A long wood bench, carved from a single tree trunk, provided a shady place to sit and wait for General Farris. The men needed a break from their saddles, so he gave the order to dismount. A clear water pump over beside the train depot became a popular spot to congregate.

"Ahh, smells fresh and clean here. All innocent-like. No gunpowder or burnin' buildings." Fitz took in another deep breath before searching the clear blue sky. "Even them little Georgia birds are flittin' around up there, purty as you please."

Fitz's colorful observations were as familiar to Ian as the way he scrunched his nose when he talked. Short and stocky, but tough as a wire brush. Since he'd joined Ian's regime two years ago, he'd proven his worth time and again. There was no better sharpshooter or friend in all of the Army of Tennessee. His sure aim had saved Ian's life more than once.

"Just look at that big ol' bell up yonder." With a nod of his grayed head, Fitz pointed out what Ian assumed was the belfry of the Methodist church. "In another month or two, she'll be gone. One side or the other will take her down and melt her for the metal. War ain't got no regard for nothin' holy."

Ian had spoken several times at the church before the war. Back when he was a student and scholar from Yale Seminary in Boston.

A lifetime ago.

"A sad sight for sure." Ian worked to keep his impatience in check. Scanning the crowd for any sign of Farris or the mayor, he barely glanced at the view Fitz described.

"Oh, Colonel Saberton!"

Ian came to his feet to greet a small woman in a wide bonnet and parasol scurrying up the walkway toward them.

"Oh, my!" Her eyes grew round as he came to his full height. "We've got ourselves a tall one. You *are* Colonel Saberton, I presume?"

"Yes, ma'am. And this is Lieutenant Fitzpatrick. Miss ....?" She had him at an obvious disadvantage. He'd never laid eyes on the woman before today.

"Mrs. Cora Dobbs. Wife to *Mayor* Walter Dobbs of Macon." Her smile relayed her satisfaction as recognition of the name caused Ian to tip his head and offer his hand.

"A pleasure to make your acquaintance, Mrs. Dobbs."

"A pleasure to be sure." Fitz stood as well. "We were just discussing what a right purty town you have here, Mrs. Dobbs." Clasping his hands behind his back, he puffed out his chest. "Puts me to mind of my beloved Tennessee. Shame to see it—."

"Allow me to escort you to better shade, Mrs. Dobbs." Ian took the lady's elbow and turned her away before Fitz could scare her with his ominous predictions.

Turning from his grasp, Mrs. Dobbs called out to a pair of ladies across the road. "Elizabeth! Eliza Jane! Come meet the new Colonel." The lady looked past them to another set of women exiting the mercantile two buildings down. "Ya'll come over and meet the Colonel." Making a complete circle, she waved in every female within shouting distance. "The new Colonel is here. Where's Abby? Someone see if she's over at the hospital."

Fitz cast a dubious eye at Ian as they were suddenly surrounded by chattering females.

"He's a looker," one said none too quietly behind her lace fan.

"And unmarried. Let's not forget that," said another sending a pointed look at Mrs. Dobbs.

"Ladies, please." Fitz stepped forward once again, his hand on the hilt of his scabbard. "You kin all have a good talk with the Colonel after we've settled in a bit. Maybe go make some coffee and biscuits whilst you're waitin'."

"Elizabeth, where's Abby?" another woman interrupted.

"Yes, Elizabeth. Where's Abby?" Several others chimed in as they completely ignored Fitz, continuing to push forward toward Ian.

With baffled expressions, the soldiers formed a half circle around their commander and the town's ladies.

"Penny Jo, run fetch her." A woman standing near the hitching post spoke to a school-age girl in braids.

"Who?"

"Abigail!" Cora Dobbs insisted before taking the girl by the arm. "Remember what I told you. Tell her we have a Colonel here, and he's a Code One!"

The hitching post woman clapped her hands to hurry the girl along. "Run now! Time's wasting, child."

With that, the girl trotted off across the street. Ian watched her over the heads of clamoring females vying for his attention.

Fitz stepped to Ian's right. "Just what are you supposin' a

Code One is? Is that some kind of secret Georgia talk?"

Ian had no idea what these women were talking about. His brow furrowed as the girl in braids ran to meet the gray-dressed woman he'd seen earlier when she stepped out from the ally.

Both of them turned toward him and the little girl pointed. Was she Abby? Why would the refined ladies of Macon want him to meet a working girl from the red-light district? Perhaps a Code One was some kind of test to measure his men's moral fiber.

"...and Eliza Jane Stratton has made her mincemeat pie for you. You've never tasted mincemeat pie like hers in all your born days."

He'd never tasted *anyone's* mincemeat pie in all his born days. He'd avoided the vile smelling concoction most of his life, and he wasn't inclined to change that now.

Glancing again in the direction of the town, he tried to spot the woman in gray again, but she wasn't where he'd last seen her. The memory of her unusual green eyes made him want to see them again. Up close.

Just as his arm was nearly tugged out of socket, he spotted her hurrying up the street, heading his way. With concentrated effort, he pressed past the swarm surrounding him.

"Need help there, Colonel?" One of his heftier soldiers called out from across the way.

"Tend the horses. See that they get water." His tone was sharper than was called for, but he wasn't used to disorder. Ian ran a tight command, and he wasn't going to let a few women be his unravelling.

The closer she came to where he stood, the more interesting she became.

Some women needed frills and finery to enhance what God

had given them, but this one, in plain, practical gray, carried herself like a champion thoroughbred. Beautiful mane held high with a graceful, confident stride.

Her extraordinary eyes rose to meet his, and he froze. Green with a hint of gold, framed by dark lashes. What was wrong with him? He'd seen pretty women before. Plenty of them.

Dismissing the odd reaction, Ian pinched the bridge of his nose and pressed his tired eyes shut. The past several days, jostling undetected through the pines, had his head in a fog. A good night's rest would have him thinking clearer.

When he reopened his eyes, he caught her smiling broadly at something one of the other women said in passing and he was right back to staring again.

Whoever she was, her smile lit up everything around her.

Macon's socialites sure were a lot friendlier toward the district women than he remembered.

A hush settled over the boardwalk as the women quieted, watching her approach the post where Ian stood.

The green-eyed woman's careful inspection of him was brazen and without apology.

"Pardon me, sir." She stepped to the side and peered around him as if hunting for someone else.

Apparently, he was not what she was searching for. Ian moved aside to let her by.

Fitz tipped his hat in greeting, but she barely gave him a glance.

Her attention was now centered on his men, who refilled the horse troughs with buckets of fresh water. This had gone far enough. The troops were in no condition to resist such blatant temptation.

"Excuse me." Ian stepped in front of her to block any more

scrutiny of his men.

Tipping her head to look up at him, her focus returned to Ian. With a careful touch, she reached out and ran a hand over the insignia on his sleeve then made a visual study of the stars on his collar.

"One, two, three." Her lips pursed in concentration. "So, you must be the colonel."

Ian wasn't sure why he let her finish her inspection, other than he was curious now to see what she was up to.

"You look fine to me," she said.

Ian felt her gaze glide over his torso.

"Nevertheless, please unbutton your shirt."

The few men who stood within earshot snickered loudly, and he heard a lady gasp behind him.

Ian silenced them with a hard look.

"I'm afraid you're mistaken, Miss ..." He still didn't know her name.

"Abigail McFadden." Confusion shone in her eyes, but her resolve didn't waver. She once again reached for the fastening of his uniform.

"Well, Miss Abigail, you're wasting your time." He caught her by the wrist, stilling her indecent probe. "My men and I are on a mission. We have no interest in consorting with public women."

Her eyes widened, and he could swear the green darkened a shade. With a sudden yank, she freed her arm from his grasp. "I beg your pardon?"

"There will be no visits to your brothel while we—."

Quick as a flash, Abigail McFadden grabbed a wooden bucket from the hands of a private and tossed its contents, soaking Ian from head to foot.

*"A thousand years may scare form a state. An hour may lay it in ruins."*

~ Lord Byron

## Two

*A*bby held her breath, intensely aware of the man she'd just doused. If he hadn't been wounded before, surely he was now.

"Well, that didn't go as planned." Elizabeth Lambert directed a weary look at Cora Dobbs before turning to the dripping Colonel. "Our apologies, Colonel Saberton. Abby can be a tad hasty."

"Don't stand there gawking." Cora waved at the stunned corporal holding the horse's reins. "Go get the colonel a towel."

"Abby's not a …" Mable Lea Thompson's eyes were huge behind her thick spectacles. "Did you hear that, Cora? He thinks Abby's a …"

Giggling trickled through the crowd.

"That's because she's always going down to the whorehouse." Penny Jo piped in.

"Hush your mouth, Penelope." Elizabeth Lambert, ever the

well-behaved Southerner, put up with no nonsense out of her two daughters. Or as Cora referred to them, "two of the sassiest young women this side of the Mississippi."

Abby cherished Elizabeth's support. From the day she'd begun work at the Floyd House Hospital, the Lamberts had taken her under their wing like she was daughter number three.

"I'm certain Colonel Saberton has a perfectly good reason for making such an absurd assumption." No one missed the irritated side-glance Elizabeth threw his way. "At least he better have."

The colonel drew his hand over the dark beard covering his jaw and flung water off into the muddy ground at his feet. "My apologies if I've offended you, Miss McFadden."

The man towering over her was staring so hard it was unnerving. Trying again, she refused to let him intimidate her. "You may call me Abby. Nurse Abby."

He removed his hat and gave a quick toss to his shaggy hair, sending water droplets showering over her.

Squinting, she wiped the moisture from one eye to clear her vision.

She couldn't prove it, but was not at all convinced he hadn't done that on purpose.

"All right, then, *Nurse* Abby. I've apparently made a grave mistake." He slid the slouch hat back over his brow and settled it onto his head, looking every bit as arrogant as he had when he'd been completely dry. "For that, I most humbly apologize."

"That still don't answer why you thought the colonel needed a good dampening down in broad daylight." The grizzled lieutenant leaning against a hitching post shared a laugh with the soldier next to him. "Best run. She'll be tryin' to bathe us all."

"I was told he was ill." Abby sidestepped the mud to avoid

ruining her best work skirt.

"So, you slung a bucketful of water at him?" The older soldier guffawed. "That's mighty curious medicine."

"Did I look ill?" The way the colonel spoke directly to her as if half the town wasn't standing there listening felt a little too cozy.

"Not necessarily." Looking him over now, she could see he was in fine form. Broad shoulders, well-defined muscles in his legs and arms. "Do I look like a soiled dove?"

His brow rose and so did hers. Abby refused to look away.

"Not necessarily."

Somehow, she got the feeling his denial wasn't as gracious as hers had been.

"I was told to come quickly." Abby tried to clarify. "Penny Jo said a Colonel here was desperately ill."

"Mrs. Cora told me to," Penny Jo offered in her own defense.

"My exact words were, 'there is a colonel here in need of desperate attention'." Cora patted the tortoise shell comb atop her tightly wound chignon. "And to hurry because he was a 'Code One'."

Penny Jo knelt to pet the dog. "I told her."

"What's a Code One?" The older soldier asked.

Cora Dobbs' clandestine code for handsome, *unmarried* gentleman. Though Abby refused to be the one to explain it.

"See? And was I wrong?" Cora stepped forward and gave Abby a know-it-all nod.

Abby looked closer and decided he was younger than she'd first thought. At least younger than most colonels she'd ever seen before. Most were well into their forties or fifties. This one might easily be thirty or even younger.

The colonel gave a half smile that softened his features.

Thankful for the breeze blowing her hair, she lifted her face to cool the sudden warmth in her cheeks.

"Now that all is forgiven, let's begin again with proper introductions. Miss Abigail McFadden, meet Colonel Ian Saberton." Elizabeth Lambert nudged her forward.

"He's here to take General Farris's place." Cora added.

The ladies began to clap excitedly.

"What in blue blazes is wrong with this bunch o' hens?" The gray-headed soldier took a couple of towels from General Farris's assistant and tossed them to his commander. "You ain't said nothin' about coming down here to take over for no general."

"And that's Lieutenant Something-or-Another." Cora Dobbs dismissed him with a wave of her lace-gloved hand.

The other soldiers gathered around, clearly confused by Cora's announcement as well.

"Ladies, please." Colonel Saberton swiped the towel over his face one last time before tossing it back to the assistant. "I'm not taking anyone's place, and this has gone far enough."

"You forget, Colonel, I am the wife of our city's mayor. I am privy to these things." Cora insisted. "General Farris is past his prime and needs to move on. If we are to fend off those tiresome Yankees, we'll need someone with a stronger constitution than that old walrus. You'll do nicely."

"So, do we get to keep him or not?" Penny Jo threw a stick across the road for her pup to fetch.

"That's none of your concern. Run on home and take that yappy animal with you." Elizabeth gave her daughter a swat on the backside to send her on her way.

"But Mrs. Cora promised. She said if I'd fetch Abby, she'd give me a nickel. Said she'd make it a dime if Abby could convince him to stay and be our new general."

All eyes turned to the mayor's wife, who appeared contrite for only an instant before resuming her normal no nonsense manner. "You'll get your dime. Now go do what your mama says."

"Just look at all of these poor men, near starving to death." Elizabeth shook her head. "Ladies, we must go and prepare our soldiers a decent meal."

"Don't have Abby cook." Penny Jo called back as she skipped down the center of the road. "She'd kill them all dead."

Abby folded her arms and turned to the mayor's wife. "A dime, Cora? Really?"

"Have I mentioned Abby is a fine nurse?" Cora looked past Abby to address the colonel. "She truly is. Simply the best."

The other ladies offered their full agreement.

Abby was fairly certain he was aware by now that she was a nurse. Although, she'd be interested to know why he made such a presumption otherwise.

As she was about to ask, Elizabeth cut her off. "No denying it, dear. You have a certain way about you most gentlemen find utterly charming. Those soldiers at the hospital won't rest at night until you tuck them in."

Now, that was just ridiculous.

"Colonel Saberton." A courier called out, running over from the depot. As he approached, he saluted the colonel. "Sir, General Farris requests that I deliver you to the Dobbs' house for a meeting as soon as your troops are settled into camp."

He then turned to Cora. "Mrs. Dobbs your husband asked that I remind you the new troops will need a home-cooked meal delivered to their camp as a gesture of Macon's hospitality."

"No, you can't go!" Cora Dobbs moved around Abby to

delay Colonel Saberton from leaving. "You tell Walter, Abby will bring the colonel over there just as soon as she shows him around a bit."

"Our orders said we'd be meetin' here at the courthouse." Lieutenant Fitz looked up at his commander, squinting against the sun.

"Thank you, Mrs. Dobbs and ladies, for welcoming me and my men. Now if you'll excuse us, we have business to attend to." Colonel Saberton tipped his hat and gave no room for argument as he immediately issued orders to saddle up.

On his way to his horse, Lieutenant Fitz clapped the courier on the back. "You're a veritable Godsend, boy. I was certain the whole pack of them were fixin' to skin him alive."

"Oh, go on. You're dismissed." Cora huffed at Farris's messenger, clearly put out that her plans were going awry. "Abby will bring him."

The young courier looked to Ian, who issued a formal dismissal.

"We are simply doing our civic duty." Cora spoke to no one in particular. "Strategizing is what women do best and our initiatives will turn the tides of this war. You mark my words."

Several women agreed with an "amen."

"Head out!" Colonel Saberton sent the company of soldiers off toward the river to set up camp. Only he and Lieutenant Fitz remained.

"Come along, ladies." They all fell in line behind Cora. "Abby, it's your civic duty to see the colonel to the meeting. Personally."

Marching off in formation, they headed back toward town.

Abby sighed. The ladies were harmless enough, just bored and desperate to help bring an end to the war so their husbands, brothers, fathers, and sons could come home.

Glancing over at the colonel, she decided it was best to start over. "I'm Abigail McFadden. My friends call me Abby."

"Then Abby it is." Colonel Saberton flashed a smile.

Lieutenant Fitz gave her a fatherly wink. "My friends call me Fitz, and I'd be honored if you did as well."

Abby watched the colonel pick up an apple from the road, bringing it to where his horse was tied. Soothing the animal, he fed it from the palm of his hand. He hadn't eaten the fruit himself, which surprised her. Fresh fruit beat fermented peaches from a tin can any day.

Even with shaggy hair and a jaw full of stubble, she could see this Colonel Saberton wasn't without his share of masculine appeal—it would be hard not to notice. But watching him there with his horse, she wondered if maybe he wasn't quite as arrogant as she'd first thought. He was fairly quiet, except when issuing orders. The man, Ian Saberton, was either a deep well of thought, or he was a tad bit on the shy side. She couldn't decide which. Maybe both.

The way he spoke soothingly next to his horse's cheek gave the impression he was a kind man when he chose to be.

Turning toward her, as if he sensed he was being watched, a hint of a grin lifted the curve of his mouth. He evidently was keenly aware of everything going on around him.

She'd watched his men obey his slightest directive with no hesitation. Therefore, she concluded, he must be a trustworthy man as well.

General Farris, by contrast, led by intimidation and coercion. No commander in the entire Confederate Army seemed inclined to confront his malignant behavior or put a stop to his cruel ways. He had no concern for anyone, man nor beast, other than himself.

Would Colonel Saberton be any different?

As if reading her thoughts, the colonel's gaze lowered to hers and stayed there until she looked away.

A daring man to boot.

Beneath the dishevel and road grime, his intelligent dark eyes spoke of wisdom, the discerning kind.

Abby reluctantly admitted he piqued her interest.

Although his manner was quiet, the man was bold. A little too bold for her comfort. Intriguing and unnerving at the same time.

Abby decided to meet her apprehensions head on. "So you're a Colonel?" She called over to him and immediately regretted it. Of course, he was a colonel.

A small button on his cap caught her eye. A Latin cross like the one chaplains wore at the hospital.

"For now." With a final pat on his horse's flank, he came around to where she stood.

"I'm sorry for … that." Abby pointed at his wet shirt beneath his open frock coat. Thankfully, the warm breeze seemed to help in drying his clothing. "Mrs. Lambert is right. I sometimes act before I think things through."

"And I should not assume before I have all the facts," he conceded.

"How's about we go find Farris and get this meeting over with so we can eat." Fitz returned and began to untie his horse.

"If you'd like, you can leave your horses tethered here in the shade. The Dobbs' house isn't far." Abby pointed up Main Street. "To the left, there on College Street."

"I believe you've been appointed our guide." The colonel held out a hand for her to precede them. "Lead the way."

More out of curiosity than any real need to go that direction, Abby agreed. Her shift at the hospital didn't start for another forty-five minutes.

"You don't sound like you're from around these parts." Fitz scratched his ear with a finger. "What brings you down to Georgia?"

A familiar dread seeped down her spine and just as quickly she admonished herself to ignore it. There was no reason to panic every time it was pointed out that she sounded like a Northerner. She was one, for heaven's sake.

"I was raised in Ohio." Abby swept a pinecone out of her path with a foot. "But nurses are needed wherever there are wounded. I was passing through and Doc Lambert convinced me to stay and help. I've been here for a year and a half."

"Wouldn't you rather be home with your family?" Ian asked, no malice in his tone.

"I have no living family to speak of." Abby gazed up at the clear blue sky. "My parents were missionaries. They were killed by Cayuse Indians when I was five. A family of the church took me in."

"I'm sorry." The colonel's condolence sounded so sincere, Abby looked over to see if it was her imagination.

His expression was gentle and oddly comforting.

He would make a good chaplain, she decided. The pin on his hat was most likely in honor of a fallen friend or relative, but she decided he must be a compassionate man as well.

"What you reckon those ladies will be makin' for dinner?" Fitz patted his flat stomach. "I could just about eat a bear."

"I heard them say something about meatloaf." Abby smiled.

Fitz licked his lips. "Makes my stomach growl just thinkin' about it."

"Do you see that house on the corner, with soldiers milling about?" She directed their attention to a two-storied home with a porch running all the way around. "That's Harbor

House. The Ladies Aid Society took up donations and purchased the place. It's now a rest stop for weary soldiers. They serve coffee and pastries all day long and dinner every evening. The ladies gather daily to knit socks and sew blankets. It's remarkable what they've done there."

"Cora is the mayor's wife. So, Elizabeth Lambert is the Doctor's wife?" As if putting the puzzle pieces together in his mind, Ian squinted off into the horizon before looking down at Abby.

"Yes. Doc Lambert is Surgeon In Charge at Floyd House Hospital."

"That means the little braid girl is a Lambert as well." Fitz took a stained hankie from his pocket and mopped at the back of his neck.

Abby nodded. "Penny Jo, the youngest. Eliza Jane is their oldest. And they have a son serving in the infantry up in Virginia."

"Them women sure beat the doors down lookin' for you earlier." Fitz shook his gray head. "Yes sir, they were set on you meetin' the Rev. I suppose all the rest of Macon's women must be spoken for."

Abby found it interesting that Fitz referred to the colonel as Rev. His regalia was that of a cavalry colonel and his men were clearly under his command. So where had he parted ways with his calling?

Realizing that Fitz was expecting an answer, she gave him a friendly smile. "Most of them are." Abby reached down to pick up another apple and tossed it to a boy standing in front of the telegraph building. "The ones who can still chew their own food anyway."

Fitz snickered.

"Is that the Saberton Colonel?" The boy called out to Abby.

"Yes, Hickory. Would you like to come and meet him?" She called back.

Hickory trotted out to where they were walking under the shade of the arching live oaks. He produced an envelope from the pocket of his overalls. "Are you Colonel Ian Saberton?"

At Ian's nod, Hickory handed him the envelope. "Wire came for you, sir."

"Thank you." Ian handed the boy a coin in exchange for the telegraph message.

Hickory ran back to the Mercantile, beaming at his good fortune.

As the colonel read, then reread the missive, Fitz made small talk about the heat.

"... yes, sir. A Tennessee summer can be a scorcher, but this beats all I ever saw."

Abby wanted to ask the colonel where he called home, but he was still preoccupied with his correspondence.

She detected a change in him as he read.

By the time they turned onto College Street, she noticed he was more than a bit distracted, a cool indifference had settled over him. The slight flirtation—whether real or imagined—was gone. Whatever was in his message had his undivided attention.

"But I tell you what, the little Tennessee women are the purtiest around." Fitz closed his eyes as if savoring a fond memory. "'cept Abby here. You done put Georgia on the map."

"I see." Colonel Saberton checked his timepiece.

Oddly enough, it irked her that he hadn't heard one word of Fitz's unique compliment.

"Bad news?" Abby ventured.

Ian didn't answer. She couldn't tell if he had heard her question or if it simply didn't deserve an answer.

He finally realized she'd spoken when Fitz nudged him with an elbow. "Hmm?"

Well, at least he wasn't ignoring her anymore. Although, she almost preferred being ignored to the distracted glint in his eye beneath the shade of his hat.

"Your telegram." She tried another approach. "Bad news?"

Again, no answer.

"Your colonel's not much for conversation." Abby's wry observation slipped before she could stop it.

Fitz wagged his gray head. "He's busy thinkin' like he does." Pressing his lips together, he looked off to the north. "Like it or not, them Yankees are comin' this way. The Rev's got a heavy task to make folks ready."

Fitz's revelation was sobering.

Abby had read in the Macon newspaper that after taking Atlanta the Union forces would most likely swing back north to Nashville. But to think that the frontline was instead moving south toward Macon sent a shiver of apprehension over her.

She'd witnessed firsthand the aftermath of battle. Envisioning the beautiful city, full of people she cared for so deeply, ravished and in ruin made her stomach turn.

They approached the wrought iron fence surrounding the Dobb's grand estate. Whispy willows swaying in the warm breeze flanked either side of the two-storied portico. Six white columns set in front reminded Abby of pictures she'd seen of the White House. No doubt that had been Cora Dobbs' intention when she'd had the house built.

"The General and Mayor Dobbs will be waiting for you." Abby patted Fitz's arm. "There's a train due in with more wounded, so I'll say goodbye."

"Would you like to come inside?" Colonel Saberton paused to address her. "I'm sure the conversation will be much more to your liking."

She started to decline, but noticed the edge of his mouth twitched as if he were trying not to smile. Just what did he mean by that?

"Thank you, no. I'm expected at the hospital." She raised a brow. "I found my chat with Lieutenant Fitz very enjoyable."

He did smile at that.

"Besides, I've had more than enough of General Farris." The last thing she needed was to have to endure him today. "They'll be looking for me at the hospital."

"Fritz can escort you there." Colonel Saberton gave a nod and a smile before starting up the brick steps.

"I appreciate the offer, but I don't need an escort." She turned to go, but stopped before she'd reached the end of the wrought iron fence. Thinking it over, she thought it best to warn him. "Colonel, watch your back. Farris has been known to undermine new commands."

His features sharpened. "Thank you, Miss McFadden. I'll certainly keep that in mind."

Waving, Abby headed back down College street.

Now she had to pray he was an honorable man.

*"A lie that is half-truth is the darkest of all lies."*
*~ Alfred, Lord Tennyson*

# Three

*A* curving walnut staircase rose beyond the polished foyer. Columned doorways on either side of the grand entry, with arched glass transoms, stood open to reveal a richly furnished drawing room. On the opposite side, a library with gleaming chessboard floors begged to be explored.

Every space an intentional reflection of the owner's good taste. Cora Dobbs no doubt assembled such opulent possessions for the sheer pleasure of boasting about their rare value. Ian removed his hat and tossed his frayed gloves inside.

Most would say Brechenridge, the Saberton family estate high on the Savannah river, was every bit as elaborate. Though it had never felt this pretentious. Three generations of Sabertons had put all their worldly goods and a lifetime of hard work into their land.

After three years on the battlefield with nothing but the threadbare uniform on his back and his prized horse, he'd experienced far too much death, destruction, hunger, and deprivation to regard such excess with anything more than disdain.

Since his father's death in the Mexican war, Ian's mother had turned her knack with thoroughbreds into a thriving operation which now helped supply the Confederate Army with fresh, healthy horses. No slave labor. No selfish gain.

"This way, sir." A corporal met them at the door rather than a houseman.

Just like his home, Ian couldn't help but wonder how many more changes this ostentatious old house might endure before the war of the states declared a victor.

A mouthwatering aroma hit him as soon as they stepped farther inside, and Ian's stomach quickly reminded him he'd had nothing substantial to eat since they'd broken camp in Atlanta. From the look on the Fitz's face, he'd had much the same reaction.

They followed voices coming down a hallway that led to a large dining area. Set up as a temporary office for the Confederate cause, the Dobbs' ample dining table was now littered with newspapers, letters, and maps. Silver candelabras and an arrangement of withered flowers were discarded haphazardly to a corner over by an elegantly draped window.

"Here they are." The announcement came from a man Ian didn't recognize, but assumed was the mayor by his forced smile and elaborate hand gestures. "Come in, come in, gentlemen. Walter Dobbs, mayor of this fair city. Colonel Saberton, you can be seated next to the General and your lieutenant will sit next to me and take the minutes."

Ian waited for the General to acknowledge his salute. Instead the commander sat at the head of the table reading a newspaper with a scowl on his face.

Dobbs knocked on the table as if it were a door causing the general to look up. "Our guests have arrived, General."

Farris gave a half-hearted salute and waved at the seat next to him. "Sit. Both of you. What's this malarkey about Sherman storming into northern Georgia? The lily-livered Governor has taken to the Atlanta papers calling on all Georgia citizens to be prepared to defend themselves against an inevitable invasion. How do you think that looks to the wretched Northerners? Sounds like we're powerless. A bunch of ne'er-do-wells preparing to hand it all over."

"It'll never happen." Dobbs insisted. "The North's propaganda has simply infiltrated the big city newspapers. Tell him, Colonel."

"It will happen." Ian removed the wire he'd gotten and placed it on the table. "And *is* happening as we speak. Union troops advanced past Picket Mill to take Allatoona Pass this morning. Sherman now has the railroad. Supplies and ammunition will be able to reach his men by train. Our troops have essentially been cut off."

Dobbs' face blanched.

"Where's Johnston's forces?" Farris bellowed as he shifted his ample weight and the chair gave a loud creak. "He's made it a habit of retreating."

The sour stench of alcohol was unmistakable every time Farris moved.

"Hear tell reinforcements are bein' called in." Fitz contributed, though not given permission to speak. He rarely passed an opportunity to tell what he knew. "Including them Texans of Granbury's. Ain't no army able to stop that brigade. So far anyhow."

"Rain is moving in. That will hold them back for a few days, but both sides have suffered crippling losses." Ian watched the general closely. The man refused to look him in the eye. "Sherman will want to move in as soon as possible to take advantage of our weakened defenses."

"Do they pay you to make guesses, Colonel?" Farris lifted his coffee cup to summon a refill. A young boy standing by the kitchen door was quick to respond.

"They don't pay me for anything right now." Ian's answer was harsh. "None of my men have seen a dime in months."

"Pity." The general responded, monitoring the amount of coffee being poured. "Might I suggest you refrain from making any foolish predictions, until you are better informed to do so."

Fitz's hand stilled from the minutes he recorded.

"I believe Colonel Saberton is here on orders from General Lee, himself, Farris." Dobbs came to his feet. "He's obviously got the General's ear. It won't be to anyone's advantage if you start things off by offending him. Besides, I wouldn't think you'd like to call attention to yourself with all you have going on."

General Farris took a long sip of coffee before setting his cup down in its saucer with a clatter. "Of course, no offense intended." He nodded in Ian's direction without looking over at him. "And I believe news that I've had a new bakehouse built at the fort to better prepare rations for the inmates would be welcome news to Lee and his cohorts. They're sending dozens upon dozens of blue-bellied prisoners daily and expect me to find room for them. I expect they'd like to know the rations—which they have not upped—are being distributed best as can be expected." He swirled a finger at Fitz. "That, you may write down."

Dobbs again took his chair. "Yes, but you might want to leave off the fact that the grease from your new facility is being emptied into the creek branch upstream of the stockade polluting their only source of water."

Ian caught Fitz's questioning glance. He nodded to his lieutenant to record the meeting verbatim.

Farris didn't bother to refold the newspaper, flinging it to the floor instead. "Someone must keep them humbled. I'll not chance an uprising."

"I've no love for the enemy and that is a fact." Dobbs pointed at Farris, emphasizing every word with shake of his wrist. "But those Yankee prisoners have only been coming here for three months. You have most of them wishing they'd died out on the battlefield."

Farris smirked, clearly pleased with the analysis of his prison camp.

Ian decided to get straight to the point. "General, my orders are to set up camp beside the Ocmulgee River. I'll reposition the gold from the depository to an undisclosed location. We will disassemble the stock machinery of Macon Armory immediately to be sent to an armory in Columbia. Arrangements will be made for all surplus, spare machinery, and tools not required for immediate use to be transported to Savannah as soon as possible."

For the first time, General Farris turned a bloodshot eye toward Ian. "Your orders are to leave us unarmed? With no cannon or spare rifles to defend ourselves?"

"Your soldiers are well-equipped to defend themselves, Sir." Ian stretched a leg and rested a fist on his thigh, saddle weary and in no mood to coddle a disreputable general. "We are removing the excess to prevent enemy forces from using them against you or the good citizens of Macon."

"Has it come to that, Colonel?" For once, Dobbs' hands were still as the seriousness of Ian's mission began to sink in. "Has Sherman got us outnumbered?"

Natural empathy for the man threatened to rise inside of

him, but Ian was adept at tamping it down. There was no room in this war for sentiment. Only a clear head, without the sloppiness of emotion, would get them all out alive.

"We'll certainly do everything we can to see his troops held back. But you'd just as well know with northern Georgia blocked off into Tennessee and without the railroad to help bring in supplies, it's just a matter of time before Sherman makes good on his threat to take the rest of Georgia."

The room fell silent. Even the house help was still.

Like so many in the South, Georgians had witnessed the war from afar through distorted lenses. Commentaries in Confederate newspapers were geared to keeping up morale despite the unthinkable number of casualties and provisions that had been lost.

The Rebs could deter the North only so long, outwitting them with creative tactics, but eventually, the ammunition would run out. Along with food, hospital supplies, and transportation. Once the telegraph wires were cut, there would be no communication and they were as good as sitting ducks.

Ian's job was to see they understood the dire consequences of losing such a battle. Raiding troops, if given half a chance, would lay everything to waste within their broad path. His cavalrymen would ride out to persuade the hundreds of people from surrounding countryside to leave their homes and take refuge in the city. There was strength in numbers.

"Bring food." General Farris barked and the young house boy scurried into the kitchen. "So all by yourself, you will be handling our country's gold. You're sending our valuable armory to South Carolina and all other surplus to Savannah. Isn't that where you hail from, Colonel? Savannah is your home, is it not?"

What could he possibly be insinuating?

"It is." Ian's response was measured.

"And didn't I just read about a Saberton somewhere in South Carolina doing something of importance? Could he be a relation?"

"What the ..." Fitz was forgetting himself again and Ian held up a hand to silence him.

"My brother, Rear Admiral Nicholas Saberton. Commanding officer of Fort Sumpter in Charleston."

The mayor dabbed his forehead with his handkerchief. "Everyone in Georgia knows the Sabertons. What exactly is your point, Farris? Surely you don't mean to imply Colonel Saberton would steal Confederate resources for personal gain." Dobbs waved off a plate of food, so the boy placed it in front of the general instead. "What you're suggesting is a serious offense. Defamation of character. I'd have to be a witness to your false accusation. Cora wouldn't like that one bit."

"No, no, of course not." The general answered with his mouth full. Ian's empty stomach took a turn. "You misunderstood me completely. I was merely pointing out what I am certain are minor coincidences. Just small talk. Eat, Colonel. You must be famished."

"I'll eat with my men." Ian pushed away from the table and retrieved his hat.

There was no misunderstanding. Farris was intentionally trying to create suspicion concerning Ian's integrity. Most likely to defer attention from his own.

The meeting had gone far enough. Ian had delivered the information as instructed. Now he was ready to help set up camp.

Fitz scrunched his mouth, replacing the cap on his ink bottle. Shaking his head, there was no guessing what his thoughts were about the odd turn of the meeting.

"Thank you, gentlemen." Dobbs stood and extended his hand. "You'll have the city's full cooperation, Colonel. Please let us know if there's anything you need. I believe the ladies are planning on having supper brought out to your men this evening."

"We'll look forward to it." Ian accepted the mayor's hand and prepared to take his leave.

General Farris waved off the mayor. "Dobbs, see the lieutenant out. I have one more thing I need to discuss with Saberton. In private."

Ian tilted his head, stretching the tight muscles along his neck, silently summoning patience.

As soon as Dobbs and Fitz were out of the room, Farris shifted his weight back in his chair. "Please sit. I saw you through the window when you arrived. Was that Abigail McFadden you were with?" Farris gazed out the window as if looking for her still.

"Miss McFadden kindly showed us the way." Ian preferred to stand.

"How accommodating of her." The general mindlessly tapped on the table with a finger. "Did she say anything that I should know about?"

"Not that I recall."

"How well do you know Abby?" Hearing him say her name with such familiarity grated Ian's nerves.

"We've just met."

"A beauty, is she not?" The general took on the slow grin of a fat cat. "I have information about her that might interest you."

Ian didn't bother to respond. The general was either drunk or completely addlebrained.

"If you'll notice, she doesn't speak like a Southerner. Does not hold the same respectful manners as our good Southern ladies."

In other words, she'd probably spurned his advances and told him what to do with his own bad manners.

"I've had her mail intercepted. She received a letter from Ohio not long ago." General Farris sucked his teeth clean with a disgusting slurp. "The sender wrote that she missed Abby terribly. Spoke of praying for her most honorable relative, who carried the burden of directing the tides of the war. What does that tell you, Colonel?"

"That you broke the law to intrude on a private exchange." The very last ounce of Ian's patience had just run out. "Now if you'll excuse me, sir—."

The general slapped the table causing the sugar bowl to turn over. "She's a Yankee through and through. Probably the illegitimate daughter of Lincoln himself. Here to report every move we make and lead the blue devils right to our doorstep."

"You got all that from a woman's letter asking for prayer?" Ian's voice was raised before he could stop himself. "Miss McFadden's personal business is none of my concern. Keep in mind, it's against protocol to falsely accuse without sufficient evidence. Especially if you damage a lady's reputation in the process."

"Unless that woman is a Yankee spy." The general persisted. "In a military court of law, whose word do you suppose they would believe? Mine or that of a common nurse?"

Ian settled his hat on his head. "General Farris, if there is nothing else, sir, I'll see to my troops."

"Think, Saberton!" Farris rose to unsteady feet. "If our secession prevails, you could retire with honors. All the more so if you were to help expose an enemy agent." Coming around the table, he stood between Ian and the door. "If you were to intercept her communiqué, get her to talk. Thousands of good Southern lives could be spared. All because you, Ian Saberton, chose to look past a pretty face to expose the ugly, black heart of an underhanded Yankee."

Farris was full of hot air.

Abby was a bit impulsive. She'd proven that well enough. But she was not underhanded nor malicious. In seminary, Ian had spent countless hours studying true black-hearted souls and Abby was nowhere near the same ilk.

He couldn't help but wonder what she'd done to earn Farris' heedless contempt. She must've dumped the whole water trough over his head.

Ian stifled a grin.

All considering, he wasn't the best one to be giving advice about Abby McFadden. "I'll be fully occupied for the next several weeks. The Federals are on our heels. There's no time for delay."

"She's sweet on you." The general again stepped in front of Ian as he made his way to the door. "Use it to your advantage. Catch her in the act. I can make it worth your while."

Ian turned on the general, whose eyes grew wide. "Permission to speak candidly, sir."

"Granted." Farris tottered backward.

Ian lowered his voice in order to remain calm. "Let it be noted that I will not be a part of any scheme to entrap an innocent civilian. Having just met Miss McFadden, I have no knowledge of any nefarious actions on her part, nor do I intend to know her long enough to ever make such a bold accusation. Are we clear, sir?"

Not waiting for an answer, he stepped around the general. Hopefully, the matter would end there.

Opening the heavy wood door, Ian heard Farris call from

behind.

"If you know what's good for you, you'll stay away from the McFadden woman."

That sounded suspiciously like a threat. Abby's warning to watch his back made much more sense now.

Readjusting his hat, Ian moved on without looking back.

*"There is no charm equal to the tenderness of heart."*
*~ Jane Austen*

# Four

"Abby has plenty of worthwhile qualities that would make for a fine wife." Elizabeth Lambert leaned over a colorful quilt, stretched on a wooden frame in front of her. "Granted, she can't cook to save her life, but with a touch more practice, she'd do just fine."

Wiping her hands on a towel, Abby came farther down the stairwell.

Six ladies in all were seated in the downstairs receiving room of the hospital knitting socks, gloves, and sewing coverlets for the wounded. They met every day at Harbor House to cook and provide comfort for well soldiers. But Friday mornings were set aside to visit the wounded, contribute to the war effort, and indulge in the latest gossip.

"I'm perfectly happy in my spinsterhood, thank you." Abby took an empty chair next to Elizabeth. It felt good to be off her feet. She'd been tending the new arrivals since before dawn, and this was the first opportunity she'd had to sit.

"Oh, you don't know what you're saying." Cora Dobbs

dismissed Abby's statement, never looking up from the embroidery hoop in her lap. "And who cares if she can't cook, Elizabeth. We have people who can do that for her."

Elizabeth's fingers deftly wove her needle in and out of the red material, making a delicate scroll design. "Some of us prefer to cook and clean for ourselves."

"Posh." Cora Dobbs smoothed a hand over her perfectly stitched flowering vine applique.

"Ow!" Penny Jo pricked herself with an embroidery needle. Lifting the offended finger to her lips, she threw her sampler aside. "Why do I have to learn to sew? I'm never getting married. I'm going to live on a farm with lots of animals and they don't care if I can make a straight row."

"Horses and dogs still need blankets, too, you know." Eliza Jane, at barely twenty, still bickered shamelessly with her younger sister.

"Well, if you're not going to pay attention to your sampler, I suggest you go on home and work on your spelling lessons." Elizabeth pointed at her daughter's discarded needlework. "And take that with you."

"I'll come cook for you, Abby. And, Mama, you can do your sewing. What else is there to running a household?" Eliza Jane shrugged. "As for finding a man, that you'll have to do on your own."

If life were only that simple.

Eliza Jane was younger than Abby by only four years, but sometimes the girl made her feel ancient. She'd married her husband, Will, at seventeen, just before he was called up to serve in Virginia. They'd been sweethearts since they were old enough to care about such things.

With Will off to war, Eliza Jane still lived at home with her mother. She had no experience running a household of her own, but her dearest friend in all the world certainly felt free to offer advice anyway.

"I've done just fine without one." Abby took a deep breath. Though they meant well, she was tired of hearing about how badly she needed a man.

Abby's father had doted on her mother. They had adored one another. Fair or unfair, Abby refused to settle for anything less. If that meant she was destined to do without a man of her own, so be it.

"Well, if you're ever going to win the heart of our new colonel, Abby, you're going to have to try harder." Cora wasn't going to let it be. "Elizabeth, make her understand a woman's duty."

In the two years since Abby had arrived in Georgia, she'd unexpectedly found a home here. These people had taken her in like she was one of their own.

She had no formal medical training, but her father had attended Medical College of Ohio before she was born. Before he and her mother traveled west to set up a mission for the Cayuse. Abby's earliest memories were accompanying him as he tended to the medical needs of the Indians.

Those had been solitary days, but so contented.

"I didn't get a chance to talk to him, but I hear he's nice." Eliza Jane was saying. "Did you talk to him, Abby? After you half drowned him, I mean."

"Who?" Abby had not been following the conversation.

"Oh, for pity sake." Cora cut her thread with an irritated snip. "You see what I mean, Elizabeth? Someone needs to explain to Abby the urgency of our endeavor."

On a heavy sigh, Abby laid her head back against the carved wood of the crimson parlor chair. The last thing she was looking for was a husband. Especially not a Confederate colonel. She was on her own mission of sorts, and it did not involve tying herself down to any man.

"So, what's he like?" Eliza Jane asked again.

"He was tall. We all saw that much." Elizabeth offered.

"And fairly handsome, didn't you think, Abby?" Cora rethreaded her needle.

"No, not especially." Abby answered honestly and immediately regretted it when all hands stilled. Eyeing the women one at a time, she knew she had just dashed their hopes for ousting General Farris. "But ... I couldn't tell with all the road dust covering him. Who knows what he looks like under all that?"

The older women shook their heads, clearly put out that she wasn't even trying. It had been two days ago. Surely, honesty counted for something.

"What I saw was pretty nice to look at." Eliza Jane reiterated.

"You all leave Abby be. If she's not interested, she's not interested." How was it Elizabeth Lambert's innocent shrug was more shaming than an earful of Cora's ranting?

Elizabeth was an expert at mothering.

Abby had learned much by watching her handle her own daughters. She was fair but firm. Fiercely protective, but gave them plenty of room to discover life on their own. Eliza Jane and Penelope Jo were confident, beautiful young women because of it.

Eliza Jane with her lovely auburn hair and her penchant for cooking. No one made pastries and pies as delicious as hers. And Penny Jo with her love for animals and riotous headful of blonde curls.

"Don't act like you didn't notice him, Abby McFadden." Cora came over and took the seat next to Abby, sweeping her wide skirts around her. "Now, you'll need to know how to embroider, so pay attention. You may know how to tie off a wound, but needlepoint is done with skill and finesse. Every Southern wife knows when to take up her needlework."

Eliza Jane bit her thread to sever it, chuckling under her breath.

After a few minutes of Cora's instruction, Abby vowed never to pick up a sewing needle again. Having to back out to start over more times than not, it hadn't taken long to admit she wasn't cut out to be a Southern wife.

"Abby, are you feeling well, dear?"

Catching Elizabeth's concerned expression, Abby laid down the quilting hoop Cora had placed in her lap. "I suppose. It's been a tiring day."

"Pick it back up and pay attention to your stitching." Cora wound her thread three times around the needle and stuck it into the center of a flower-shaped design. "There. Now, you do it."

Abby didn't want to do it. But humoring Cora Dobbs was easier by far than bucking her.

"Finish off that row, then I'll come back to see how you've done." Cora returned to her own seat and took up her quilt square once again. "You all will never guess what I heard. Those brazen Yankees not only dared to cross our borders, but now they've taken Atlanta!"

The ladies twittered all at once like a nestful of sparrows.

"Walter says General Braggs has done everything in his power to stop them but their Commander What's-His-Name managed to slip past our guard, and Atlanta is all but under siege."

Abby's pulse quickened and her breath caught in her throat.

Memories of the battle lines sickened her stomach. These dear women had no idea what they were up against.

The front door to the hospital opened and in walked Mayor Dobbs with another army officer.

"Why, look-y here. Walter has brought our very own Colonel Saberton for a tour of the hospital." Cora announced as if she hadn't planned every minute of it.

Abby glanced over, then quickly looked again.

The man taking up most of the doorway couldn't possibly be the same man who'd ridden into town last Wednesday. Clean shaven, except an oddly-appealing narrow strip of beard going from just under his bottom lip down his chin. A closely trimmed moustache further framed his well-shaped mouth. Dark brown hair gleamed in the sunlight, falling to just below his collar.

Abby sat forward in her chair, staring openly. The man's bone structure belonged in an art gallery. On a statue somewhere.

"Afternoon, ladies." Even his Southern drawl seemed more pronounced.

"Good afternoon, Colonel." Women's voices sounded in unison as they cut their eyes toward her.

The only thing these Macon women enjoyed more than sewing together was matchmaking. Call it what you will ... war, strategizing, duty ... what they had in mind would put Cupid to shame.

He strolled into the room to stand beside her chair.

"Colonel Saberton, we were just talking about you." Cora smiled. "Weren't we, Abby?"

"What? No." Abby tried to argue but it was useless.

"Good things, I hope."

At least he was paying attention, Abby noticed. Better than

when she'd left him.

"All good, of course." Elizabeth smiled and snipped her thread with a dainty pair of stork scissors. "Colonel, I'd like you to meet my husband. He's upstairs. Abby can show you the way."

Abby didn't move.

Elizabeth leaned over and gave Abby a discreet whisper. "Stand up, Abby, dear. You haven't greeted our new colonel. You don't want to be rude."

It wasn't her intent to be rude. She just didn't want to give the impression she was interested when clearly she was not.

Looking up, she hoped to get a better look at him without the sunlight in her eyes.

Colonel Saberton regarded her with a hint of amusement tugging at the corner of his mouth. One brow lifted before he unleashed a full smile, offering a hand to help her stand. "Good to see you again, Miss McFadden."

"Gabby-Gail. Er… Gabby—Abby." Closing her eyes, she chided herself to get control. "Good to see you, too, Colonel."

Another prod from Elizabeth reminded her to stand. As soon as she did, a loud tear sounded in the room.

Looking down, she was horrified to see that she'd embroidered the quilt piece to her best dress. The hoop dangled precariously from a telling rip in her skirt.

While the other women snickered, Elizabeth reached over and gave the thread a snip with her tiny stork scissors.

Abby McFadden's pert nose lifted a notch while the other women giggled behind her. Her wobbly smile was the only indication that she was affected at all.

He admired her resilience. Abby was oddly self-assured

considering her frilly undergarments were showing.

"Please, call me Ian." He pulled aside his frock coat to settle a hand in his trouser pocket. "I apologize if I startled you."

"I wasn't expecting you ... like that." She looked him over before seemingly remembering herself. A blush brightened her cheeks quite becomingly.

The women were back to their needlework, but their interest in the conversation was far from removed.

Mrs. Lambert tacked the torn place in Abby's skirt before calling up to the top of the stairs. "Hickory, please ask Doc Lambert to join us, dear. There's someone I'd like him to meet."

For just an instant Ian caught sight of a small copper-colored head peering from the top floor before disappearing to do his bidding.

"Forgive our manners, Colonel. I believe you've met most of these ladies the other day. This is my daughter, Eliza Jane Stratton. Her husband and our son serve in the Georgia 15th Infantry in northern Virginia."

"Under General Lee?" Ian was genuinely impressed.

Elizabeth Lambert nodded. "And Penny Jo, our youngest, is at home, hard at work on her schooling."

Cora opened her mouth to comment, but Mrs. Lambert cut her off with a shake of her head. "And if she's not, I don't want to know about it."

"She's running around upstairs with that little wild child, Hickory." Cora Dobbs answered anyway, poking her needle up from the bottom of her quilt square and pulling the thread taught with a flourish.

Abby crossed her arms, a fond smile on her face. "Hickory's not a wild child. He's very polite and actually better at reading and arithmetic than most his age."

"Well, maybe he should see Penny Jo does her schooling then." Cora made a face. "Instead of chasing after him and a bunch of cats and dogs all day."

"May I?" Ian pointed to the stethoscope around Abby's neck. "I read about Cammann's binaural stethoscope in a medical journal." In Tennessee, he had studied the effective use of such an instrument in one of the many journals he'd subscribed to before the war. But had never examined one first hand.

"It came in last week." Abby removed the instrument and handed it to him. "It's the newest model and the resonator is three times more sensitive. Lately, I've used it to monitor babies' heartbeats in utero."

Ian was intrigued. "You can detect a baby's heartbeat?" Ian took the stethoscope and turned it over in his hand.

"Like this." Abby placed two end pieces into his ears. Then she took the bell-shaped amplifier and carefully laid it against his chest.

He listened, in detail, to his own heartbeat. Looking down into Abby's unusual eyes, he heard the pace quicken considerably.

Abby met his excitement with a happy grin. "They say when it's twins, you can hear two separate fetal heartbeats."

"Fascinating." He still held her gaze. No longer speaking about the remarkable instrument.

The ladies began to murmur.

"I take it Hickory's not the only one. You sound as if you are quite a reader yourself, Colonel Saberton." Mrs. Lambert observed with a pleased smile. "Abby loves books as well. Especially the medical catalogues. She assists my husband in seeing that babies in Macon are born strong and healthy."

"She's more than an assistant." A thick set man stepped from the last stair into the large reception area. "Especially when it comes to childbirth. I have too many soldiers to tend to. Abby takes care of the babies."

"Meet my husband, Dr. Jebediah Lambert. He's in charge here at Floyd House Hospital." Elizabeth smiled graciously, then affectionately took her husband's arm. "Honey, this is our new Colonel, Ian Saberton."

"Good to meet you, Colonel." For a doctor, the man had the beefy handshake of a lumberjack.

"Abby's an invaluable help to me. With more and more wounded and less supplies to tend them, I've had to lean heavily on her. The soldiers have taken to calling her their Angel of Mercy."

Again, Ian spotted the kid looking down at him. "I see you have another assistant."

The doctor followed his gaze and called for the boy to come down.

"Hickory's one of the war orphans." Abby's voice softened. "He stays down at the shanty settlement outside of town, and he's very precious to me. I won't have him bullied."

Ian lifted a brow. It wasn't his imagination. Miss McFadden had just issued him a direct warning. "Agreed and accepted."

The same boy he'd seen at the telegraph office popped down the stairs and came to a stop in front of Ian. There was something familiar about him, but Ian couldn't place when or where he might have known him.

"Hickory, meet Colonel Saberton." Doc Lambert encouraged the boy to shake Ian's hand.

"I met him already. Twice. I brought him his important war telegram and he was there once when I saved a lady from a rattlesnake." Hickory had an engaging smile. "Killed it with my slingshot."

That's where Ian had seen him before.

His sister-in-law, Tori, had benefited from the boy's protection about four years ago. But Hickory had disappeared into the brush before Nicholas could properly thank him.

"You are correct, Sir." Ian shook his hand. "My family owes a debt of gratitude to you for your heroic bravery that day." Ian noticed the kid had grown a few inches and had all his teeth now, but otherwise still looked the same. He must be about nine or ten years old now.

"Penny Jo, you may as well come down, too. I see you peeking at us from up there." Her mother called out and the girl promptly obeyed.

"Would you like to have a look around?" Clearing his throat, Doc Lambert prepared to show Ian around the hospital. "This building used to be a home. The army took it over when they needed more space for a hospital. There are four hospitals in Macon." Turning he called over to the mayor. "That reminds me, Walter. Got word this morning to prepare our wounded to move over into Alabama. What do you know about this? I have some that wouldn't survive the trip."

Walter Dobbs looked like a man caught in a whirlwind. For a politician he certainly didn't have much to say.

"Yes, Walter, that sounds like it needs some serious discussion." Cora glided over to her husband in her hoop skirt. "Why don't you and Doc go put your heads together. Abby can show Colonel Saberton around."

With a nudge to her back from a town lady, Abby teetered forward. Ian put a hand on her elbow to steady her.

"Not much to show. Abby got 'em all settled down and most are taking a nap right now." Hickory beamed at Abby much the same way he had with Tori that day in the woods.

Abby caught a wayward strand of her hair and smoothed it behind an ear before sweeping a hand toward the stairway. "We have forty-eight soldiers right now. Nine are in isolation with typhoid fever. Most aren't critical, but there are a few where gangrene has set in."

Ian could tell that this tour had not been her idea. She was probably supposed to be off for the day. But she was being gracious, and he appreciated her effort.

Hickory and Penny Jo tagged along behind them.

The hospital was set up with the whole second floor lined with cots where the patients were in various phases of recovery. The third floor held surgery rooms where stains on the hardwood floors left little wonder to the use of that space. Baskets of bandages and bottles of medicines were tucked on shelves in what used to be a hallway.

Ian had seen many army hospitals both in camp and in buildings much like this. One thing was evident, Doc Lambert kept his numbers to a workable few. Most hospitals north of here had half the space and ten times the wounded, with supplies at a bare minimum.

"And that's about all there is to see." Abby walked him back to the staircase with Hickory and Penny Jo close behind. "I hope you'll be able to come back sometime when you can sit and visit with the soldiers awhile. It would mean so much to them."

"I'll make it a priority." Ian promised as he returned to the first level. "Thank you for an insightful tour. Now I must return to my men."

This time none of the ladies tried to stop or redirect him. They looked more like cats who'd just shared a juicy mouse.

"Good day, Colonel." Cora called after him as he walked

out the door.

With a hand in his pocket, Ian stepped onto the sidewalk. Long shadows fell across the road as the building was silhouetted by the setting sun.

For whatever reason, he hesitated before returning to his horse.

From where he stood, he could see inside the hospital's receiving room through the large pane window in front. He stopped to watch Abby pull Hickory in front of her as she talked with the other ladies. Tenderly, she ran her hand through his copper curls, laughing easily at something he said.

Ian was drawn to her warmth. When she smiled, it made him want to smile.

Looking up, Abby caught his eye and gave a friendly wave.

Ian nodded, then moved past the window.

*"No one is useless in this world who lightens the burdens of another."*
*~ Charles Dickens*

# Five

"Abby! Abby! Come quick!"

She was awake in an instant. Abby's heart sank as she recognized Hickory's voice.

The frantic call sounded below her window, along with the sound of pebbles pinging against the glass.

She lit a candle lamp, hoping to clear the drowsy fog from her mind. Clutching a flannel robe to her chest, she pushed open the hospital's third story window, trying to detect his slight form in the dark. "Hickory?" She tried to keep her voice quiet to avoid disturbing the soldiers below. "Are you all right?"

"It's Sallie. You need to come with me, Abby. To Dove's. Hurry."

"Wait for me by the door. I'll be right down."

Abby set about changing into a workable dress, cautioning herself to remain calm. A number of things could bring Hickory out to fetch her.

No matter how many ways she tried to reason it out, she knew deep inside that Sallie and her baby were in serious trouble.

The public women, as Cora called them, were rife with sickness and disease. Not many doctors would agree to see them, certainly not in the middle of the night. So they suffered shamefully. Doc said most of them died within five years of taking up the profession.

Sallie's pregnancy had been riddled with problems from the beginning. Venereal disease spread throughout her body which had been a challenge to control without risking the health of her baby.

Sallie persistently refused treatment, complicating her situation even more. She feared owing money she didn't have. All because Farris made sure the girls were destitute, owing him more than they could ever take in.

Abby replenished a physician's bag, tossing in an extra roll of gauze, a bottle of mercury salts, and a tin of labor tea just for good measure.

The Dove's Nest was only four blocks from the hospital in a row of seedy establishments filled with gambling and drinking.

Once she had a chance to assess Sallie's condition, she'd send someone to fetch Doc. He would grumble and complain, but she knew he wouldn't refuse to come help, even if it was over at the Dove's Nest.

Abby cracked open the door, and Hickory grabbed her by the hand. "Hurry, Abby. Mama Ivy says Sallie's dying for sure." He sniffed, and the wobble of his chin evidenced his nine-year-old angst.

She held tight to his hand as they navigated the empty street.

With little coaxing, Hickory shared all he knew, mostly second-hand information from Mama Ivy. Sallie had lost her waters and from his innocent description of blood on her sheet, Abby assumed she was most likely hemorrhaging.

Despite the warm breeze, she could feel Hickory's shaking limbs. "Don't fret, sweetheart. We'll do everything we can. With the Lord's help, they'll both be just fine."

*Lord, let it be so.*

He nodded but deep concern furrowed his brow. "My Sallie can't die, Abby. She just can't."

Slowing, Abby pulled the child closer to her side, wrapping an arm around his narrow shoulders as they walked. Once again, she was stricken with compassion for the orphans forced to make their own way. Forgotten victims in this monstrous conflict.

Hickory had an unusual attachment to Sallie. Abby couldn't quite figure out why. She supposed he didn't have many friends at the shanty town, and Sallie had most likely started out there. The working girls at Dove's usually came from desperate places.

"I promise to do all I can." Abby gave his shoulders a squeeze.

Hickory had been failed by so many on this earth. Only by the grace of a loving God would his faith be restored. A faith that should come naturally to a child.

"Is Mama Ivy with Sallie now?" Abby felt him nod against her side. "I need you to run on ahead. Ask her to bring up some clean towels and some alcohol if she can find it. Whatever form she can get her hands on will do. Can you remember that for me?" She laid a palm on the side of his cheek where she felt moisture from silent tears.

Hickory sniffed and scrubbed a hand across his nose, clearly embarrassed that she'd caught him crying. "I'll tell her you want a towel and to bring you a whisky."

Abby smiled at his attempt to be funny. "Never mind that. You just tell Mama Ivy what I said. She'll know what to do." Tousling his curly hair, she sent him off.

Pumping his arms, he ran off as fast as his legs would carry him.

Abby grasped her skirts and made her way down the alley to the Dove's Nest. Bawdy laughter and loud accordion music spilled into the quiet night.

Wickedness ran rampant in the back alleys while the rest of Macon slept.

Once inside, she side-stepped a bear of a man shuffling unsteadily toward her down the stairs. Despite leers from travel-worn drifters, long in their cups, she took rickety steps to the upper landing. Focusing on the last door at the end of the hall, she prayed for guidance.

When she entered Sallie's dim room, Abby's eyes struggled to adjust.

A tarnished candleholder held a faint flicker on the bed table. Sallie lay unmoving on the rusted iron bed. Abby laid a hand on her shoulder and a muted sob escaped the young woman.

"Sallie, it's Abby."

Silence.

Moving to a window, Abby cracked it open far enough to let warm night air circulate the stifling space. "Hickory tells me your baby may be coming." She tried to sound calm and reassuring while she lit two kerosene lamps to provide better light.

Abby took quick inventory of what could be used in tending an untimely birth. A basin on the side dresser, a chipped pitcher on a chair in the corner, a threadbare sheet hanging from the end of the bed, and a tattered quilt that Sallie clung to as if it were her only lifeline.

Mama Ivy, a small woman with dark features in a white-patterned head kerchief, padded lightly into the room with fresh linens and a bottle of alcohol just as Abby had requested. With a sorrowful glance toward the bed, the elder woman shook her head.

She was a wealth of knowledge when it came to medicinal potions and homemade remedies. Though her ingredients were primitive, in some ways Mama Ivy was a far superior healer than the best physicians graduating from today's medical schools.

The former housemaid was the undisputed head of "the family" at the shanty town down by the river. Mama Ivy managed the rowdy settlement of freed slaves, stragglers, and smattering of war orphans with careful attention.

Hickory had landed on her doorstep two years ago. She'd taken him in and done her best to protect him from the seedy dealings of Macon's underworld. Abby knew she was here at his request.

Gently pulling back the quilt, Abby spoke softly to Sallie who laid curled to one side of the sagging mattress. Her hair hung in a heavy braid past her thick waist.

Most pregnancies in the Red District didn't make it this far, but Abby was determined to give this baby a fighting chance.

"I need you to listen to me, Sallie." Abby's mind raced but she kept her tone steady. "The baby is coming, and you are going to have to help it get here."

In the beginning, Sallie had insisted she didn't care what happened to the child. A baby was an inconvenience that kept her from bringing in money. Over time, she became more attached as she began to feel her baby come to life inside of her.

Unfortunately, suffocating infection wracked her body and Sallie's heart had grown weaker. Earlier this week, when Sallie had begun to show signs of early labor, she'd all but begged her to save the child.

Abby prescribed full bedrest—alone. Whether or not Sallie adhered to that advice was anybody's guess. Ultimately, the fate of this little one was in God's hands.

Doc Lambert entered the room followed by a silent Mama Ivy holding a copper vat of clear water. Hickory had obviously fetched everyone he thought might make a difference.

Abby examined Sallie's abdomen, trying to get a feel for the baby's position.

Three other Dove's Nest girls poked their heads in the doorway, craning to see what they could see until Mama Ivy firmly shut the door. "Sallie don't need no audience."

Doc rolled up his sleeves and rinsed his hands.

"Ain't no use." Sallie's thick nasal tone, most likely from crying for the past several hours, gave her voice an added raspiness, raw with emotion. "God's punishment, I suppose."

Abby listened carefully through her stethoscope.

Turning her back to Sallie, she informed Doc that the fetal heartbeat was strong and clear. But Sallie's was faint and irregular with an odd clicking sound most likely caused by a failing valve.

Caught up in another contraction, Sallie's brow dotted with sweat. With hurried hands, Abby felt her abdomen to check progress. She was in full onset of labor now, but the child was not in proper position to be born easily.

Abby took her place at the foot of the bed, to speak quietly to the doctor. "The baby's breech—bottom first. I fear trying to turn it would only make things worse for Sallie. I don't think her heart can take it."

"This could be a long night." Doc replied, easing Sallie back onto her pillow with a gentle but firm hand. "Save your strength, now. You'll be needing it."

Over the next two hours, Abby encouraged Sallie to push with the contractions. The forced exertion had her whole body shaking and drenched in sweat.

Mama Ivy quietly offered an opiate elixir to ease her pain, but Doc shook his head. "Not this time, Ivy. She's weak as a kitten. The best course will be to relieve her of this child as quickly as possible before shock sets in. She'll need all of her wits for that."

Another hour passed before the revelry downstairs settled into a sleepy drone.

Hickory knocked at the door now and again to bring re-filled pitchers of clean water. Mama Ivy accepted from the doorway, assuring him everything would be all right.

"Hickory? Is that you?" Sallie managed a breathless whisper while Abby bathed her face with a cool rag. "Did you get a preacher like I asked? A man of God. To pray. In case ..."

Abby lifted her eyes to Doc's.

"Hickory said he would get you one and if anyone can coax a body out of his bed in the middle of the night, it's that boy." Doc answered. "I imagine there's probably a preacher waiting outside the door. You can talk to him just as soon as we—."

"This can't wait." Sallie shook her head. "This baby never asked for this." She gritted her teeth against another hard cramp with a sob. "Not like this ... never asked to be born to me." An exhausted shriek tore from her throat.

Abby continued to cool her brow with a wet cloth, speaking words of encouragement with every sharp pang.

"I'll take what's coming." Sallie panted. "But the preacher can ask for lenience ... for the ..."

With Doc's guidance, the next good push became the last as a perfectly formed baby girl was born, squawking loudly to make her presence known.

Though tiny, she had good color and appeared as healthy as any Abby had ever helped bring into this world.

With tender care, Mama Ivy took the child, bathed her and swaddled her in a blanket.

Sallie barely had strength to sob silently.

Abby's heart broke for her, but there was nothing to be said. She was fading. Nothing would make up for the overwhelming loss Sallie felt at the moment.

*Lord help her find peace she so desperately needs.*

Mama Ivy stilled the baby cradled in her arms by humming a sweet lullaby. "That preacher Hickory done fetched came a while back. If you want, I can bring him in here now."

Sallie was too weak to speak above a whisper, but she begged to see the minister.

"Send him in." Doc's hard exterior was firmly in place.

Abby supposed it was his way of dealing with all the suffering he met with daily.

Still, the weariness in his voice matched the ache in Abby's heart.

Before morning, there would likely be one more orphaned child in Macon.

*"For if our heart condemn us, God is greater than*
*our heart,*
*and knoweth all things."*
1 John 3:20

# Six

*T*he tremulous sound of a baby's cry pierced the quiet hallway.

Ian pushed away from the wall where he'd been leaning in a dim corridor of Dove's Nest Brothel.

Two hours past, Hickory, in a near panic, half-dragged him from his bed insisting, "Sallie needs a preacher."

The brass cross on Ian's hat was all the evidence the boy needed to come begging on behalf of someone named Sallie. No amount of argument or refusal could deter the kid from his mission to deliver a man of God to the brothel.

Ian hadn't considered himself a man of God in a long while and was fairly certain the Almighty shared his conviction. Where prayer had once been second nature, he now struggled just to offer grace before a meal.

*Unforgiveness,* his mother had once written in a letter, *if not destroyed, will ultimately destroy you, Son. Thankfully,*

*mercy is free and forgiveness has already been provided. You
must find courage to accept.*

Dottie Saberton had a gift. She had a sense for the deep
things. To see beyond the surface, right into the heart of a
matter. Ian once shared his mother's gift. Naturally, he had
pursued a vocation with the church in response. He had a
passion for people, a desire to see broken ones made whole
again.

Until, in one fateful moment, the gift was crushed. A moment that tormented his mind and haunted his sleep.

"Can't you make them let us in?" Hickory was beside himself as he tried to peek inside the room. Unable to wait any
longer, he pushed the door open and was met by a woman in a
crisp headscarf.

"Hickory, you listen to Mama Ivy. I'll let you in, but you
gonna have to be quiet as a mouse, you hear? Sallie needs her
rest. Reverend, you can come on in, too." The door opened
wider and Ian let the boy go ahead of him.

While Hickory took a closer look at the tiny bundle in the
woman's arms, Doc Lambert waved Ian over to the side of a
dilapidated bed.

Frayed curtains moved on a heavy breeze but did nothing
to clear the stale air inside the room.

Death.

The stench was unmistakable. Whether in a field hospital
or an open battlefield, Ian recognized the tang of blood and
disease that hung in the room like a fetid beast.

A frail woman, pale as the bedsheet beneath her, was far
too young to be surrendering to death's cold grasp. Her
tormented expression suggesting she sensed it, too. Her hollow
eyes were stark against the ashen features of a surprisingly
pretty face.

A vision of another pair of eyes, dead and lifeless, flashed in his mind.

Ian gritted his teeth.

The woman fighting for her life on the bed in front of him deserved his undivided attention. He may not be able to sort through the brambles of his own conscience, but he knew how to help ease hers.

Abby McFadden washed her hands in a basin in the corner. When she turned, she tilted her head as if she was surprised to see him.

No doubt she'd been expecting a minister, not a Cavalryman.

"This is the preacher, Sallie." Hickory spoke behind Ian. "He has a cross on his hat, so I brought him like you asked."

"Is that that truth?" The young woman rasped. "You a minister?"

"Credentialed, yes." Ian's answer sounded forced.

Sallie turned her attention to Hickory and gave the boy a weak smile. "Hickory, did you see the baby?"

"Yes'm." Hickory's voice was thick with emotion. "Mama Ivy showed it to me."

Mama Ivy brought the baby over to the bed, but Sallie refused to take her.

"I can't." Sallie slowly shook her head.

"The baby will need a home, Sallie." Doc McFadden was all business. "She can't stay here."

Ian watched Abby continue to pack up a doctor's bag in silence. In the dim light, he thought he saw moisture on her smooth cheek.

"This little darlin' will have a home. Don't you worry yourself about that." Mama Ivy resettled the baby in her arms.

"As much as I know you'd do your best, Ivy, the shanty's

no place for a newborn. Especially not this one. She'll need monitoring for a bit to make sure the infection has not been transferred." Doc ran a beefy hand over his jaw. "Weather's going to be turning cold soon. She'll need somewhere dry and warm. The hospital's full to overflowing with men. We haven't a cot, nor the staff to care for her there."

"Couldn't Elizabeth take her in for a short while?" Abby spoke quietly with her back to Sallie, but Ian heard every word. "Eliza Jane could help with her, too. Would give her something to do to help take her mind off of Will."

Doc Lambert released a long breath and shook his head. "We aren't equipped to handle an infant."

"Then I suppose she comes to the hospital. She can stay with me." Abby stood firm until the doctor gave her a look of exasperation.

"Sallie, it's best if Mrs. Lambert and I take your baby in for a bit." He nodded to Mama Ivy to bring the child to Abby. "She'll be taken care of."

"Reverend, pray for her first." Sallie's plea was barely above a whisper. "I'll take my punishment. But not the baby. She don't deserve this." When she could say no more, she turned her head. Tears trailed down her gaunt cheek. "I need to … make sure she don't have to pay for none of my wrong-doings."

"Babies are innocent." Ian knelt on one knee on the side of the bed to where Sallie wouldn't have to strain to see him. "They're all precious in God's sight. Same as you are. No one is beyond His forgiveness."

"Pray." Sallie implored with every bit of strength she had.

Abby stood on the opposite side of the bed holding the small bundle in her arms. Hickory sidled next to her, wide-eyed and somber.

"I'll pray." Ian opened his hand to her and was surprised when she placed unsteadily fingers on top of his. "But the most effective prayer for this baby will be from you, Sallie." Ian's other hand covered hers. "There's no sweeter sound in heaven than that of a mother praying for her child."

"God and me don't talk." Her hooded stare told him her time was growing short.

"Good thing He can read what's in your heart." A stab of truth pierced his own soul. "And He has a special fondness for broken ones."

At that, Sallie lifted her teary gaze to his, trying to focus on his face. Clearly, she searched for something solid in his words.

"There is nothing you've done that He isn't willing to forgive." Ian spoke quietly. "Nothing you do or say will ever make Him love you less."

Sallie began to weep. "My mama used to tell me He loves me."

Ian slowly nodded. "Your mama was a wise woman. He loved you then, and He loves you now. He's never going to stop. It's just up to you whether you're going to accept it and love Him back."

Sallie closed her eyes and trickles of moisture fell to the pillow. "Please, pray."

Ian prayed for her and for the baby. And when he heard Hickory's wrenching sobs, Ian prayed for him, too.

He asked for God's unmerited love and forgiveness on Sallie's behalf and felt her give his hand a faint squeeze. The smallest of gestures, but one that held great eternal consequence.

Upon the last amen, Ian realized Sallie's hand had gone slack. She'd crossed into eternity, but not alone. She had a Savior waiting to escort her there.

Ian stood and let Doc check her wrist for a pulse.

Mama Ivy made her way around the room blowing out all but two lamps. A soft rain had begun to fall, and the patter against the window added to the surreal mood.

"Is my Sallie gone asleep?" Hickory looked from Doc to Abby, a rise of panic in his voice.

Doc didn't answer, he simply shook his head.

"No! Mama, no. Don't leave me. I'll take care of you." The boy's cries felt like a punch in Ian's gut. "I'll be good, Mama, please come back."

Hickory threw himself across Sallie pleading for God to send her back.

Abby handed the baby to Mama Ivy and slipped an arm around the boy's shuddering back.

Without a word, Ian placed his hat upon his head and prepared to return to his troops.

Three years of theology and honors at the top of his class. Still, nothing had prepared him for this. When he left Yale, he thought he knew all there was to know about ministering.

But tonight proved he had much to learn about loving and caring for people.

Glancing back, he watched Abby hold Hickory in her arms, rocking him as his tears were spent. Renewed admiration for her soared through him. He'd been humbled beyond belief by the tender way she cared for Sallie—a woman who would have been shunned by most of his colleagues at seminary.

Abby's honest care for her was a crucial reminder that Sallie was every bit as valuable to God as anyone else in this city. He'd mastered Yale's academics and was skilled to the teeth in hermeneutics. But it took the unconditional love of a nurse with green eyes to show him how to tend to a real heart.

*"I try to avoid looking forward or backward,*
*and try to keep looking upward."*
*~ Charlotte Brontë*

# Seven

*A*n array of summer color splashed up against raised porches all along Mulberry Street. Abby had come to love that about Macon. The gardens were vibrant this time of year. Towering trees canopied over residential drives providing just the right amount of shade against the sweltering sun.

Most Sundays she enjoyed her walk to church, but barely a week had gone by since Sallie passed, and her heart was still heavy. Hickory hadn't come around the hospital like he usually did, and his duties had gone to others.

Abby missed him.

Since the Confederates suffered a decided defeat up in Northern Georgia, the hospital had been inundated with casualties. Her days, and some nights, had been occupied with tending to the wounded, preparing those able to be moved for transfer to Alabama.

She'd had no opportunity to go out to the shanty town to check on him.

Hickory's new little sister was thriving with the Lamberts even though Elizabeth had, at first, been hesitant to accept Sallie's baby into her home. As lovely and genteel as Elizabeth Lambert was, she feared the stigma of embracing the child of a public woman. Her sparkling reputation could ill-afford such a scandal.

Eliza Jane, however, had been smitten with the tiny infant from first sight.

One look at the baby's cherub face and she'd embraced her as if she were her own. Abby put together a special formula devised from a recipe in the latest medical journal to keep the baby fed and healthy. Eliza Jane provided the snuggles.

Abby hoped word had gotten out to the shanty children that the church was having dinner on the grounds today. Hopefully, they would gather down by the creek to meet her, in hopes of garnering a few leftovers.

She hoped to lure Hickory out of hiding as well.

Passing the General Store where the postmaster was located, a familiar sadness settled over her. There was no use going inside to check for news from home. She'd stopped expecting any months ago. Her correspondence had all but ceased since Farris put her every move under constant scrutiny.

The last letter she'd written to Mrs. Pearce was back in February a year ago after finding record that Malcolm had been stricken with smallpox, treated at Ocmulgee Hospital in Macon, then shipped back home.

Whether his mother had ever received the letter, or had simply chosen to disregard it, remained to be seen. As far as Abby knew, the woman still blamed her for the boy's disappearance in the first place. A source of uncertainty she struggled with, herself.

Since following Malcolm's trail to Georgia, Abby had been

given no choice but to stay. Most of what she earned at the hospital was in the form of room and board. With only a few coins of Confederate currency, she was unable to travel home without a pass issued by General Farris or his Provost Marshal. The general savored what limited control he had over her. He'd made it perfectly clear that as long as she was within his jurisdiction, he, alone, held the keys to her fate.

Abby wasn't willing to pay the steep price he wanted in return.

Until she could find another way home, she was stranded behind Confederate lines.

If not for favor granted by the Dobbs and Lamberts, she would have fled months ago. Elizabeth and Cora took her in and saw to it she never missed a meal. Eliza Jane had become a close friend who always found a reason to gift her with skirts or blouses whenever Abby wore the same one too often.

The women of Macon lifted a united front against Farris' harassment and each time Abby had been tempted to run away, they had reeled her back in with an abundance of kindness.

By the time Abby slipped into the back pew of the church, the congregation was well into the second verse of *Bringing in the Sheaves*. With great zeal they sang, impressing one another with having memorized all the words.

Cora Dobbs ended the hymn with her usual high-octave trill that never failed to give Abby a momentary eye-twitch.

Taking the pulpit, Reverend Baxter gave instruction for the people to be seated as he began his welcome.

Abby wondered if Colonel Saberton would be in service today. Though he'd never attended before, the ladies were providing a special dinner today to honor him and his men.

Before taking her seat, she took a casual look around but

didn't come across him.

Over the past month, all the church ladies had been sure to mention how charming Colonel Saberton was. How likeable and debonair. How he was never out of sorts and had a persuasive way about him.

You'd think the man was straight out of a classic fable.

Abby wouldn't deny she'd seen glimpses of it herself. He definitely had a charisma about him. But she couldn't help but wonder about the real man behind the glib tongue and easy grin.

The man she'd been with at Sallie's bedside. He had been exceptionally comforting and candid. He'd handled Sallie's imminent death with wisdom and a certain grace that could not be put on.

Maybe she'd misread him.

On the surface, he was every bit the self-assured colonel of a renegade cavalry. Strong and charming as he traded pleasantries with locals on the street. But when given the chance to try her new stethoscope, he'd revealed a curiosity, a hunger for knowledge, which she'd found much more attractive.

Abby wanted to believe she'd only seen facets of the man as a whole. A man she found herself thinking about throughout the day—and sometimes well into the night.

"... and the passage goes on to say, 'the people in one accord gave heed unto those things which Philip spake and saw great works in their midst as a result.'" Heads nodded all over the building among dozens of "amens" as the pastor closed his sermon.

Precisely eleven fifty-nine. Pastor Baxter was a stickler for routine. Abby imagined he'd done things the same way all eighty-something years of his life. He certainly wasn't about to change now.

No wonder Hickory hadn't been able to summon him or any of the other pastors in town to come pray over Sallie. In the past, they'd made it perfectly clear that the goings on in the red-light district were none of the church's concern.

Abby traced a finger over the pink satin flower on her hand-me-down bonnet as empathy for Hickory once again tightened her throat. The child had lost his mama. She'd always suspected Hickory was related to Sallie in some way, maybe an aunt or distant relative. But it had been a shock to learn that the young prostitute was actually his mother.

"My Sallie," she'd heard him say.

Every time Abby had been around them, Sallie distanced herself to the point of pushing him away. Her reasons were understandable. The brothel was no place for a boy of nine years old. Or anyone for that matter.

She'd insisted he call her Sallie for his own protection. If anyone, especially Farris, had suspected the boy belonged to her, Hickory would have been in immediate danger. Everyone was a pawn to Farris to be manipulated until they were no longer useful.

Then again, Hickory wasn't one to be rejected. Always around the corner, waiting to see if Sallie needed anything or if she might, by chance, want to see him for any reason. In his heart, she was his mama no matter what she wanted to be called.

Hickory had done everything in his power that night, frantic to see her taken care of. Calling upon all three ministers in town, but not one was willing to get out of bed. In desperation, he'd gone for Ian.

And Ian had answered the call.

The weight of his compassion for the boy caused her breath to catch.

Abby closed her eyes against unexpected tears stinging her eyes, still hearing the heart-wrenching wails of a child left with no one. Begging, as if everyone who deserted him did so of their own volition.

"Please stand for the blessing." The pastor's voice sounded even more monotone today. Or maybe, in the humor she was in, Abby simply refused to believe the man capable of feeling any emotion at all.

Spiteful thinking, deserved or not, wouldn't help the situation.

She'd need to pray about that.

As everyone stood, Lieutenant Fitz caught her eye from across the aisle and gave her a wink at having been caught with his eyes open during prayer. There, next to him, stood his broad-shouldered commander.

Ian glanced at her briefly with a lazy grin that made her heart skip a beat. She couldn't help but smile back.

Tall and freshly groomed, he held his hat in one hand and the other hand other rested easily on the hilt of his curved sword. He resembled an illustration she'd seen in Malcolm's literature book of a French musketeer. His mustache was closely trimmed with a thin patch down his strong chin. His longish hair curled at his collar with a fresh shine. Though worn in places, his black cavalry boots were polished to a high shine.

He looked as if he was born to lead men.

Her eyes rose to find him watching her and he held her gaze until her cheeks warmed and she looked away.

Flutters, not altogether unpleasant, took over her stomach. Only with concentrated effort could she avoid looking back again.

She should probably pray about that, too.

"Amen." As soon as the pastor finished his prayer, a couple of boys were the first out the door and the ladies all sprang into action. The grounds were set up for a Sunday social, which meant plenty of good food and fellowship.

The women spent most of yesterday cooking. Abby had gone by to help after her morning rounds. Before long, just like every other time, she ended up at the sink washing dishes instead. Which suited her just fine. She had no patience for cooking.

Nevertheless, these were some of the best memories she'd take from her time in Macon. It had been a long while since she was part of a family. She'd missed the laughing and teasing and sharing from the heart. Her adopted home in Ohio had moments where she'd felt included, but never to the degree she'd been accepted here.

Abby hung back as the rest of the congregation passed her by.

"Was that not the best sermon you ever heard in your life?" Cora, with Mable Lea by her side, made a bee line to block her escape.

Abby turned to exit the row from the other end.

"How would she know? She was busy makin' eyes at the Colonel." Eliza Jane hemmed her in before she could clear the back row.

Abby had no choice but to endure the interrogation that was sure to follow.

"I saw him looking at you." Eliza Jane had that droll look and sing-songy tone she took on when she thought she knew something no one else did.

"Who?" Abby received impatient smirks from all of them.

"Who do you think, silly?" Eliza Jane held the baby, stroking her hair with one finger. Clearly, she was not budging until she got the reaction she was looking for. "Colonel Saberton. And what's more, I saw you smile back."

That little tidbit got their full attention.

"Well, then, you must have eyes in the back of your head." Abby crossed her arms and lifted a brow at her. "Besides, church is hardly the best place to pursue a man."

"What better place could there be?" Cora waved her off with a flick of the wrist before dissolving into an artful fan flutter. "He can't run off, so he's yours for the taking."

"Abigail!" Elizabeth Lambert entered the sanctuary from the back. "Abigail McFadden!"

The pastor's mousy wife dashed in behind her wringing her hands, looking panicked.

Eliza Jane stepped aside and pointed to where Abby stood. Traitor.

"Abby what on earth have you done?" Elizabeth brushed past Eliza Jane and took Abby by the arm.

"I –I don't ..." Abby was trying to make sense of the sudden alarm. Was someone hurt?

"The mashed potatoes! Yesterday, when I told you to salt the potatoes, what did you put in them?"

Wracking her brain to remember, Abby began to recite what she recalled. "You said grab the salt off the shelf. I took the yellow can marked salt next to the baking powder. Your recipe called for a pound so I put it in there."

"No, no, no! Oh, merciful heavens!" Elizabeth headed for the window, looking out across the church grounds. "The recipe called for a pinch. P is not for pound, it's for pinch."

Cora fairly flew to Elizabeth's side. "Has it been served?"

"That's not the worst of it." Elizabeth's face turned ashen. "The recipe called for table salt. The blue can. The yellow can is Epsom salt. Abby, you put a *pound* of Epsom salt in the mashed potatoes."

Eliza Jane stifled a giggle behind her lace-gloved hand. "Epsom Salt? That's some stout potatoes. Doesn't father use that for—?"

"Yes! Good heavens, don't say it." Elizabeth's hands flew to her temples. "As soon as I had a taste, I knew there'd been a grave mistake. I took up the bowl before any more was served."

The ladies all returned to the window.

Whether Elizabeth wanted it said or not, Epsom salt was made up of magnesium sulfate, a well-known colon stimulant. And a pound could send a whole army to the outhouses for a week.

Abby only remembered seeing salt on the can. Kitchens were not infirmaries, why would Epsom salt be kept with the food products? *This* is why she hated to cook.

"Did you say it's already been served?" Cora practically screeched.

"Now, simmer down, Cora. We mustn't get upset." Elizabeth straightened her back. "They insisted the new colonel, General Farris, and Pastor Baxter be first in line. I'm afraid they had already gotten to the potatoes before I could."

"What'll we do?" The pastor's wife continued to wring her hands.

"Where are they?" Cora scoped her prey from the window. Quickly, she turned back to the other women. "Colonel Saberton hasn't taken a seat yet. Pastor Baxter is saying grace, and General Farris is seated at the head of the table by the rose bushes. He's already started eating, and the prayer isn't even over. The heathen. Eliza Jane, go tell Penny Jo to distract Farris. Do whatever it takes to get that plate away from him." Cora gave marching orders like a three-star general. "Sister

Baxter, go tell Pastor you need urgent prayer. Make him put down his plate and pray in earnest. Mable Lea, take his plate and dump it in the scrap pile while he has his eyes shut. Abby, you go distract the colonel. Shake your tailfeathers, that'll get his attention. Whatever you do, don't let him eat those potatoes!"

They all quickly disappeared, anxious to perform their duties.

On a heavy sigh, Abby glanced up at the hefty oak cross hanging on the back wall.

She supposed she'd need to pray about this, too.

*Lord, forgive my blunder and if any of them do by chance eat any potatoes, let them eat enough to get a good, thorough cleansing. Amen.*

There was just no good way to pray about such things.

*"It was her chaos that made her beautiful."*
~ *Atticus*

## Eight

" *T*hese Georgia women are loonier 'n a cock-eyed bean counter!" Fitz swiped at the gravy stain spreading down the leg of his gray trousers.

Next to him, another soldier agreed, raking collard greens from his hair.

Ian stood before his men at the head of the table, food everywhere but on their plates, trying to assess the cause of the mad commotion going on under the church's red-striped canopies.

Initial evidence pointed to Abby McFadden who appeared to have started it all when she'd sashayed pretty-as-you-please past his table with a come hither look in her eye. Every head at his table turned when she'd reached out and caressed Ian's cheek as she walked by.

None had been more stunned than Ian.

Just as Ian was about to call her back to find out what she was up to, a little woman with thick glasses came from behind and whacked his glass of lemonade over onto his food, sending the whole plate skidding into Fitz's lap.

The chain reaction was fast and fierce.

Ian leapt to his feet. Lemonade splashed in Fritz's eye. He flung a spoonful of greens onto the man next to him, who bobbed and hurled his chicken leg across the table knocking a coffee cup from the hand of another soldier, scalding two more down the line.

At the same time, over on the other side of the large tent, Ian caught sight of General Farris juggling his own plate and drink as he tried to fend off a bushy-tailed cat that scampered up his back.

Doc Lambert's youngest daughter, Penny Jo, whistled and the animal leapt from atop the General's head to settle in the girl's arms, accepting a piece of cheese.

In a pink frock, with her bonnet pushed back behind her neck, she looked the picture of innocence. No one would believe such a mess was orchestrated by the little girl with deep dimples.

On closer inspection, however, Ian watched Elizabeth Lambert toss her daughter a satisfied wink as she handed the general a dishtowel.

Over by the food tables, Ian noticed all the ladies wore similar looks of satisfaction. One or two openly giggled before hiding behind waving fans. If he didn't know better, he might suspect these fine ladies of executing a highly organized maneuver to completely disrupt the church social.

Ian bent to retrieve his plate from the grass, where a pup sniffed the soggy heap of food. Oddly, the dog turned up his nose and ran off, leaving the scraps untouched.

"Water! I've been poisoned!"

Ian spun to see General Farris red in the face, waving his empty goblet. Choking and sputtering dramatically, a large hunk of cornbread in his other hand.

"Nonsense!" Cora Dobbs approached his table with regal authority. "It's a new flavor of mashed potatoes. It'll probably do you some good."

"How'd he get mashed potatoes?" Fitz wondered aloud.

"Arsenic I tell you!" Farris hurriedly drained his cup and held it out to be refilled. "The bitter taste cannot be washed from my mouth. It's probably eating at my throat. Don't stand there gawking, you imbecile, go for the doctor!"

His trusty aide scrambled to his feet.

"Wait." Abby stepped to Cora's side where the older woman immediately tried to shush her. "There's no need to bother Doc Lambert. He has his hands full this morning. A mistake on my part—."

Mrs. Lambert rushed over to join the damage control. "We used a different kind of salt, General. Harmless, really. I take full responsibility because it happened in my kitchen."

"You!" Farris pushed back from the table, pointing a finger at Abby. "I should have known you were behind this. A Yankee plot to see me killed."

Ian moved to defuse the situation. Farris threw out some serious allegations. Were he to call for Abby's arrest, there wouldn't be much Ian could do to help her.

"General, there's no proof of ill intent." Ian kept his voice calm. "We are all witnesses and the ladies have offered their most humble apologies. They've given a perfectly reasonable explanation for your tainted mashed potatoes."

Farris looked like he was near to exploding.

If he were wise, he'd let the matter drop. It would do him no good to accuse the mayor's wife, and Macon's most affluent women, of lying to cover an enemy conspiracy. If he did choose to do something so foolish, he'd better have stronger proof than just a burning tongue.

"Abby's not a hateful Yankee. That's just silly." With the baby on her shoulder, Eliza Jane moved to stand next to her friend. "She's been in Macon just as long as you have. By now she's as Southern as you are."

Ian didn't miss the pained expression on Abby's face.

She wasn't capable of poisoning the general, of that he was fairly certain. But in Ian's opinion, she was still hiding something. If she didn't appreciate being called a Rebel, why was she here? Her reasons for being so far from home were worth questioning.

"Until I have a doctor's guarantee that I've not been poisoned, Miss McFadden's actions remain suspect." Farris snatched his hat from the table and elbowed his way down to where his horse was tied by the street.

"Oh, posh." Cora waved off his threat as soon as he was out of earshot. "He'll be sotted by dinnertime and won't remember a thing."

All the other ladies fell into a twitter of giggles.

Except Abby. The crease in her brow had her looking concerned.

Ian wanted to believe her. Still, the two highest ranking officers in attendance were the only two who'd been served the questionable potatoes. That certainly didn't help her cause.

The tides of war had begun to turn against the South. He wasn't prepared to dismiss any suspicious activity at this point. Even if it meant keeping a closer watch on a beautiful lady Yankee.

As if privy to his thoughts, she lifted her gaze to meet his. "Thank you." Though her words were silent, he read them easily from her cupid bow lips.

"Tempted, Colonel?" Mrs. Lambert asked from the other

side of him.

"I ..." Ian had to stop to make sure he hadn't expressed his thoughts aloud.

"Cake." She offered a large piece of chocolate cake on a china plate with pink flowers. "Might we tempt you with a bit of dessert."

Apparently, cake was the closest he was going to get to a full meal today, so he gladly accepted.

"Your men seem to be enjoying themselves." She smiled.

Many weeks they'd spent Sunday mornings around a campfire sharing scripture and favorite songs until each one drifted off into silence. For most, their faith was what sustained them.

"Today's a rare treat. The men were able to attend church and enjoy a homecooked meal, too." Ian couldn't remember the last time he'd had cake. This one tasted especially good. "But we still have plenty of work to do. I'll be rounding them up soon."

"Oh, but, Colonel, it's so good to see them playing horseshoes and laughing without a care in the world." Her unspoiled view of his soldiers both pleased and disturbed him.

Ian had to admit it was good to see them laughing. A beautiful day, delicious food with noisy kids running and playing, served as a good reminder of what they fought for. Hearth and home.

They'd be rejuvenated for days to come.

Unfortunately, too much of a good thing could backfire. He'd lose them to homesickness if he let them stay too long. A soldier constantly pining for home was a liability and a risk for desertion.

"Surely, you still observe the Sabbath in the army." Mrs. Lambert tilted her head and rose a questioning brow. "It is still a commandment, you know."

"Yes, ma'am." Although rest on the Sabbath had become a thing of the past. That particular commandment would have to wait until the war was over. "We just observe it in shorter intervals for now."

"Oh, my. Your smile is so like your mama's." Elizabeth Lambert seemed to enjoy his surprise. "But those shoulders and build is Samuel Saberton made over."

Now Ian was genuinely baffled. "I didn't realize you were acquainted with my family."

Mrs. Lambert laughed at that and he saw a glimpse of the girl she'd once been. "Everyone from the coastal plains of Georgia is acquainted with the Sabertons. My brother attended West Point with your father, and I must admit, I had quite a fondness for him when we'd go up to visit. He was witty and engaging and more handsome than a body had a right to be." She paused to look up at the feathered clouds drifting above. "Ahh, those were such innocent days."

Ian didn't respond, but let her savor her memories.

"You know, word had it, Samuel hailed from British royalty. I can certainly believe it." As if embarrassed at having spoken so candidly, Mrs. Lambert folded her arms and gave a small shrug. "But, alas, Dottie Ramsey came along, and no one else could ever light up those dark, shining eyes of his like she did. I was terribly sad to hear he didn't make it back from the Mexican war."

"Thank you. My mother still lives on our land upriver from Savannah. My brothers and I were fairly young when he died." Ian settled his hat on his head and looked out past the city to where the Georgia pines marched over rolling hillsides and onward to Brechenridge. An unexpected wave of homesickness washed over his own tattered nerves.

"Colonel, did you know that traitor, William Sherman, was

also in your father's West Point class?" Mrs. Lambert added with a stern dip of her head. "He was once stationed right here in Macon."

His mother had never mentioned Sherman, but then, Sherman had never been worth discussing.

"And I'll tell you another thing, your father wasn't the only one who found Dottie Ramsey utterly fascinating."

Now, that he could believe. She still had more than her share of admirers.

"Do you hear from your mother? How is she doing?" Mrs. Lambert asked.

"Doing well. I received a letter about five months ago. Just after Christmas. We've been mobile since then so I'm sure she hasn't known where to send a letter."

"You must write her right away and let her know you are right here in Macon." Mrs. Lambert retied the bonnet strings under her chin as she watched Abby clearing the tables. "And be sure to tell her you plan to stay awhile." She patted his arm with a motherly smile and left him to join her daughters under a tall shade tree.

Ian had actually written his mother last week to warn her to prepare the stables, for possible enemy raiders. Over a hundred of her select mares and five champion stallions would need to be relocated to keep the bluecoats from seizing them.

Last he'd heard, his sister-in-law, Tori, and her little girl were getting ready to take a trip to visit Nicholas in Charleston out at Fort Sumter.

If the Union pressed farther south into Georgia, the next logical move would be to cross the border into South Carolina. Charleston would be even more vulnerable than Atlanta had been.

Ian hadn't known about his father's association with Sherman, nor had he known that Sherman was so familiar with this part of the South. This would require more diligence in making out his report of recommendations for removing Confederate gold and assets to a safer location.

A movement over by the food table caught his attention.

Abby held up the ends of her apron to provide a basket as she filled it with biscuits and baked goods. Clutching the apron close to herself, she turned and disappearing into a clump of trees that led down to the creek below.

Ian narrowed his gaze, scanning the trees where Abby had vanished.

A commotion drew his attention to the horseshoe pit where clapping and cheering indicated that most likely someone had scored a ringer. When the crowd parted, Fitz emerged clasping his hands together on either side of his head in true champion form.

A dog barked excitedly, chasing a group of boys that ran after Penny Jo and her friends.

Ian spotted Abby slip back over to the food tables. This time she packed her apron with fresh fruit. And just as mysteriously, she again disappeared into the winding copse of trees.

Ian was determined to follow her this time.

Circling his way around the crowd, he traced her path, entering the shade of tall pines. He lost sight of her but headed toward the sound of burbling waters coming from a high creek. Once out from under the canopy of trees he had to shade his eyes from the sun reflecting brightly off the water.

Down by the water's edge, Abby doled out food to Hickory and several other children. Excited squeals followed as she filled their eager hands.

Awestruck by the tender smile she offered each one, Ian drew closer.

*"The door that nobody else will go in at,*
*seems always to swing open widely for me."*
~ Clara Barton

# Nine

❧

" **H**ello, Colonel."
Ian's scouting skills were slipping. He'd tracked Abby, taking extra care to remain unnoticed. But she greeted him the minute he stepped toward her. Almost as if she'd expected him to follow.

She didn't bother turning, but continued to fill a little girl's burlap bag. Ian counted four other children, including Hickory, devouring turnovers beside the stream. Straightening, Abby dusted crumbs from her apron while the child ran off to join the others. When she tilted her head, the brightness of the sun brought a fiery glow to her hair.

"Did you come on your own or did General Farris send you?" Her lips held no hint of a smile.

Ian was used to direct questions. He also knew when to answer and when to keep silent. Abby would have to come to her own conclusions about his motives.

His attention moved to where the children sat with their

bare toes in the water, eyeing him with open curiosity.

"Children, this man is Colonel Saberton." She cast a side-glance his way. "He's here with the army and is sworn to protect you."

The mixed bag of kids, every color and size, didn't look convinced until Hickory hopped to his feet and came to stand beside Ian. "He's the preacher I told you about. He came to help get Sallie to heaven. Abby likes him and so does Miss Tori." Spitting into his hand, he wiped it on the bib of his overalls before offering it to Ian as token of friendship. "The Rebs elected him a colonel. That's good enough for me."

Ian accepted. He hadn't forgotten the boy's bravery in helping Tori. Any half pint kid willing to take on Nicholas for her honor was a friend worth having. "As I remember, you're quite a sharpshooter with that slingshot." Ian pointed to the hand whittled weapon hanging from Hickory's back pocket. "Have you been keeping the Yankees at bay?"

"Yes, sir!" Hickory gave him a full-face smile and ran back to take his turnover from a boy who'd already helped himself to a bite.

"I'll see you all next time. Be good and mind Mama Ivy." Abby waved and turned to the woods that led to the church.

A chorus of goodbyes followed her.

Hesitating a moment, she looked to see if Ian was coming, too. "We may as well walk back together." Wisps of hair escaped her thick braid and fluttered across her face until she smoothed them neatly behind one ear. "Unless there's some other dangerous criminal you need to follow."

He had that coming.

Ian easily caught up and held aside a vine as they entered the dark awning of trees. The odds of her having purposely poisoned Farris just dropped considerably in his estimation.

Still, Abby was taking quite a risk to bring leftover food into the woods to feed a bunch of shanty kids. She had to know Farris would suspect her of aiding escapees. Backwoods areas were no longer secure. Runaways and deserters hid out in the shanty towns, always looking to find a way up north. Shanty towns were known for the type of lawless activity that went along with desperate men who had nothing more to lose.

If caught aiding them, Farris would have grounds for Abby's arrest.

"It's peaceful here, don't you think?" Abby stopped and scanned the towering pines surrounding them. The fallen needles beneath their feet muffled all other sound but their voices. "I come to this spot sometimes when I need some quiet."

There was much he wanted to know about her.

A large moss covered stone provided a place to sit. Something about the way she gracefully swept her skirt aside before settling down, told him she had once been accustomed to wearing much finer dresses than the simple work skirts she always had on.

Ian leaned a shoulder against the bark of an evergreen and crossed his arms. "Much quieter and less demanding out here than in the hospital, I'm sure."

"Yes, it is." She studied her hands clasped in her lap. "There are days the hospital is overwhelming." On a quiet sigh, she smiled. "I'm sure you've seen your share of suffering, too. I remember the battlefields."

"Where were you close to battle?" Ian pushed off from the tree to come closer to where she sat.

When she looked up at him her eyes reflected the verdant color of the forest around them.

"A year after the war began. I left where I was living to

look for someone. I came upon the aftermath of a Kentucky skirmish. The field surgeons couldn't keep up. I stayed for two weeks to help with nursing before moving on."

"That was very brave of you." Ian slid in beside her on the rock. "Who were you looking for? A brother ... or a beau, perhaps?"

She looked off into the trees and, for a minute, he didn't think she planned to answer.

"Colonel? Tell me, why I should trust you." Her honest request came in a breathless whisper.

It suddenly occurred to him that Abby had no idea how alluring she was. Otherwise, she wouldn't be alone in the woods with a man twice her size. Ian felt an obligation to protect her from her own naïveté. "If I were a threat, I would have asked whether the field surgeons you assisted wore blue or gray."

Abby ran a finger across her brow to tame a stray strand of hair caught by the breeze. Taking a deep breath, she looked up at the swaying branches above. "Fair enough." Her gaze returned to his and she gave a hesitant smile. "I was raised in a foster home in Ohio. By the time I was eighteen, I felt I was imposing on their generosity, so I took the position as governess to the twelve year-old boy of an affluent attorney. Mainly, because it provided a roof over my head. I soon found I enjoyed working with him. He was bright and curious with so much potential to become anything he set his mind to."

Ian stretched a leg out and rested his forearm on a knee.

The way she waited for his reaction to her account told him this was not a rehearsed script. She was being as honest as she dared.

"Three years ago, my charge, Malcolm, turned fourteen. The very next day, he disappeared. I found a note saying he'd run off to enlist. His mother was distraught, and absolutely furious at me." She shook her head slowly as if trying to remove the memory. "With good reason."

"Why?"

Abby frowned slightly as she studied the folded hands in her lap. "Malcolm was asthmatic—shamelessly coddled by his mother. I tried to encourage him to be more independent. To convince him he could do anything the other boys could do if he'd just get over being afraid." With a slight groan, she looked away. "What I failed to realize was that Malcolm had set his mind on going to war. He thought to win his parent's respect by coming home to a hero's welcome."

"So you ran away, too." Ian watched her closely and could tell immediately he'd struck a nerve.

"No, I went after him." The dare in her eye made him grin.

"Malcolm's nanny went traipsing after him?" Ian tried not to laugh, but couldn't help it. He imagined the reaction of his own troops if she'd marched into camp to drag a young soldier home by the ear. The poor kid would have taken less harassment in front of a firing squad.

"Governess." Abby corrected. "Nannies are goats."

Ian could tell she was offended.

"And stop laughing." She scooted farther down the rock.

"Abby, that was a reckless move—even for you." Ian enjoyed the bright color glowing in her cheeks and green fire in her eye. "What were you thinking?"

"I was thinking a boy had set out to do a man's job he was completely unprepared for." She was up on her feet with a hand on her slender hip. "And he really was sickly. His mother had a valid concern."

"All right, all right." Ian took her other hand and pulled her back down beside him. "What's done is done. Just tell me this. You obviously didn't find him or you wouldn't be all the way down here stranded in Macon. Assuming you are stranded."

"I am." Abby sighed heavily, before meeting his pointed look with a challenging one of her own. "General Farris refuses to sign my travel pass for the railroad and border barricades. So unless I decide to set out on foot and somehow slip past the guards, I can't leave. Working at the hospital gives me a place to lay my head, but I pray every day General Farris doesn't come up with some concocted reason to send me to prison."

Ian settled a fist on his thigh. The longer he was in Macon, the more he'd come to despise the city's highest commander. "Why do you suppose the general wants you arrested?"

At that, she shrugged and looked the other way.

Ian instantly knew he'd hit upon the crux of her dilemma. With a careful hand, he reached over to cup her chin, gently turning her face back to him. "What has he done?"

Again, she hesitated.

Ian got the feeling if she shared what she knew, it would be detrimental in the wrong hands. His thumb caressed her jaw. "You'll have to trust me."

He watched her inner struggle play out in the shadows of her face. Finally, her eyes lifted to his. "I may have caused him to lose a great deal of money."

"You may have? You don't know?" Ian's brow quirked.

"Not for certain." She moved her chin from his grasp. "But from what Sallie and the Dove's Nest girls told me, he's only bringing in a quarter of the amount that he had been before."

"Before?" Ian felt like he was on a winding trail up a steep mountain.

"Before they started keeping more of what they earned. Farris used to keep it all for rent."

"Wait, General Farris owns the Dove's Nest?" Ian was fairly sure that bit of information hadn't come up at the general's promotion interview.

"He owns most all of the red district. The women at the Dove's Nest all started out owing him money after he found them without a home or in the shanty towns. He offered them lavish loans, then turned on them. They were made to sign indentures of servitude to work off repayment." Abby's voice quieted and Ian could tell she was having second thoughts about confiding in him. "I suppose you already know how they are forced to work."

He needed to validate her story. If what she said was true, the general was in serious ethical violation.

"Why does he blame you?" Ian was still trying to put all the pieces together. How had Abby become involved?

"Well, when I had a look at their servitude contracts, I noticed they were only committed to four years of service. No specific amount of money was indicated that needed to be repaid, only an agreed upon term of service in exchange for food, clothing, and shelter."

A grin tugged at the corner of Ian's mouth.

"So I helped them figure a fair price to be paid for those necessities, and they handed that amount over every month." Abby tucked her hair behind an ear. "And ... they kept the rest."

She gave a small shrug as if it had just been that simple.

"No wonder Farris would like to put you away." Ian grinned.

"He hired some ruffians to intimidate the women into giving their full earnings, but I threatened to go to his commanding officer. I doubt he wants all of his dirty dealings brought out in a court of law."

"You are either extraordinarily brave or completely senseless." Ian wasn't certain which.

Abby stood and shook out her skirt. "I had no intention of reporting him. I wouldn't even know how to go about it. But someone needed to help them."

"So why does he insist you are a Federal spy?"

"He started intercepting my letters and quickly discovered I was from Ohio. He's been trying to sway public opinion against me ever since."

His gut told him every word she'd said was the truth.

Ian leaned forward with an arm across his knee, watching the wind ruffle her hair. Abby McFadden was a most peculiar female. Whatever circumstance she got herself into, she acted with all of her heart. Most times she dove in headlong without much thought, but with her heart just the same.

Noticing the sun lowering in the sky, he came to his feet. His men would be finishing up their field exercises by now. "Come on. You need to get back to the hospital before people start to talk."

Ian took her hand and led them back to the edge of the church grounds which was long deserted by now. A quiet rumble in the distance warned of an evening shower to come. No campfires tonight. The men would be forced to play cards or write letters inside their tents, which always made for a quiet opportunity to get caught up on his field reports.

Before they parted ways, Abby stopped him with a hand on his arm. "Ian?"

He liked the way she said his name. Glad she'd moved past calling him, "colonel." As if she'd finally come to regard him as a man not just another soldier.

Abby's serious expression caused him to pause.

"I do trust you." Her quiet confession warmed him. Made

him want to earn more of her trust. "And to answer your question, I didn't notice."

He had to think about what she was talking about.

"Most of the time the field surgeons had their jackets off while we worked. We saved men who wore gray and men who wore blue. It didn't matter what they had on. They were mortals in desperate need of care."

Abby let her hand slip from his arm and walked away.

*"I dream of a better tomorrow where chickens can*
*cross the road*
*and not be questioned about their motives."*
*~ Ralph Waldo Emerson*

# Ten

*A*s September progressed, the sweltering temperatures they'd experienced all summer were finally beginning to cool. The mass of green foliage covering the city had taken on touches of red, orange, and gold. According to the locals, the abundant rainfall Macon experienced this summer was a sign that winter would be an especially harsh one for middle Georgia. Some predicted they might even see some snow this year.

Abby missed winters back home in Ohio. Especially the Winter Carnival with long sleigh rides and wassail with nutmeg.

Winter was very different here.

Last year the church had put on a Christmas Festival complete with a nativity play put on by the children. Abby implored the church committee to include Hickory and the shanty kids, but was met with her first real taste of class discrimination. Watching the disappointment and hurt on their little faces, most not old enough to understand such rejection, had been like a thousand daggers to her heart.

Of course, she'd witnessed slavery and social segregation even in Ohio. Her father had been an avid supporter of treating all God's children as equals. Even the wild heathens who'd set fire to the mission that caused his death, Abby had no doubt, would have been considered brothers in her father's eyes.

Abby took her time walking back to the hospital. Transfer of the wounded from Atlanta had begun. Floyd House Hospital was full to capacity. Serious cases were moved to the larger Ocmulgee Hospital, such as the soldier she'd just accompanied there with gangrene destroying the flesh to his hip.

Abby was caring for triple the number of soldiers now than when she'd first come to Macon. There were days, she never stepped outside the hospital walls.

Today, she'd jumped at the chance to steal away for a few minutes. Especially thankful when Doc had suggested she stop by Harbor House for a bite to eat before reporting back for her evening shift.

As she rounded the corner from Mulberry to First Street, a gust of wind blew in from the south, whipping her skirts around her legs. Abby heard thunder roll in the distance as she surveyed dove gray clouds billowing up on the horizon with the promise of a cooling rain.

A sergeant on horseback, tipped his hat in passing.

Abby immediately wondered if he was one of Ian's men. All of Macon appreciated Saberton's cavalrymen. Ian demanded his troops treat civilians with courtesy and good manners. They were never intimidating or demanding like General Farris' officers could be. In both cases, she supposed, the unit reflected its leadership.

Thinking back on their conversation under the soaring evergreens, Abby couldn't help but think she might have divulged more than she should have. But she was a firm believer that everything happened for a reason. Ian followed her to where she met the children. They had been so excited to see her, mostly because she'd brought more food than they'd probably eaten all week.

It had been a chance for Ian to see them for himself.

The two of them had enjoyed easy conversation, and Abby was comfortable spending time with him. He was opinionated, and teased her freely, but he wasn't malicious or dishonest. On a whim, she'd decided to confide in him. If nothing else, she was glad to get it all out in the open. Other than the town women, who talked big but were essentially powerless against Farris' bullying, Abby hadn't spoken about it to anyone.

Now, she would wait and see.

If Ian Saberton was the man she hoped he was, prayed he was, he'd take what she'd told him and find a way to help her. Or if by chance, she'd grossly misjudged his character, she still wouldn't be any worse off than before. General Farris would still nip at her heels and look for ways to destroy her.

Crossing Cherry Lane, Abby noticed a commotion in front of the Lambert House on the corner. Both of Penny Jo's dogs barked in the yard with Eliza Jane standing between them, broom in hand and ready for battle.

Abby picked up her pace and called to her from the front gate.

Eliza Jane couldn't hear her over the ruckus, but she pointed at the front window and yelled, "That crazy cat is loose in the parlor again."

Abby hurried up the steps to see if she could help.

Elizabeth shooed the feline away from a tray of cheese and biscuits, scattered all over her cabbage rose rug. The nervous animal laid its ears back and hissed before clawing its way up the draperies.

Elizabeth quickly lifted the baby to safety from where she wailed in her cradle next to the sofa. Snuggling the infant next to her chest, she called for Penny Jo to come tame her pet.

Abby grabbed the fireplace poker, determined to steer the little troublemaker out the open window. Unfortunately, the dogs were making such a fuss under the window pane, the cat chose to hop a side table instead, knocking a brass oil lamp to the floor.

Elizabeth took an audible gasp as it leapt to the high mantle where it crouched low beside one of her grandmother's porcelain vases.

"Penelope Jo." Elizabeth's voice was low and strained, trying not to further upset the baby. "Get that demented creature out of this house."

"He's only scared." Penny Jo whistled but the cat didn't move. Moving around the fainting sofa, she held her arm up to the mantle. "It's all right, Mr. Whiskers. I won't let them hurt you." She cooed softly until the cat allowed her to pull him down into her arms, nibbling at a tea biscuit in her hand. "See? He just wanted a snack."

Through the window, Abby could see Eliza Jane swatting at a dog playing tug-of-war with her skirt.

"I don't care what he wanted, this house is no place for barn cats." Elizabeth motioned for Eliza Jane to come inside. "And I don't intend to say it again. Now put that flea-bitten animal outside and get up to your room this instant."

"Yes'm." Penny Jo left with her squirming companion, but not before making a face at Eliza Jane as she passed her in the doorway.

"Mercy sakes. I don't know how many times I've told that child not to bring home stray animals." Elizabeth handed the baby over to Eliza Jane and hitched her skirt to kneel beside Abby who was busy picking up scattered food off the rug. "One day I half expect to come home to a grizzly bear sitting at my dining table."

"Penny Jo's hardly a child anymore, Mama." Eliza Jane took the baby over to a rocking chair. "She's nearly ten. High time she stop acting like a boy and start actin' like a lady."

"She's still my baby." Elizabeth returned to her chair and jabbed a needle into her tapestry with an impatient hand. "You'll understand one day. It doesn't hurt a thing to let her enjoy her childhood while she still can."

Penny Jo was the last of the Lambert children to grow up and move on. Being a nurturer at heart, Elizabeth was determined to hang on to her little girl for as long as she could.

A grandchild would certainly help ease that void. Abby watched Eliza Jane talking to the baby with tiny fingers curled around her own.

Eliza Jane glanced up and caught Abby's eye. "Mama, did you know I saw Abby and that new colonel down at the creek a while back?"

Abby threw her a shrewd look.

"Alone." Eliza Jane continued with a mischievous gleam in her eye. "Just the two of them."

"How awfully observant of you." Abby laid the poker aside and dusted off her hands. "Considering you probably had to push through a horde of soldiers, leap over three tables, and borrow Mable Lea's spectacles to witness such a thing."

"Never you mind, I want to hear all about it." The excited look on her face told Abby she was happy to have something scandalous to talk about. "Did he steal a kiss?"

"Did he … No, of course not!" Abby felt her cheeks warm.

"Who's been kissing?" Penny Jo rejoined the group, scrunching her nose at the odd conversation.

"Colonel Saberton." Eliza Jane answered, rubbing the baby's back. "And Abby."

"You're horrible." Abby pointed to her friend, who rocked slowly with wicked grin.

"Well, if he didn't, he should have." Eliza Jane nestled the sweet head next to her cheek. "He missed a perfect opportunity."

"What, pray tell, went on in that thicket?" Elizabeth put down her needle and adopted her best mother's face.

As nice as it was to be cared for, Abby knew if Elizabeth suspected foul play, someone would answer for it. She'd be the first to inform Cora Dobbs and the Self-appointed Female Vigilantes would have them married by sundown.

Abby wouldn't let that happen. Ian had never been anything less than a gentleman.

But she knew she'd have to give them something else to chew on or they wouldn't let the matter drop. "I told him why General Farris has been doing his best to pin a spy charge on me."

"Penny Jo, I said go to your room." Elizabeth snapped.

"Aw, why can't I stay? I never get to hear the good stuff." The youngest whined as she flounced back out of the room.

"And I better not catch you listening through the cracks either." Elizabeth waited until she heard footsteps going down the hall. "Abby, dear, shut the door, and tell us everything."

Abby prepared herself for the endless questions to come.

As soon as the pocket door was pulled into place, both women beckoned her to sit beside them, encouraging her to finish her story.

"There's really nothing to tell. I hadn't planned on telling him, but it was apparent that Farris had already begun to fill his head with lies about me." Abby brushed a burnished curl from her cheek. "Ian followed me because he wanted to know the truth. I appreciate that he came directly to me."

"Mama, can Hickory come over for supper?" Penny Jo called from the other side of the door.

"Hush up, you goose, and get to your room." Eliza Jane called back causing the baby to startle. "What else, Abby? You didn't tell him the whole truth, did you?"

Elizabeth laid aside her needlework. "Is there more you two haven't told me?

Abby had never told either of them *everything* there was to know about herself. Even Eliza Jane didn't know her most guarded secrets.

Some things she must never tell.

"You told him the general propositioned you most inappropriately?" Elizabeth waved her fan to stir the warm afternoon air.

"No. I didn't mention that." Abby glanced at the clock on the mantle. She had ten minutes to get back to the hospital.

"And did you tell him you walloped Farris for it?" Eliza Jane asked.

Abby shook her head. "No, I might have spared him that detail, too." Moving toward the door, she decided to try and make a quick exit. "I'm due for my shift at five, so—"

"You can't just leave it at that." Eliza Jane stood and laid the sleeping baby back in her cradle. "Finish your story."

"That's about all there is to the story. Ian left me at the churchyard, and we went separate ways."

"Ian." Eliza Jane nodded at her mother, who nodded back.

Abby resisted the urge to roll her eyes.

"Don't deny that you find him attractive." Eliza Jane wasn't going to let it rest.

"He's not repulsive." Abby was finished with their questions.

"No, he definitely is not." Elizabeth set her tapestry in a sewing valise next to the sofa. "And I've seen the way he watches you."

Nothing escaped Elizabeth's notice.

Just thinking about his intense gaze caused a twinge in Abby's chest and a faint smile to cross her lips.

Elizabeth came over to where Abby stood by the door and took her hand. "Dear, there's no shame in admitting you're attracted to a man. I know you've been left alone too many times to count in your life. But don't be afraid to give your heart. When the right man comes along, you'll be able to trust him with it. And he will cherish your gift and protect it with his life."

Eliza Jane nodded in solemn agreement.

Abby felt as cornered as Penny Jo's cat.

They both expected her to make some grand confession but doing so would be pointless. Ian would never fall for a sworn enemy. Especially not one with Yankee ties that could tangle around his neck someday.

Releasing a pent up breath, Abby decided to give them just enough to satisfy their curiosity and hopefully leave her be. "Yes, the colonel is very handsome. I enjoyed talking with him very much. But that's all there is to it."

"Well, that's just plain silly." Eliza Jane was clearly put out that Abby wasn't going to fess up. "And I don't believe a word of it, Abby McFadden. No woman gives a man that much time in her day unless she's at least a little interested."

"Eliza Jane, we mustn't meddle." Elizabeth came to her feet and smoothed her skirt. "Abby doesn't owe us anything. She doesn't have to admit her feelings for the man to us, or him, or anyone else." The woman was an expert at casting guilt. "Granted, by the time she comes to her senses, he may be old and gray with a wife and fourteen grandbabies. But she absolutely has the right to deny it all day long."

This time, Abby did roll her eyes.

*"I cannot consent to place in the control of others
one who cannot control himself."*
~ Robert E. Lee

# Eleven

14 September, 1864

𝓜idmorning found Ian directing wagonloads of priceless cargo into storage sheds lined up behind the railroad depot. A constant procession of freight cars rolled in filled to capacity with furniture, family relics, and valuables from surrounding farms and plantations.

Middle Georgia newspapers reported blasts of gunfire heard as far south as McDonough. Hordes of defenseless civilians fled the countryside in fear of Federal raids.

The fall of Atlanta brought a sobering haze over Macon.

Ian dispensed twenty-three companies into the eight counties surrounding the area to bring in as many refugees as would come to seek shelter in the city. The trains began to arrive a week ago, teeming with anxious residents. While Macon's good citizens took in relatives and acquaintances, tents were set up to house those who could not secure rooms at a hotel.

"Colonel, a message for you from Mayor Dobbs, Sir." A

young courier stood on the other side of a pack of mules being led to the stables by one of Ian's horsemen.

Fitz, logging inventory at Ian's side, shook his head. "We're a little busy here, Son." Lowering his voice to a mutter that only Ian could hear, he added, "tell ol' mutton chops you'll see him at election time."

As always, Ian chose to ignore Fitz's commentary, reaching for the sealed envelope. His aide de camp was too useful to cite him for insubordination every time he opened his mouth.

A grin spread across Ian's face as he read the short message.

"They're bringing in a new commanding officer. Fitz, keep the men busy filling warehouses until I return."

Not waiting for a surly reply, Ian took up his jacket and began to roll down his sleeves. This was what he'd been waiting for. As he approached his horse, he glanced down at the note one more time.

*Report to the Dobbs House at once.*
*Governor has advised a change in command.*
*General Hawthorne to replace General Farris.*
*The Honorable Mayor Walter Dobbs*

Hopefully, Macon would be in better hands, and Abby could finally rest easier.

The letter he'd sent to Georgia's Governor Joseph Brown detailed the city's susceptibilities. Now that the Union had broken through the Georgia lines, it was Ian's opinion, and that of his commander, General Wheeler, that the Yankees would carry their campaign south.

The city's most glaring defect, Ian had advised, was the ham-fisted command of General Farris and the numerous threats he issued to his men and civilians alike on a daily basis.

Morale was low within Farris' camp. Ian observed no motivation among his troops to perform routine duties.
Statements were documented, under the guarantee of anonymi-
ty, that food and basic necessities were withheld as petty
punishment, dependent largely on the mood the general found
himself in at any given moment.

A high rate of desertion had been recorded, as well as an
unthinkable number of Farris' soldiers who had applied for
exemption to escape another year of service.

The citizens refused to heed his relentless orders. He seized
property and dry goods at will, with no record for payback.

Governor Brown had been a friend of the Sabertons long
before his four terms as presiding officer of the state. A
respectable attorney and conscientious statesman, Brown was
one of Nicholas Saberton's most trusted friends. Though not
always popular, the family shared the governor's middle of the
road views.

Nicholas had become a popular voice at the Governor's
mansion as he stood against secession with Brown, and many
other governors over the southern states. They proposed to let
the process of democracy strengthen the laws and ultimately
weed out the greed and injustices that split the country.

Ultimately, to no avail.

Governor Brown had expressed hopes that Nicholas would
one day take a government position, but as far as Ian knew, his
brother had no political aspirations.

On Ian's suggestion, the governor had hopefully sent Farris
back to the battlefields.

From high in his saddle, Ian spotted Abby a block away in
the wide yard of Floyd House Hospital. Under a sprawling
oak, she helped a man stand from his wheelchair to sit on a
granite bench. When she smiled up at the soldier, encouraging

him to take a step, he gave it a try with no argument.

Drawn by her compassion, Ian reined in. Sitting a minute, he watched her unnoticed.

A white sling holding the man's arm prevented him from holding a pen, so Abby knelt on the grass, primly tucking her skirt around her, and used the bench as a writing desk to write a letter as he dictated.

To most the kind gesture would seem an unimportant detail. But to Ian, her selfless desire to serve the man with her full attention stirred him deeply.

Abby pulled a thin shawl closer around her shoulders. The breeze had turned cold. Still, she smiled patiently, allowing the young soldier to unburden his heart into a letter back home.

Nudging his horse, he continued on.

Hopefully, in this new change of command, Abby would find relief from Farris' constant harassment, and maybe even receive the documents she needed to get back home.

The intensity of that thought caught him off guard.

He didn't want to think about never seeing Abby again. Truth was, he enjoyed her company. He'd sorely miss their evening strolls as they walked over to Harbor House for dinner each evening.

The way she smoothed her hair away from her face as she spoke so adamantly about the orphans. The way she smiled, just barely but honestly, if her hand accidently brushed against his. So many things he would miss about Abby McFadden.

Still, he'd let her go, just the same.

The war stripped him of any misconceptions he'd had about love. He simply wasn't capable of giving love the way Abby deserved. She should be free to go back home to Ohio. Marry herself a doctor, or attorney, or some ruddy-nosed cleric destined to be a saint someday.

His mood had soured by the time he pulled up to the group of horses gathered in the road out front of the Dobbs House. Ian dismounted and took the steps two at a time.

As soon as he removed his hat in the hallway, he heard a heated conversation coming from the back dining area where Farris had set up office.

"This is outrageous! I will not be sequestered away to guard Yankee vermin while your bother-in-law steps in to take credit for everything I've worked for here in Macon." By the time Ian walked into the room, Farris was in a red-faced rage. The mayor beckoned him to join them. "And if I find out you've had anything to do with this Saberton, I'll—."

"Hold your tongue, Farris." Another general stood at the mayor's right with his assistant taking meticulous notes at the table. "I'd be careful about further incriminating yourself with slander. These minutes will be sent to the Secretary of War for permanent record."

Farris's jaw slammed shut, and he fell hard into his seat.

"Colonel Ian Saberton, meet General George Hawthorne." Quick with the introductions, Dobbs ignored Farris' scowl. "George is our new commanding officer in charge of overseeing Macon."

"General." Ian gave an easy salute which was immediately returned.

"Meet Cora Dobbs' brother." Farris crossed his arms over his protruding belly.

"George has led his men through many a victorious battle throughout the Eastern theater. A general most worthy of our respect." Mayor Dobbs sat at the other end of the table from Farris. "It took some convincing, but George finally agreed to come home to Macon."

General Hawthorne sat next to his aide. "Have a seat,

Colonel."

"Thank you, Sir." Ian removed his gloves and pulled out a chair across from Hawthorne.

"I'm sure General Wheeler has you busy with special missions, so I won't keep you." It wasn't hard to detect family similarities between Hawthorne and Cora Dobbs. Their no-nonsense manner and prominent brow mirrored one another. "I've heard glowing reports of Saberton's Cavalry. Fast and elusive. Expert trackers with all the courage and bravery of young lions."

Ian laughed at the whimsical interpretation of his regiment. They were all risk-takers and a few were half wild. Because of it, they followed him into impossible situations without question.

"I can't tell you how impressed I was at hearing your regime intercepted not one, but two raids headed for Macon in August. Sherman was sent back to Atlanta with his tail between his legs." General Hawthorne tapped a pencil against the table to emphasize his words.

It was not common knowledge that his cavalry had been the main deterrent on that mission. But Ian was pleased that Hawthorne had taken the time to read his briefings.

"I will convey your kind regards to my men, General."

"You are very well-spoken. Where did you attend school?"

The man taking notes paused and pushed his spectacles up on his nose, looking over at Ian for the first time.

Farris pounded his fist on the table. "What has this got to do with my removal from this post?"

He reminded Ian of a child not getting his way.

"Yale University, Sir." Ian didn't usually discuss those days, but he took an immediate liking to General Hawthorne. "Divinity School actually."

"Ahh! A man of the cloth." General Hawthorn also appeared to ignore Farris's tantrum. "I imagine you are called upon to speak regularly for our troops."

Ian remained silent.

He'd not offered a sermon since giving up the Chaplaincy early in the conflict. "Gentlemen." Farris's nostrils flared like an angry bull. "Shall we?"

"Certainly. You are reassigned to oversee the prisoners at Camp Oglethorpe. I will be taking over your duties, in addition to others, here in Macon. Captain Cuyler will remain as Arsenal Commander, as will the laboratory stay with Lieutenant-Colonel Mallet. Colonel Saberton remains in charge of Special Forces."

"Outrageous!" Farris again took up his tirade. "I shall write to Brown, myself."

"The changes were instigated by Governor Brown with full cooperation from the Secretary of War." General Hawthorne smoothed his long graying beard, and Ian could almost swear he had done so to cover a smile.

"Camp Oglethorpe is overrun with blue-bellies. Not enough resources to feed and house the ones they have. They're expecting hundreds more in days to come." Farris had resorted to whining.

"Then, I suggest you get creative and find some solutions, Farris." General Hawthorne flipped through some documents in front of him, clearly not pleased with the role he'd just inherited. "We do what we must to see this war come to a favorable end. Rally your troops and put your best foot forward. Or your next reassignment may have you peeling potatoes in a mess tent."

The closing of the front door reverberated down the hall and energetic clicking of heels pattered against the wood floor.

"Walter? Georgie?"

Cora and an entourage of ladies marched in with wicker baskets dangling from their arms. "We've come bearing goodies to welcome our new General."

Every man stood out of gentlemanly respect.

With great fanfare the women each laid their basket on the table nodding at the general and his assistant. Ian was the only one who noticed Farris grab up his hat and leave the welcoming committee to their task.

Mayor Dobbs reached for a sugar biscuit, and Cora shooed him back with a lace-gloved hand. "Just for the soldiers, Walter. We've made plenty extra at Harbor House. I'll see some are put aside for you."

"Ladies, this is indeed a treat. Thank you. And for the next several weeks, we look forward to making Macon our home." General Hawthorne prompted his assistant with a shuffle of his boot.

"Y-Yes, ma'am. Thank you." The young soldier sounded like he was from the backwoods.

Most likely fresh from a schoolyard somewhere. His grin widened when Cora removed a slab of brown sugar fudge just for him.

"Speaking of Harbor House, Colonel, I believe it's just about time you meet Abby for dinner." Cora clasped her hands in front of her.

Bonnets bobbled all over the room.

"So it is." Ian was grateful for a reason to be dismissed. "General, if that's all?"

Saluting with one hand, a sweet roll in the other, Hawthorne gave him permission to leave.

On his way out the door, Ian looked up at the clear blue sky. He couldn't help but offer a word of thanks. For the

Governor's quick response. For sending a commander that met with the ladies' approval. For a more secure Macon.

Glancing toward the hospital, Ian settled his hat low on his head.

Most of all, for answering Abby's prayer.

*"It's a matter of taking the side of the weak against
the strong,
something the best people have always done."*
~ Harriet Beecher Stowe

# Twelve

*M*acon quieted for the evening, just as things were getting
busy at Harbor House. By five o'clock, soldiers in
transit and officers from every division were seated to enjoy a
home-cooked meal.

Abby saw weariness on every face, even so the men remained courteous, grateful for a respite from camp fare. As
usual, the ladies worked tirelessly to see them fed and encouraged before sending them on their way by seven.

Tables were cleared, and the noise of hungry soldiers
waned. Only the sound of cicadas high in the trees, buzzed
through the open windows on the cool night air where Ian and
Abby were the last ones seated.

Under the watchful eyes of the ladies washing dishes in the
kitchen and wiping down tables around them, she knew this
was a safe place to enjoy his company without compromising
her reputation. She had no parlor to entertain guests and the

hospital lobby was closed to visitors after six p.m..

Here at Harbor House, a table for two was always set up for them in the back corner with a vase of fresh flowers. Quaint and beautifully furnished, every room in the house had been transformed into dining space. Sofas and armchairs were laid out in groupings against the walls and in front of the fireplaces. Perfect for the men to relax with a cup of coffee and a piece of Eliza Jane's pecan pie.

The kitchen out back had been expanded and the carriage house provided covering for tired horses.

The front door swung open and Mayor Dobbs came through with his acting city manager, who was at least ninety years old—too old to serve in battle but eager to contribute, nonetheless.

"Cora, I'm back, dear." The mayor called toward the back then turned to shake the old man's hand. "I believe that's the last of our business, Ned. Go on back and see if there's any pie left before you go."

Closing the leather binder in his hand, the mayor strolled over to Abby's table. "As you know, our esteemed president, Jefferson Davis, will be here in Macon to give his speech from the train in one week." He accepted a steaming cup of coffee from one of the women. "George has given his approval for the Harvest Festival to go on as scheduled in October."

Abby watched a look of doubt cloud Ian's expression. "Supply trains have become scarce. Even the ships are having a hard time getting their cargo this far north." He leaned forward with arms on the table in front of him. "By then, we may not have anything coming in at all."

A newspaper man followed Walter inside and took notes at another table.

Mayor Dobbs approached him, and shook the man's hand

with a pat on the back. "According to our polls, most Maconites were against celebrating Harvest this year with so many farms out of commission. Folks have become weary of this conflict. But as I always say, when faced with hardship, all the more reason to celebrate."

Abby took a sip of her coffee to keep from saying what she was thinking.

The mayor needed to take a field trip to Atlanta to see what hardship was really all about.

"We must celebrate." As if to draw an audience from the ladies lingering in the dining rooms, Mayor Dobbs became animated, talking with his hands. "We must keep up the morale. It's up to us who remain on the homefront. We must see that life goes on as usual."

Stunned, Abby bit back the questions that immediately formed on her lips.

What, exactly was usual? Overnight, the country became divided, so thoroughly torn apart that nothing was usual anymore.

Her beloved country would never be the same.

Abby rubbed her arm as a shiver of apprehension chilled her to the bone.

"I was hoping I could count on you to serve on our Christmas Pageant committee this year, Abby." Walter Dobbs stood smiling at her.

"Christmas?" Abby looked from the mayor to Ian who leaned back in his chair. How could he even consider elaborate Christmas festivities this year?

"Yes, of course. You're very well thought of here, and we all know you have a way with children. Mrs. Horace Parker fell ill and has declined the opportunity to direct the play this year, and—."

"Mayor, you do realize there is a very real threat bearing down on your city, do you not?" Ian frowned.

"Well, yes, certainly. I'll leave that in George's capable hands. In the meantime, folks need a diversion." He brought a fist down into his other hand, side-glancing at the newspaper man. "As long as I'm mayor, I'll see that our good citizens are not deprived of the small joys they're accustomed to here in Macon."

"I'm sorry, Mayor. The hospital is overflowing with wounded. I'm much too busy right now." Abby kept her expression closed. As long as Hickory and the shanty town kids weren't welcome to participate, he'd have to find someone else to be on the committee.

"Abby, I do wish you'd reconsider." The mayor took a chair at the table across from theirs. "Cora, make her reconsider."

Cora entered the room from the back, putting on her satin gloves. "Walter, she turned you down last year, too. And you know why." Tying her purple hatstrings under her chin, she came to stand next to Ian. "We all love Abby, but she's stubborn as a mule. Especially when it comes to those little ragamuffins she's so fond of out at the shanty town. That's what this is truly about." Clicking her tongue, she gave Abby a scolding shake of her head. "Until Walter agrees to let *all* children in the area be included in our Christmas Pageant, including that little scamp Hickory, she refuses to lift one finger to help."

The mayor joined his wife in shaking his head. "If Macon is going to survive all this unpleasantness, we must take a strict approach to protect our population. Letting those hooligans loose on the city would be asking for lawlessness to abound. I'll not have it."

"How does a nine-year-old pose a threat to Macon's population?" Abby removed the napkin from her lap and tossed it to the table. "We're talking about children here, Mayor."

The mayor gestured helplessly to Ian. "She's completely unreasonable."

"I admire her determination." Ian finished the last of his coffee and set the cup on the table. "Abby's passionate about what she believes in and sticks to her convictions."

"Where there are questionable children, Abigail, there are questionable grown persons." Cora's familiar argument was grating.

"It's a Christmas play for pity's sake. Where is the goodwill?" A thick curl fell across Abby's cheek and she swiped it behind an ear. "The children have no say in the difficulties they're born into. Truthfully, it's my hope that once the children become involved, the questionable grownups *will* follow. Isn't that what Christmas is all about?"

When she glanced over at Ian, he nodded with an arm casually hooked over the back of his chair. Something in his indulgent grin bolstered her courage.

"And I'll tell you another thing. I hope to see every person in this county given an equal opportunity to worship together in that church of yours one day." Her daring words were about as effective as whistling in the wind.

Cora ignored her completely. At least they didn't seem inclined to string her up for speaking her mind like Farris would.

"Maybe we should put her on the election ballot." The newspaper man laughed as he put his notepad in the front pocket of his jacket before walking out the door.

Abby had forgotten the man was in the room.

Now, Walter Dobbs looked dejected, and Cora scorched

her with an angry glare.

Abby went to where Cora spread a fine lace shawl about her shoulders. She'd need to appeal to her good qualities to get out of this mess. "Cora, you've been so wonderful to me. Please, don't think I'm ungrateful. You've shown me such kindness." Cora turned from Abby, throwing one end of the shawl over her shoulder with dramatic flair. Clearly, she was going to make Abby work harder for her forgiveness.

"You're charitable and generous. And you truly love the people here."

Again, Cora turned from her. Abby persistently followed. "So, I know you understand that banishing the children just because they live in shacks outside of town is heartless."

Cora continued to smooth the lace, dismissing Abby as if she were a pesky fly on the wall.

Her impertinence finally worked Abby's dander into a dither, as her father used to say. Resting a hand on either side of her waist, she stepped in front of both Cora and Walter as they prepared to leave. "Do you even care that those babies go to bed hungry every night?"

"Abby ..." Cora's gave an exasperated sigh. At least she had the woman's attention. "I agree. It's a sad state of affairs those children find themselves in." Cora gently pushed Abby's shoulder aside to clear her path so she and Walter could be on their way. "Most every soldier in camps all over the land are going to bed hungry tonight, too. It's a shame, but until the last battle is over, I'm afraid this is their plight."

"Soldiers are grown. They signed up for this. The children did not." Abby's huff was highly unladylike as she pursed her lips. Her indignant look was lost on them, however, as Walter hurried to follow Cora out the door.

They never looked back.

After a long minute, Ian picked up his hat and well-worn gloves. "Come on. Let's walk." Abby took a deep breath. Her temper had gotten the best of her again.

This wasn't Ian's fault that the children weren't going to be invited to the Christmas Pageant again this year. Unfortunately, he'd had to witness her rant just the same.

She really should apologize for snapping at Cora.

"Irish?" His question took her by surprise as they stepped out onto the porch.

"Me?" Of course, he was talking to her. Abby felt her cheeks warm. "Yes. My father was Irish."

"I should have known by the way your hair takes on strands of burnished copper in the light o' the sun." His flattery came in an impressive Irish clip.

"Lovely to look at whilst waiting for a wee bit o' wisdom ta turn it gray." The memory of her father's favorite saying made her smile in spite of a need to be annoyed.

Ian unhitched his horse and led him along as they walked back to the hospital. "That would explain your fiery temper." Ian had the audacity to wink at her.

Abby put on a scowl to tell him what she thought of that.

When he laughed, she sucked in her cheeks to keep from smiling, which made him laugh all the more.

The night sky was enchanting with its vast glittering of stars. A cool breeze ruffled her hair, sending unruly curls stirring around her face. With so many camps lit up surrounding the city, a warm glow haloed the outbuildings at the far end of the street.

Without warning, the smell of smoke assaulted her nose and a familiar rise of panic gripped her throat. The air was thick from smoldering campfires on every side.

"Abby?" Ian stopped and steadied her with an arm around

her shoulder. "What is it?"

Embarrassment flooded her as she fought to regain her composure. "The smoke." Her mouth had gone dry. Running her tongue over her lips, she tried again. "I guess it caught me by surprise."

"The smoke from camp? Are you bothered by it?" Abby didn't have to look up to know he was concerned.

"No." She quickly reassured him. "I mean, yes, it bothers me. But not how you think."

She'd give anything to take back her unreasonable reaction. Talking about her childhood fears was something she avoided at all costs.

"Then, why did it shake you?" Ian's question was low. The warmth of his arm around her was as comforting as a soft blanket.

Her resolve to keep her reasons to herself shattered the moment her eyes met his.

Moonlight reflected in the dark depths and she was unable to look away. "My mother and father were killed in a fire that destroyed the small village where we lived. I don't remember much, I was very young. But I do remember the smell. I couldn't get away from it. Couldn't wash it from my hair." Her explanation came in a breathless whisper, not entirely the fault of smoke.

Ian wrapped his other arm around her and pulled her into a warm embrace.

Years had passed since she felt as secure as she did in that moment. Closing her eyes, she tried not to move, content to simply rest in the safety of his arms.

"Tell me about them." Ian stepped back and she immediately felt the void. Folding her arms in front of her to replace the warmth, she resumed their walk, keeping her attention on the road ahead.

"My father was a trained physician but had a proclivity for ministering. My mother was a natural care-taker. When they married, they applied to the missionary council, and set out to build a mission for the Indians in the mountains out west." Abby's memories of them were rare. Mostly, the conjured images in her mind were figments of her own imagination. She'd lost the ability to remember actual details of their faces a long time ago.

"You mentioned they were killed. Indians?"

"There was an Indian uprising. The mission was burned to the ground." Abby told it as if she were retelling a story she'd once read in a book. "I'd gone with Brother Benjamin, a young novice missionary, to get food and supplies from the fort nearby. As we came back over the rise, we saw huge black billows of smoke. The mission was fully engulfed in the valley below."

That image was forever burned into her memory.

"And your mother was with him?" Something akin to sadness shone in Ian's eyes.

"She was." Waves of sorrow still washed over her when she thought about them. Her life would have been so different had they lived. She would have stayed out west and had their love to guide her. "My mother taught the Cayuse children, and they adored her. She was a model of human kindness."

"Much like her daughter." Ian would never know how much his casual remark meant to her. "You were their only child?"

Abby gave a slight smile. "Yes. My mother used to say that I was a special gift to her by God. He'd given her a dream that she would one day have a red-headed angel. She said from the first moment she laid eyes on me, she knew her dream had been fulfilled."

Up until four years ago, Abby couldn't tell the story without choking up. She wasn't sure if she had matured over time or just grown more impervious to its affect.

"My hair has lost most of the red I was born with. It's more golden like my mother's now." She gathered the thick braid down her back and brought it over her shoulder.

"How did you end up back in Ohio?" Ian's horse tossed his head, wanting to stop and have a taste of the grass.

Abby pulled her wrap tighter around her shoulders. "After my parent's death, I became a ward of the church. My father had no family in this country and my mother's family was scattered. I briefly stayed with the local minister and his wife, but they were older and ready to retire. They were not prepared to take in a grieving six-year-old."

"So they gave you up?" Ian's brow furrowed.

"I ran away." Abby answered quietly. She'd been so young and disillusioned. She'd gone searching for a life that didn't exist anymore. "I was placed twice more before staying with my foster family at thirteen."

Abby lifted the hem of her skirt and stepped lightly over a rut in the road. Those were lonely years she'd put out of her mind.

She felt him looking down at her as they walked. "Why did it take four tries to find you a suitable home?"

Abby shrugged and tucked a stray curl over her ear. The truth was the truth. There was no way around it. "I kept running away."

Pointing to the sky, she made an attempt to change the subject. "Oh, look! A falling star." In the limitless universe up there, surely a star must be falling somewhere. She cut her gaze to see if he was following her new train of thought.

Ian's lips quirked at her lame effort. "We can talk about the running away another time." He spoke louder to be heard above the clop of his horse's hooves when they turned a corner and the dirt road became brick. "I'd like to go with you to visit the shanty town."

Abby stopped abruptly.

He shouldered the horse to keep him from running them over.

"You would?" Abby had to keep herself from becoming too excited. Maybe she hadn't heard him right. No one ever wanted to go with her out to the shanty.

"I would." Ian urged her on with a nod of his head.

"We can go tomorrow. My shift ends at midnight tonight. I'm on surgery duty at seven in the morning, but we should be done by noon. I won't have to be back until nine."

"Hold on." Ian laughed. "Tomorrow I have plenty to do. Maybe some—"

"Tomorrow." Abby smiled up at him, nearly beside herself with excitement. "I'll have Eliza Jane pack us a lunch and we can eat along the way."

"All right, Angel. Tomorrow."

Abby froze.

No one had called her Angel since the last time she'd kissed her papa goodbye.

~

Not sure if it was her unwavering confidence in him or her infectious smile, but Ian finally relented to go with her out to the shanty. General Wheeler was expecting a headcount from the surrounding settlements, so this would not be a trip wasted.

"They are good children. Most are war-orphaned except Hickory." Abby strolled leisurely beside him as she continued to talk. "They are healthy. Mama Ivy and I have seen to that. Essentially, they'd make a loving addition to anyone willing to give them a home. But how will the people ever see what wonderful children they are if they're shunned from every event?"

The sincerity shining on her face humbled him.

Abby wasn't asking for great amounts of money or fame to further a career. She only hoped that every child be given a chance to find love and acceptance.

A passing carriage caused them to move closer to the walkway.

"Generally orphaned children are taken in by family and friends. But those with no particular pedigree or surviving relatives have been left to themselves. They end up like these kids, abandoned and alone." He liked the way Abby reasoned things aloud. She had a quick mind and a compassionate heart. "The church is fragmented. In no condition to care for them. Unfortunately, the war continues to add dozens more orphans by the day."

Ian could easily see her concern. "Promise me you'll give it time. All the good intentions in the world won't transform centuries old problems in a day." Ian spotted a lady peering at them from her parlor window. She waved with a pleased smile. "Only a deep change of heart can bring about the difference you envision."

"Yes, but they haven't the luxury of time." Abby's shoulders fell with a heavy sigh. "Hickory's nearly ten years old. The army's determined he's eligible for the draft in five years. Two older boys don't know from day to day what their fate will be."

Without thinking, he took her hand and tucked in the crook of his arm. "Keep advocating for them, Abby." He searched the starless sky. "Maybe God made you stubborn as a mule for a reason."

Abby cast an impish grin his way. "If it makes things better for the children, Cora can call me whatever she likes."

A low chuckle rumbled in his chest as they stopped at the steps of the hospital. "See you tomorrow then."

On impulse, Ian ran the back of two fingers down the delicate curve of her cheek, enjoying the silken contour of her skin. Smoothing a stray wisp of hair from her eyes, he tucked it behind her ear as he'd seen her do so many times.

Abby turned her head into his touch.

"After drills in the morning, I'll meet you at the stables about noon." Ian let his hand drop to his side.

"I'll be over as soon as I'm free. And thank you." With that, she stepped away and disappeared through the hospital entrance.

Ian watched her leave, then swung up into his saddle. "Quite welcome, Angel."

Gently prodding his horse, he turned toward camp.

*"It is easier to build strong children than to repair broken men."*
~ Fredrick Douglass

# Thirteen

*L*ifting her face to the sun, Abby took in living, breathing color in every direction.

Fields of emerald green grass with soaring southern pines lined the western horizon against a cerulean blue sky. Orchards to the left were laid out in rows with brightly colored leaves dotting their branches surrounded by rolling hills, teeming with trees in various stages of yellow, orange, and red.

The fifteen minute ride just northeast of the city didn't usually take an hour, but every so often Abby would see a look of concentration come over Ian's face as he slowed the horse and buggy. She could only imagine the responsibility he carried in keeping a step ahead of the Union armies. Knowing the safety of every person occupying this area was on his shoulders.

Abby was thankful he'd agreed to come with her at all.

Watching Ian look over this country, Abby could easily see the pride he took in this beautiful land he called home.

"If I remember, it's just up the road here." Ian surveyed the hills to the north.

"Yes. That wagon trail just beyond this field leads to a train trestle." Abby pointed with her gloved finger. "The shanty town is set up below. The shacks are so close to the tracks, it's deafening when a train crosses over."

"Dangerous for a bunch of kids to be playing under." The irritation in his voice was unmistakable.

This was as good a time as any to ask him about something that was bothering her. "Ian, the army would never use the shanty children to do anything dangerous, would they?" She shaded her eyes with a hand to take in his response.

Ian pulled in the reins and pushed his hat back on his brow. "No, of course not. What makes you ask?"

"I don't know it for a fact, but Hickory said a while back some soldiers approached the boys about carrying explosives for them. Apparently, they're the only ones who could fit in the crevices of the trestle and ferries. Surely, the army doesn't plan to blow up bridges with people living beneath them. They offered the boys a dollar per explosive. That is a lot of money to these children who have nothing."

"Abby, are you certain?" Ian turned the horse's head from grazing with his reins and gave a nudge to keep him moving.

"Ask Hickory about it. He can give you more details." Relief flooded her at hearing Ian's men were not the ones who'd approached the boys. Abby couldn't rest until she knew they would be safe. "Who do you think they were?"

A frown creased his brow. "I can say for certain they weren't Rebs. My men are the only ones responsible for destroying the railroad lines around here. But that won't happen until there's a clear danger of Federals moving in. And never if any children are around."

"Well, that only leaves deserters or ..." Maybe if she didn't say it aloud, it would keep them from coming.

"Or the Union army." He said it for her as he quickened the horse's pace.

They rode in silence the rest of the way, each deep in their own thoughts.

Having seen firsthand what explosives could do to a grown man, she refused to consider what they might do to a boy Hickory's size. What kind of man would ask a child to take such a risk?

When the trestle bridge came into sight, Ian slowed the buggy.

"Down there." Abby let the wretchedness of the place speak for itself. "This is where dozens have sought refuge."

Below, men of all sizes, shapes and race milled about the dark lean-tos. An older boy pumped a handle while a little girl filled a tin bucket with water. Clothes and towels, hung out to dry, crisscrossing throughout the wooden beams.

The two of them sat unnoticed in their buggy watching in silence for a good five minutes. The clean scent of pines and harvest grasses gave way to the smell of bacon and burned coffee grounds. Goats roamed freely and chickens pecked at discarded ears of corn while a couple of roosters strutted among them.

Abby adjusted her bonnet to better shade her eyes. "The larger tent in the middle belongs to Mama Ivy. The children all sleep there, too."

"Our stables at home are better shelter than this." His admission caused her to look over at him to see if he was teasing. His dark eyes beneath his hat held no sign of playfulness. From what she could tell, he was completely serious.

With a flick of the reins, Ian guided the buggy down the

broken trail. When it dipped in a washed out rut, he laid his arm across her lap to make sure she was steadied.

Abby smiled to herself at his protectiveness, even though she wasn't used to being given special treatment. The consideration Ian showed her made her feel as if he genuinely valued her.

Once on level ground, they followed the path forged by others from the upper bank.

Two or three canvas tents were set up on the point bar. Otherwise, shabby lean-tos scattered around the outer flats.

"Lady!" A dark-skinned boy, knee-deep in the uneven creek, dropped the tin cup in his hand and trudged to where Abby climbed down from the buggy. "Lady, you came. You bring somethin' good to eat?"

"That all depends. Have you been working on your numbers like I showed you?"

"Yes'm." He nodded emphatically. "I got all the way up to my four by's."

"Abby!" Hickory stuck his head from a tent and ran to greet her. "I thought Doc had you working today."

"I finished at noon." Abby answered even though his attention was clearly on Ian. "Is this your day to help at the telegraph office?"

His lips were cracked from being too long in the sun, so Abby reached for a small jar of aloe balm from the pocket in her skirt.

Shaking his head, he was unable to answer while she applied a liberal amount of the salve to his puckered mouth. As soon as she let go of his chin, he answered with a sour look. "Not until tomorrow. I'll get my money then."

The first boy stuck his lips out for some balm, too.

When Abby complied, he swiped his dingy sleeve across his

nose. "Is he gonna put us in jail?"

"No, this is Colonel Saberton."

Ian led the horse down to the murky water for a drink.

Taking the boy's hand, Abby brought him over for a proper introduction. "Ian, I'd like you to meet my friend, Little Jon."

"A pleasure, Little Jon." Ian held out a hand, but the boy hesitated to offer his own, looking up instead at Abby for reassurance.

Two other children came over with their hands out to have a turn.

"This is Molly and this is Paco."

Paco had lost another tooth up top since Abby had seen him last.

"Colonel Saberton is a good man to know." Abby smiled as Paco skewed his lips to one side and took the offered hand without looking up at Ian.

"Boy!" The bellow came from inside a tent, but Abby didn't need to see a face to know they'd stirred the wrath of the man they called Mo.

Quick as a flash, Little Jon retrieved his cup and was back in the water.

Ian's hand was on the hilt of his sword as a frown wrinkled his brow.

"That's the self-appointed camp boss, Moses." Abby folded her arms while watching the others duck their heads and continue their tasks. "He's a deserter and mean from what I've seen. The children are half-terrified of him. He won't cross Mama Ivy though, and she makes certain they are not hurt."

Ian said nothing but swiped his hat from his head and dusted it against his britches. "How many women and children are out here?" His eyes followed three females silently scrubbing clothing with rocks against a worn wash board.

"You met Mama Ivy. Halona is Creek Indian. Mo bought her from a fur trader." Abby couldn't hide the disgust in her voice. "And Mrs. Oberhaus is the other lady. She and her husband came for gold in the mountains north of here. From somewhere up near the great lakes. But Mr. Oberhaus got typhoid fever and died a few months back. She has the two little girls playing there beside her. Since they have no home and no money, they stay here. She helps Mama Ivy with cooking."

Ian gave a sweeping glance at the men milling about the camp. Some had come out to have a look at the visitors. One had a pick axe in his hand.

"There are about twenty men total." Abby provided. "Other than the two women you see here and Mama Ivy there are no other women. Any woman who comes seeking shelter usually ends up at the Dove's Nest courtesy of Mo."

Ian gave his head a toss before smoothing his hat back in place. "How many more children are up here besides Little Jon, and Hickory?"

"Six. You've met them all except Mrs. Oberhaus' girls." Abby followed as Ian led the horse to a tree and flung the reins over a branch. "They are the only ones who have living relatives."

When Mo emerged from his tent, Ian reached over and took Abby's hand into his own.

"Miss Abby?" Someone tugged at her skirt. Abby found four-year-old Inga Oberhaus impatiently waiting to be noticed. "Miss Abby, did you bring us something to eat?"

"Eat!" The two-year-old wearing only a diaper echoed her sister.

"I surely did." Abby retrieved a small paper package tied

with twine from the buggy as they both clapped for joy. "Be a big girl and carry this over to your mama for me, please."

"And do you think you two can eat an apple turnover all by yourselves?" Handing juicy pastries to Molly and Paco, Abby got excited squeals in answer.

When she turned back to Ian, he watched her closely, but she couldn't read his expression.

Smiling, she took another heavier package down from the buggy and began to walk down to where Mrs. Oberhaus waved to her. "I haven't been able to come often, but I try to bring salt, flour, bacon ... that sort of thing. And a few treats for the children."

Ian took the packet and hefted it up on one broad shoulder. "That's not happening again."

Taken aback, she stared at him as he made his way down the slope to where Mrs. Oberhaus and Mama Ivy waited.

Hitching her skirt with one hand, she quickly caught up with him, practically running to match his long strides. "If you're worried that Mo will harm me, you can put your mind at ease. As long as I bring food and supplies, he's happy to leave me alone. He likes to eat like the rest of them."

Tossing her curls over her shoulder, she cast a leery glance at Mo who sneered at her with arms crossed. Truth be told, he was a bit scary. But she never came past dark and never stayed long enough for him to bother her.

"I've only come a couple of times, and I keep my stay to a minimum so he has no reason to take it out on Hickory or any of the others after I leave."

"Hickory's coming with us." Ian looked around. "Where is he?"

Abby placed a hand on Ian's arm. "Hickory can't come with us."

"My men are in the process of setting up refugee camps within the city. I'll set aside three for the women and children. They will get rations and the camps are secured by patrols. Fitz will make arrangements for transfer as soon as we get back."

Ian wasn't used to having his orders questioned.

Abby proceeded carefully. "You don't understand." She lowered her voice to avoid being overheard. "Just like Farris owned Sallie, he now has possession of Hickory."

"What?" Ian didn't bother to keep his volume down.

Abby shushed him and pulled him over to the side out of the children's earshot. "Farris has a piece of paper saying so. He bought Sallie as an indentured servant, but after her death, her contract was not fulfilled so he's decided Hickory will serve it out. Two more years. His provost marshal signed it and put his seal on it."

Abby watched Hickory's carrot top appear from under his lean-to when the girls showed him their pastries. A sweet smile split his face as he waved to Abby.

"I've long suspected Farris tries to take all the money Hickory makes at the telegraph office and hospital, too." Abby spoke quietly. "I've seen him pass off coins to Penny Jo. She probably has them in a sock tucked away under her bed for him."

Mo watched their every move.

Abby turned to see if Ian noticed as well, and found him staring the man down with a dangerous look in his eye.

Desperate to divert a storm, Abby made an attempt at small talk. "Hickory once told me he was named after President Jackson. He seems proud of that."

"Abby!" Mrs. Oberhaus waved her down to where she, Holana, and Mama Ivy were waiting for them.

Ian went before her as she continued down the slope. Mrs.

Oberhaus greeted her with a hug. "Thank you for bringing us supplies. I know this didn't come cheap."

"Mrs. Oberhaus, meet Colonel Ian Saberton."

"A real Colonel!" She clapped her hands together much like her little girls had done.

"Pleasure to meet you, Mrs. Oberhaus." Ian gave a forced smile, and the dear lady blushed.

"Holana, I brought a bristle brush for your hair." Abby lifted a wooden brush from the packet and brought it to the solemn woman. "It's like the one I told you about. My friend has beautiful long hair like yours, and a brush like this makes it shine."

Holana remained guarded, but turned for Abby to whisk the brush through the end of her braid.

"You did what you came for, Nurse Lady. Now be on your way." Mo hollered from his place outside his tent.

The brusque way he refused to address her by name never failed to rattle Abby's nerves. "Holana, get over here." As usual, his tone was angry.

When she didn't move fast enough, Mo came over and snatched the brush from Holana's hand. He ordered her inside the tent with a jerk of his head. His large belly was barely covered by a faded red vest with a revolver tucked inside the waistband of his pants. His hair, black as coal, bushed out on either side of his head and his straggly beard fell down to his chest.

The malice in his black eyes was a force of its own.

Abby stood directly between Ian and Mo. The tension between the two was palpable.

Mama Ivy apparently felt it, too. "Children. Get inside the tent." Her tone was calm but firm.

Abby decided she needed to act quickly to avoid the

mounting hostility.

"I'm here to bring supplies." Abby lifted her chin and walked over to where Mo stood, refusing to be intimidated. "And treats for the children."

She held up the sack of pastries Eliza Jane had sent, knowing he would reach for them.

When he did, she moved it just out of his reach. "And a hairbrush for Holana." Holding out her other hand, she took a chance that he would be willing to trade.

A slow smile crept up his pock-marked face, showing blackened teeth as he began to laugh. "Of course." Though he smiled, there was no humor in his eyes as he snatched the sack and tossed the brush her way.

Ian caught it in midair to keep it from hitting her.

"Who's this? Your body guard?" Mo laughed until he choked.

"Colonel Ian Saberton." Abby paused to let it sink in. "At the snap of his fingers, he can bring you in on a string of charges."

She expected Ian to act a bit more appreciative of her defense. Instead, he seemed irritated.

Mo turned his head and spewed a stream of tobacco juice into the dirt. His eyes narrowed, as he summed up the much taller man at Abby's side.

"We don't need no army up here." With that, he flung back the flap of his tent and called back from inside. "You brought what you came for—now leave."

Abby handed the brush to Mrs. Oberhaus. "Please see that Holana gets this."

"He's a nasty one." Mrs. Oberhaus said none too quietly. "But I'll keep it in my tent for her to use. He knows better than to look for it in there. Mama Ivy will see to that."

With a wave to the girls, Abby and Ian started back to their buggy.

"It's always a struggle to leave them to Mo's bullying." Each time she came she wanted to bring them all home with her. The problem was, she had no home to bring them to.

"Has he ever laid a hand on you?" Ian helped her up the incline.

"Never." That was the honest truth. Mo had no control over her, and he knew it.

"Hickory?"

Abby couldn't put into words the cruelty she'd seen in the angry welts across the boy's hind quarters on two separate occasions. So she just nodded and left it at that.

"There's one more pastry." Abby lifted it from a brown paper on the buggy seat. "I'll bring it down to Hickory."

"Mind if I take it to him?" Ian watched Hickory over her shoulder, and Abby followed his gaze.

The boy kept his attention on her, probably hoping she hadn't forgotten him.

"Tell him there's more." Abby handed Ian the pastry. "I gave them to Mrs. Oberhaus. She'll give him another one later."

Ian nodded, and went to where Hickory stood beside his makeshift home. Crossing her arms, Abby watched Hickory eagerly accept the treat from Ian's hand.

Ian took off his hat and removed the Chaplain's cross pinned there. Reaching over, he tacked it to the shoulder strap of Hickory's overalls. She couldn't tell what was being said, but Hickory's face lit up, and he gave a wide grin.

With a ruffle of the boy's bright hair, Ian bid him farewell and waved once again to Mrs. Oberhaus and her girls before meeting Abby at the buggy.

Abby's heart swelled thinking about his considerate treatment of the shanty camp waifs. Honestly, she hadn't known what to expect. Ian Saberton surprised her at every turn. He was more like her father than she ever would have imagined. Even to the point of silently simmering when he was mad.

Now to figure a way to divert the fury working that muscle in his jaw.

*"True love cannot be found where it does not exist...
nor can it be hidden where it does."*
*~ William Shakespeare*

# Fourteen

*I*an never wanted to take another man's throat into his
hands as badly as he had when that degenerate openly
leered at Abby, slowly taking in her every curve.

Call it chivalry, or suspicion. Call it whatever you please.
The memory still curdled his blood. To think Abby had made
the trip out there alone in the past, several times, sent a surge
of irritation through him like he'd never known.

Brandishing the reins to get the ancient stable horse moving
past a snail's pace, Ian avoided looking over at her. He needed
to get his temper under control first.

Abby McFadden was exasperating.

Without a doubt, she was the most hard-headed woman
he'd ever encountered. Even Dottie Saberton, who was known
for her gumption, could learn a thing or two from this one.

The way she'd sauntered down there to confront that coward. Flagrantly daring him over a hairbrush for Halona. The
woman had more mettle than brains.

Shanty towns were a haven for outlaws and renegades. No place to give free rein to her reckless impulses. She'd get herself killed. Somehow, Ian was determined to make her see it. He refused to think what might have happened if he hadn't gone with her today.

It was imperative he get back to send a dispatch out to General Wheeler as soon as possible. The information Abby had inadvertently passed on was crucial and needed to be acted on immediately. His soldiers hadn't been the ones trying to solicit the boys into planting explosives, so that could only mean the Union forces had forged south. Most likely planning to take down the railroad to prevent troops and supplies from coming in.

But first things first.

Before she left this buggy, Abby would understand that from here on out, she was banned from going back to the shanty camp. She'd better know he had the authority to enforce it, too. And wouldn't give a moment's hesitation in doing so.

He'd have the women and children, including Hickory, removed to the refugee camp before tomorrow evening. If Farris had a problem with that, he could come ask about it himself. Ian would relish that conversation.

Steering the buggy onto a rocky flat, overlooking a cascading stream, Ian set the brake and propped a boot up on the footboard, fully prepared to have this out once and for all.

"Ian? Is everything all right?" Abby asked quietly.

This was for her own good. He'd get the children out of that filthy hovel without losing Abby to her own foolishness.

Then he made the mistake of looking over at her.

Reddish-gold wisps danced about her shoulders from where her long hair was pulled back into a ribbon at the back of her neck. His gaze wandered over the soft curls blowing in the breeze around her, and he suddenly wondered how they would feel between his fingers.

Sitting back, Ian rested one arm on the back of her seat, the other on his bent knee.

"No, Abby. Everything's not all right." His plan to remain calm gave way as soon as he opened his mouth. Only by heaven's grace was she was sitting here at all. "What were you thinking back there? Do you have any idea who these people are? Desperate criminals, that's who. Desperate enough to slit your throat and toss your remains in the river without a shred of remorse." His voice rose steadily until he was practically yelling. "I can guarantee Mo has killed for much less than what you just did. Making an utter fool of him in front of the whole camp. If something happened to you, who would look after the kids then?"

He watched for tears, but Abby didn't intimidate easily. Soldiers twice her size had backed away from such fierce questioning.

Instead, Abby straightened her back, crossed her arms, and lifted a perfect brow. "Now's a fine time to care. Some of those children have been wandering aimlessly for years. And not one person has seen fit to take them in."

"You're not going back." Ian countered just as adamantly.

"Not with you, I'm not." She huffed and looked out the other side of the buggy. "You can count on that."

Ian gritted his teeth to keep from snapping a direct order of "silence!" Soldiers were infinitely easier to keep subordinate than a headstrong female.

Drawing a cleansing breath, he decided to try again. This time he'd put personal feelings aside to simply present the facts. "For your own protection, you will not leave the city. I will arrange to move the women and children to a camp in Macon. A meeting place within city limits will be established for you to provide sweets or hairbrushes or whatever your little heart desires to a representative of the shanty be it Hickory or Mama Ivy—anyone as long as it's not that buffoon, Mo. Is that understood?" Ian gave his order in the same tone that brooked no argument from his men.

Why was she laughing?

"You're serious?"

When Ian assured her that he most definitely was, she only found it more amusing. "I will come and go as I please. I've not broken any laws."

"I have no time for this, Abby." Unfastening the reins, he steered the horse back onto the road. "You will heed my orders, or there will be consequences to pay."

"I would think that you of all people would recall that I do not like to be threatened, Colonel." Bold and unyielding, the challenge in her eye was unmistakable. "General Farris can brief you on that."

Ian chose to ignore her bluster.

Tense quietness between them stretched on for a good ten minutes, broken only by the steady clopping of the horse's hooves. Finally looking over, he saw that she was watching a couple of squirrels playing tag on the outer bank.

"They seem to be getting along better than we are." Abby offered without looking at him.

"I just want you safe."

That was as close to an apology as she was going to get. The thought of losing her knotted his stomach. Admitting it, however, was more disturbing than dealing with her anger.

"I know you do." Abby turned to him. "But they depend on me." Her hand slipped over to lightly clasp his. "Ian,

Hickory depends on me."

Ian nodded, scanning the blue sky. "He's a remarkable kid. Has every reason to have lost faith." His tone softened considerably with her hand in his. "But the boy's steady as a rock."

"He counts on me for more than just food and an occasional treat, you know." She let go of his hand and Ian instantly felt the loss. "With Sallie gone, I'm his last link to a life outside the shanty. A buoy in the storm so to speak." Deep concern shone in her eyes. "I won't abandon him."

Ian slowed the horse to a stop and turned to better see her. "Abby, I'm not asking you to abandon him. You can see him as often as you need to. I just won't risk you going to the camp alone anymore."

Abby got quiet for a minute before she went on. "Without his mother, Hickory needs to know I won't leave him. That I'll still be here for him, wherever he may be."

Endangering her right along with the children was not the solution.

"Once I get back this afternoon, I'll look at the camps. We'll make room for Mama Ivy and the children in army issued tents closest to the hospital. Will that make you feel better? You can go see them as often as your schedule allows."

That was closest to a full concession that he was willing to go. In truth, his mission in Macon included gathering vulnerable citizens into supervised refugee camps. That included Hickory and his friends.

In her excitement, she leaned toward him, and Ian folded an arm around her.

Her expression suddenly fell. "But Farris has made it clear he won't let him go."

"Farris' piece of paper means nothing. General Hawthorne

has the authority to bring Hickory under local supervision with sufficient evidence of neglect and mistreatment. You and I will both attest to that. I'll speak with him this afternoon."

Her smile was back. "Thank you. Promise me when this war is over with, you'll find a permanent place for Hickory. And for his baby sister, too. You know people in Georgia who might take them in."

"Like your foster family did for you?" He lifted her chin to bring her eyes up to meet his. Shimmering green with splashes of gold.

"Yes."

"I give you my word."

For the briefest moment, Ian lowered his head. His mouth hovered over hers, as he struggled with his conscience. Allowing his lips to brush her lips in a soft caress, he could taste her sweet breath. He was unmistakably drawn to her. But he knew one simple kiss would be offering a promise for more. And with so many uncertainties, he had nothing more to offer her.

Ian sat back into his seat.

He could see she mistook his hesitation for rejection. Hurt shone bright in her eyes.

"I could kiss you right now. And believe me, I'd enjoy every minute of it." Without thinking, he traced the pout of her lower lip with his thumb. "But, your heart's been broken far too many times in your life. I won't be the cause of another."

Abby caught his hand and placed a sweet kiss on his palm. "Then don't be."

He smiled at her simplistic reasoning.

"Let's get you get back to the hospital." Releasing the brake, Ian snapped the reins. "And stop thinking so much about kissing."

Abby side-glanced his way. "Is that an order, Colonel?"

Ian raised a brow at her question. "Would you obey if it was?"

A shrug and faltering grin were her only answer.

~

Abby made a concentrated effort to appear unaffected, but her pulse was racing. If she were capable of catching a thought, she'd try to make sense of what just happened.

Maybe it hadn't happened at all. Maybe she'd simply imagined it.

Resisting the urge to touch her lips, she decided it had indeed been real. When she closed her eyes, she could still feel the intensity that had passed between them in that fleeting moment when his lips brushed against hers. Like nothing she'd ever experienced.

Unfortunately, it only left her wishing for more, though not exactly sure what it was she wished for.

Despite the fact that neither of them spoke, it was more sad than awkward. If only they'd met five years ago, things would have been so different. They'd most likely be married by now and could kiss all they wanted to.

But given who she was and what he was, there could be no future for them. Ian had made that fairly clear. Times were perilous, only God knew what the future held for this land or anyone who lived within her shores.

Just as they entered the outskirts of Macon, Abby noticed a rider barreling toward them. As he neared, his Confederate gray uniform became more distinct, and Ian pulled on the reins.

Lieutenant Fitz skidded up alongside the buggy. "Rev, you're needed at headquarters." Catching a breath, he yanked the kerchief from around his neck and swiped at the perspiration dripping down his face.

In two steps, Ian leapt from the buggy and approached Fitz's horse. "What's happened?"

"The Yanks got to the storehouses. Raided two of 'em. They tried to set 'em ablaze but we shot one full of minnies and they took off."

"Lieutenant, are there other wounded?" Apprehension furrowed Abby's brow.

As it was, every hospital in town was well over capacity. If fighting broke out, they'd soon be short on supplies and horribly understaffed.

"See Miss McFadden back to the hospital in the buggy. I'll take your horse."

Fitz slid from the saddle, and Ian swung up in his place. "Abby, my apologies."

"No. Absolutely, go." She was fully aware of the heavy mantle of responsibility that drove him.

Wheeling the animal, Ian leaned low and sent the horse dashing toward town.

Fitz climbed in next to Abby and took up the reins. No flippant remarks or engaging stories today. He appeared every bit the dogged soldier that Ian's cavalry was known for.

"Did anyone see how many raiders there were?" Abby asked, hoping to get some answers for Doc and the others at the hospital who would be asking. "How did they get past the guards?"

"You're sure a curious little thing, aren't ya?" Fitz shook the reins and gave a click of his tongue to get the horse moving faster.

Unfortunately, the rented nag was not inclined to go any faster than a snail's pace.

At first, she thought to dismiss his gruff as understandable, given the circumstances. But something about the way he narrowed an eye at her made her realize that Fitz was as unsure of her as Farris had been.

Anything she said right now in her own defense would only make matters worse. There would come a time when her innocence would be proven, but while the city was reeling from a Union attack was not that time. Truthfully, she couldn't blame them. What did anyone down here know of her really? Besides her name, her skill for nursing, and possibly her love for children orphaned by the war.

If they did—truly know her—they'd surely hate her as fiercely as they hated the worst of the dreaded Yankees.

"Can you tell me what was taken?"

Fitz refused to look at her, so she hurried to explain. "I only ask because the hospital counts on those storehouses for supplies. We won't be getting another shipment anytime soon and with so many patients ..."

Fitz veered the buggy to the left and circled to deposit her at the front steps of the hospital. She thought he was going to completely ignore her question, so she prepared to leave him to his duties with no further questions.

"Valuables." He finally answered. "And lots of 'em."

"Civilian's?" Abby looked back over her shoulder.

"Everything they had. Well, anything worth keepin' anyhow. Entrusted to the CS army for protection."

"Oh, no! Fitz, that's awful." Abby gave him a sad smile before scooping her skirts and stepping down from the carriage. After thinking on it she turned and spoke from her heart. "I'll pray that you and your men are quick to recover every bit of it. And the truth of who's behind it be revealed."

Fitz seemed to contemplate her words for a good long minute before setting the old nag back in motion.

As he rode off, her heart was heavy.

As hard as she tried to fit in, times like this reminded her she was still considered an outsider.

*"I have thought a sufficient measure of civilization
is the influence of good women."*
~ *Ralph Waldo Emerson*

## Fifteen

❦

The mayor called an emergency meeting between five key commanders of the Macon area.

General George Hawthorne, Commander in Chief of Macon,

General Buford Farris, Commander of Fort Oglethorpe,

Colonel Ian Saberton, Confederate States Army Special Forces,

and Major General E.G. Baker, Georgia Militia Field Commander out of Forsyth.

By the time Ian got to the community house, his mood was as black as the starless night.

Contrary to the rabid scuttlebutt firing through the streets of Macon, triggering panic at every turn, the allegations of a shrewd Federal raid just didn't add up. With intense battles going on seventy-five miles north as Sherman's army began to push its way down past Atlanta, no Union officer worth his salt would sacrifice even a few men to raid a storehouse full of family heirlooms and trinkets. Such a frivolous move made no strategic sense.

And if the evidence was to be believed, only someone familiar with the layout of the old cotton storehouse would know how to get in from the broken aeration vent. The grading bin was removed from the outside. Just last week, Ian had issued a request to Mayor Dobbs that the owner have it sealed at first convenience.

In the meantime, an iron rod had been put in place from the inside to prevent unauthorized access. That rod had been removed.

With lanterns in hand, anxious citizens came from every direction to surround him as his horse drew up to the hitching post.

"What have you to say, Colonel, about today's Yankee attack? Is enemy siege impending?" A reporter Ian recognized from *The Macon Telegraph*, with tablet and pencil, gave him no room to pass.

Ian stood head and shoulders taller and easily brushed past him to the wide brick-paved steps of the city's community center. He was in no mood for interviews. Especially not by an ambitious newspaperman trying to make a name for himself.

"Sources say you were seen with a Yankee Spy earlier. Can you confirm her involvement?" The words slammed into the back of Ian like a runaway freight train.

Stopped in his tracks, though refusing to turn around, Ian inspected the tall windows of the building in front of him. As wildly satisfying as it would be to lay the halfwit out for his careless accusation, it wouldn't help Abby's cause in the least. Hard as it was, he'd still be better off to ignore ignorance than justify it with an answer.

"Colonel, Oh, Colonel!" Cora Dobbs pushed through the

crowd to Ian's side. "Hazel, stand back, I have official business."

A woman whose hair was pulled into a severe bun stepped aside but peered over Cora's shoulder looking like she had chewed a lemon.

Cora latched onto Ian's arm and half dragged him up the steps. "Colonel, with you in attendance, we now have a deciding vote."

"Deciding on what, exactly, Mrs. Dobbs?" Ian held the door open.

Cora entered, pulling her skirts in as she passed through the doorway. "Turn the lock. Make sure no one follows us."

The crowd had already moved up to the top steps as Ian slid the lock into place. With the reporter out there sensationalizing the event, they could easily become a panicked mob within minutes.

Hawthorne needed to assemble a special guard.

"You'll have to admit, the driving force in this resistance has and will continue to be the ladies left behind to defend our own homes from Yankee ravagers. We're committed and efficient. None are more invested in keeping those marauders from taking our land than the very women who sent our men off to fight for the right to defend it. And we demand to be supplied with weapons the same as any male reservists."

"Driving force might be a bit of an overstatement." Ian was not inclined to smile but did anyway when her fierce defense of the ladies' right to bear arms had her waving her parasol like a rapier blade. "But, yes, I'd say you ladies are about as well-organized as any I've seen in Virginia or down through Tennessee."

"Then I can count on your vote to allow me, as Commander of the Georgia Ladies Auxiliary Militia out of Macon, to attend this meeting?"

The lamps lit the way down a shiny wood floor to an open door with light splaying out into the hall. Ian halted briefly, knowing unless Cora was appeased, this meeting would never come to order.

She folded her arms. "We practice three times a day, sometimes with real guns. We only ask for a few bullets."

Ian pitied the man who'd oppose them.

"Mrs. Dobbs, you still haven't told me how it is that I'm your deciding vote. This is your husband's meeting. Ask him if you can sit in." Ian rested a gloved hand on the hilt of his scabbard, and removed his hat before entering the meeting room. "But I must warn you, these are confidential matters. If your husband is wise, he will not subject you to the temptation of repeating what you might hear."

"I already asked him. Walter is perfectly fine with my attending. He knows my value in strategic warfare."

Ian grinned. He'd just bet Walter did.

"And so is Georgie. It's that odious Farris and Major General what's-his-name that are putting up a fuss. Votes are tied, two to two. You, Colonel, get to decide."

A rumble of laughter started deep in Ian's chest but never made it any farther before annoyance completely choked it out.

"Between you and me ..." Cora took a step toward him and lowered her voice. "You will need me in that meeting for support."

Ian's brow rose a tad. "Why would that be?"

"Walter tells me Farris is insinuating he has hard evidence proving Abby was behind the Yankee raid."

"That's ludicrous."

"Exactly what I said!" She folded her gloved hands before her and squared her shoulders. "Well, not exactly what I said.

But your version is more pleasant."

"Abby was with me at the time of the raid." It irritated him to have to give an account for her at all.

"I know that. We all know that. Abby's plenty of things, but a Yankee spy is not one of them." Cora wagged a finger. "And if that pompous walrus says otherwise, you'll need me in there as a character witness. I don't care if she is from Ohio, she's been a Southerner for the past two years. Not another female in Bibb County has done more to ease our suffering Confederate soldiers as Abigail McFadden. Never giving a moment's thought to her own lack or exhaustion but sitting up all night sometimes at the bedside of another dying young man because he's afraid to cross over."

Ian smoothed a hand over his hair. With all he had to face this evening, whether or not Cora Dobbs had her nose in this meeting was the least of his concern. If she could possibly help Abby, he had no qualms about her being there.

With a gallant wave of his hat, he allowed Mrs. Dobbs to precede him into the room.

Farris and Hawthorne were already in a heated discussion at the back of the room. Walter and Baker played chess at a long table set in the middle. Theater posters lined the brick wall between long tall windows facing the river.

Cora marched to the head of the table. "All those in favor of my attending this meeting say, 'aye.'"

"Aye." General Hawthorn and Walter Dobbs responded in unison. Walter, never looking up from his game.

Ian pulled out a chair and turned it around, motioning for Mrs. Dobbs to be seated first. "Aye." He answered with a half grin before straddling the seat.

"The aye's have it. Let the meeting begin." If she'd had a gavel Ian was sure she would have wielded it freely.

"General, this is outrageous." Farris padded to the table. "When the time comes that we need help from our most delicate and genteel–."

"I am neither delicate nor genteel, Buford. Now, who will begin?" Cora ignored Farris' incredulous sniff.

"Let's start with the facts." General Hawthorne took his place at the head of the table, standing beside his sister's chair. "Colonel Saberton, please brief us on your findings concerning this afternoon's raid."

"Storehouse Number Twelve across from the railroad depot was burglarized at some point between noon and four p.m. Though ransacked, only one trunk and a priceless painting are missing. Everything else has been accounted for. An unknown assailant entered the warehouse through a known damaged vent accessed from the back outer wall. Their escape was made through the front where the guard on duty sustained a gash on the back of his head as he was assaulted from behind."

"Blue-belly calling card." A smug sneer indeed gave Farris the look of a walrus with the long ends of his shaggy mustache hanging down past where his neck should be.

"Actually no, Sir, it's not." Ian crossed his arms over the back of the chair. "The main purpose of a Yankee raid would be to infuse fear in the locals and cause the Confederate army to know that this area had been invaded. Therefore, they would have made a display of entering the city in formation and confronting our men at gunpoint. They would not have crept in the back but through the front of the building taking possession of everything they could carry away and burning down what was left."

"And they would have gone from storehouse to storehouse until they found food, medical supplies, or ammunition to bring back to the Union camps bearing down on Atlanta."

Major General Baker concurred. "A painting and lady's trunk would not be of particular interest."

"Priceless painting." Farris interrupted.

"Where do you suppose they would sell such a priceless possession?" General Hawthorne postured with a hand resting inside the frock coat at his chest. He made a valid point. "Unless you suppose that they would haul such a cumbersome piece all over creation to get back into Union territory, they would have to find an unscrupulous buyer south of the Mason-Dixon. Otherwise, what good would Confederate currency do them?"

"Colonel, are you of a mind that this was not a Yankee raid, after all?" Cora wanted to know, drumming her white-gloved fingers on the polished mahogany table.

"The dead Yankee would beg to differ." Farris's face turned crimson. He took a long sip from his snifter, glaring at Ian.

"It's true, Cora. They shot one down behind the warehouses." Walter Dobbs looked from Cora, to Farris, back to Cora again.

The one aspect of this incident that made no sense whatsoever.

A red patch found on the soldier's hat identified him as an infantryman for the Army of the Potomac. As far as Ian knew, they were engaged in Virginia and had never come this far south.

"Perhaps the Colonel's personal investment in this case has blinded him to the truth." Farris finished his drink with a repugnant belch.

Both of the other General's turned to Ian for an explanation.

"I have no investment, General, personal or otherwise." Ian

stood and swung the chair back to the wall. "Perhaps your bottle of cheap brandy has you mistaken."

"He was with a known Yankee spy today while the prized possessions of our good citizens were pilfered and fleeced." Farris tried to stand but fell back into his chair. "Conveniently, it was his duty to protect our trusting residents from this contemptable act of cowardice. Very convenient, indeed."

Cora Dobbs was on her feet in an instant. "Farris, you drunken old fool."

The mayor intercepted her charge toward the other end of the table. "Simmer down, dearest. You'll get another one of your sick headaches."

"Yes, dearest." Farris mocked. "We wouldn't want poor Walter to spend the night alone on the sofa again." He was the only one laughing.

"Georgie, ..." Cora began.

"You can't call me Georgie. You must address me as General." Her brother corrected her gently. "We are recording official minutes, Cora."

"General, then." She picked up where she had left off. "Don't you dare believe a word that man says. We've no known Yankee spies within a thousand miles of here. He's drunk as usual and hasn't a clue what he's talking about."

"Georgie, I believe we should order a pair of britches for your sister from the Quartermaster." Farris shook the last drops from his bottle into a cup. "She's gotten too big for her husband's."

"General, you disgrace yourself." General Hawthorne strode to Farris's side and directed him to stand. "You are dismissed. Return to your command at once. My full report will be sent to your commander concerning your behavior. This is not the first time you've attended a meeting intoxicated."

"He's even more disgraceful when he's sober." Cora dusted off her skirts and returned to her chair, retying the bow under her chin that secured her hat.

Farris set his bottle down hard and made for the door. His eyes, bloodshot and cold, skimmed over Ian as he passed. "You should be questioning your Yankee whore about how those men knew where to look for valuables. I have proof she facilitated the entire operation."

"Present your evidence then, General." Ian stood. He was fed up with Farris' accusations.

The Major General came to stand between them, facing Ian. "Saberton, he's not worth it. He has nothing or he'd have presented it long before now."

"That will remain to be seen." Farris exited into the hall and pulled a sloppy salute. "Good evening, gentlemen."

The room was quiet until they heard the door at the front of the building open and close once again. Hawthorne sent an aide to make certain it was locked.

"I don't know why that odious imbecile still walks our streets." Cora continued to grouse. It was no secret she had strong feelings when it came to Farris. He'd broken trust with her a long time ago.

Ian circled the table to look out the floor length window. While a few still milled about on the street waiting for the meeting to end, most had dispersed to their homes where they were sure to take extra precautions to secure every door and window.

Ian had no doubts Farris was bluffing. He had no proof of Abby's involvement or he'd have been happy to parade it under their noses.

"Colonel?"

Ian turned to find all attention centered on him.

"My apologies." He leaned a shoulder against the cool brick. "General Farris' intense dislike for Abby is tiresome. I've never seen her disrespect him, in fact she goes out of her way to avoid him from what I can tell."

"Is this the Abby I met at the hospital last week, Walter?" General Hawthorne asked.

"The nurse." Cora waggled a finger at the aide taking minutes. "Get this down, Abigail McFadden. Reddish-gold hair, green eyes. A mite too skinny."

"Ah, yes. Lovely girl. Very well thought of among our soldiers." General Hawthorne clasped his hands behind his back and walked to the other side of the room.

"Nurse Abby was a veritable angel of mercy tending our reservists." Major General Baker scratched his beard. "Granted, we've not seen many battle wounds but a round of measles took hold. If she hadn't put the sick ones in quarantine, and taken such good care of them, we'd never have survived it as well as we did."

Ian smiled at his choice of words. Abby was indeed an angel of mercy.

"When Abby first came to Macon, I'll be the first to admit I was suspicious of her myself. She being from Ohio and all." Cora tilted her head and regarded Ian with an uncharacteristic tender smile. "I don't think I've told you, Colonel about the night that all changed for me."

Ian shook his head. "No ma'am."

"Walter and I had an only child. A son so handsome it almost hurt to look at him." She clasped her fingers on the table in front of her. "Harrison was thirteen years old, and had not begun to live the life he was destined for when he contracted typhoid fever. Within days it was apparent he would not recover." Her voice trembled. "Abby refused to leave his side. She cared for him, prayed for him, even sang to him. When the time came, our dear boy was afraid to cross over, and Abby held his hand. She talked him through to glory, describing the wonders, and promising he was merely going ahead of the rest of us to pick out a prime spot beside the golden shores."

Ian had not known of Harrison Dobbs. Hearing of Abby's compassion for the child only confirmed what he knew of her. She was extraordinary in every way.

"When Harrison passed, Abby cried sincere tears right along with mine. I have accepted her into our fold from that day on." Cora cleared her throat and straightened her back. "And I'll not sit idly by while that drunken blowhard tries to drag her down to his level."

"Why do you suppose General Farris is so fixed on vengeance where Miss McFadden is concerned?" General Hawthorne asked.

"I'll tell you exactly why he's so fixed on vengeance."

"Now, Cora, we really shouldn't." Walter patted his forehead with a handkerchief.

"Abby sent him running out into the street with no pants and a shiny black eye." Cora sat back and puckered her lips, taking in each of their reactions one at a time.

Ian should have been stunned like the Generals were, but when it came to Abby nothing shocked him anymore. "Mind telling us how that came about?"

"As we all know, General Farris has questionable business dealings here in Macon. Abby disrupted his income from those businesses, and he was determined to make her pay. Made a fool of himself if you ask me." Cora's lips thinned as she shook her head. "One day, he had gone to, shall we say, sample the goods."

"Cora, I insist you stop this instant. This is most unbecoming." Walter warned.

"Abby was there tending the rabble." Cora went on. "Farris mistakenly approached her from behind in his red long johns thinking she was one of his business women. When she turned and saw what he was about, she grabbed a chamber pot off the table and gave him a good trouncing. Right in the eye. Chased him all the way down the stairs and out into the street. He was the laughing stock of Bibb County for months after."

"Cora, General Farris would not appreciate you airing his embarrassment." Walter shook his thick muttonchops. "You need to stop provoking him, dearest. He has far-reaching ways of retaliation."

"Oh, Posh. He doesn't scare me one whit. But I'll tell you what's unbecoming, Walter." Cora was back to wagging her finger. "The way that man has gone above and beyond to seek vengeance on Abby. His hate runs deep. And I truly believe he'd stop at nothing to see her pay."

Stark dread gripped Ian as the truth of her words took hold.

Farris would stop at nothing. Even so far as to see Abby hanged for a crime she didn't commit.

*"Keep me from the snares which they have laid
for me."*
*Psalm 141:9*

# Sixteen

*O*bby removed soiled dressings from the stump of an amputated leg. The young private laid sedated upon a cot. The forlorn way he stared at the wall undoubtedly had more to do with the healing he needed on the inside. Healing which would take much longer and require much greater finesse than she possessed.

This soldier was more fortunate than most. No gangrene or infection. He'd most likely be back at camp within a couple of weeks. Carefully rewrapping with strips of bed sheets, Abby blessed whoever had donated the coveted cloth. They'd gone weeks without a supply shipment and now depended heavily on citizens to bring in what they could spare.

"Can I get you anything, Private? Would you like to write a letter home?" Abby gently laid her hand on his arm, hoping to take his mind off of his plight.

He shook his head without looking at her.

In an odd way, she could almost imagine her mother going

from bed to bed here, administering what medicine she could and always with gentle assurance. It would not have mattered to her what state or country these men hailed from. They were all God's precious creations. She would have been determined to show them His kindness.

A familiar wave of homesickness for a home that didn't exist washed over her. They'd been gone for nearly twelve years, but little things brought back memories. Abby could almost smell the rosewater her mother wore on her wrists.

"Abby, General Farris is here to see you." An orderly passing through with a scrub bucket pointed with his mop down the long convalescence ward. "He's waiting in the examination room."

"Thank you." A rise of panic threatened to steal her breath. Encounters with Farris always ended badly. As a second desperate measure, she called back to the orderly. "Is there a Doctor on duty tonight?"

"Yes, ma'am. Doc Lambert. But he's gone down to the coroner's building just now."

Abby refused the dread that seeped to her very core. Reminding herself that she'd done nothing to justify his wrath, she removed the bloodied apron, tossing it to a pile of laundry, and smoothed her skirt.

Loud clanging echoed from the exam room disrupting the quiet aisles.

Quickening her step, she was intent on reaching him before he woke every patient on both floors. By the time she reached the exam room, she would have run straight into him had he not stopped her with a bottle filled with liquor in his outstretched hand.

The pungent swill sloshed over her bodice and she watched an amber stain spread across her sleeve.

"I was beginning to think you weren't coming, Miss McFadden." His words were slightly slurred, and Abby immediately noticed he had a hard time focusing on anything besides the splotch soaking her chest.

"What brings you to the hospital tonight, General?" She folded her arms to limit his view. "Have you run out of mercury salts?"

Her hasty comment ignited his anger evidenced by the bizarre way his nostrils flared. He reminded her of a bull preparing to charge. Eager to dissuade the attack, she chided herself to hold her tongue. Goading him would only make matters worse.

"If you've come to see Doc Lambert, I can go find him for you." Abby eyed the door, anxious to be done with this erratic visit. Given Farris' inebriated state, she was rapidly becoming more cautious.

"My intent here regards you." Farris tried to kick the door closed but instead his boot made contact with the wall, giving Abby time to get herself through the doorway.

She immediately came up against the broad form of the general's assistant who grabbed her arm to prevent escape.

"No need to fear, Miss McFadden." General Farris motioned for the soldier to escort Abby back to the exam room. "I've come to offer an olive branch as it were."

Nothing he could offer was of any interest to her. She'd already planned to speak with General Hawthorne about her travel papers just as soon as she got Hickory and his baby sister settled with a family.

A sinister sneer crept up his face behind Farris' ratty beard.

The assistant shoved her into the room none too gently. What Abby wouldn't give for a real olive branch just now to even the odds.

General Farris lifted the bottle to his mouth and took an ample swallow. "As you know, I have recently taken a prestigious position overseeing one of the largest Prisoner of War camps in the entire western theater." He stumbled but refused help from the beefy sergeant.

"Congratulations." Abby murmured. Everyone knew it was a blatant demotion, one step away from sending him back to Alabama to do clerk work.

"In my transition, I found in my possession a trinket that once belonged to a friend of yours, the unfortunate creature working the whorehouse downtown."

Though Abby tried to keep her expression closed, she flinched at the careless mention of Sallie. Was he even aware she'd died from the insidious infection he so freely spread? Truth be told, he simply didn't care.

Fumbling in his coat pocket, he produced a shiny gold chain with a coin pendant set in a gilded rope mount. "By my own generosity, I accepted this tainted bauble as payment for ... a loan."

Probably the only thing of value that Sallie owned.

"I hear the misfortunate Cyprian has mercifully passed on. Take it to her whelp." A long draught from the bottle no doubt helped soothe his conscience –or lack thereof. "And now you may show your gratitude."

Apprehension swiftly gave way to outrage.

Taking a firm hold on her courage, Abby shut the door herself, leaving the assistant to guard from the outside. What she wanted to say to the general was private and the patients need not be disturbed by any more of his drunk theatrics.

"Sallie died delivering your child. From a disease acquired by you." Abby snapped, leveling a heated gaze at the stagger-ing bore. "Yes, I'll accept this measly recompense for the baby on behalf of her mother. No generous gift from you, but an inheritance rightly deserved." Sheer motivation to have this out once and for all, spurred her on. "And at Sallie's request the child will be baptized in the Methodist church where her name will be recorded along with that of her mother's *only*."

Unbalanced by a surge of fury, he tripped over his own boots, knocking a bed pan noisily to the floor. "If the wretched woman is dead, it's only because you are no doctor. You have no business delivering Southern babies or even touching the most sullied of our confederates."

A pang of truth stayed her response.

She'd done everything in her power to save Sallie, but the disease was too far advanced. With much manipulation and grace from above, the baby passed into the world without infection.

With no warning, Farris gave a bellow and pitched the bottle to the floor in an echoing crash. Stampeding across the room, he pinned Abby against the brick wall. The bulk of his weight crushing her until she could scarcely take in a breath. "Do not provoke me, Yankee. I have tolerated your meddling for the last time." Through clenched teeth his fermented breath blew hot and sour next to her neck.

Struggling against his roving hands, Abby heard the material of her dress rip and felt the tender skin of her shoulder suddenly exposed.

With a bruising grip Farris squeezed her arm as he spoke. "I now have all the proof I need to see your feet dangle at the end of the gallows. By morning, every good citizen of Macon will be calling for your execution." His unbalanced heft shifted to allow her to jerk from his grasp and shove him backward.

"You are insane. Release me this instant." The catch in her throat belied her brave front. She had to get away from this madman.

Just as he advanced on her once again, she reached for a syringe laying on a side table and stabbed it deep into the meat of his thigh.

With a shriek, Farris grabbed at the needle, and Abby made a frantic dash for the door.

It would take several minutes before the effects of the morphine dulled him enough to render him unconscious. She had to get far enough in that time that he wouldn't be able to catch her.

She prayed that combined with the half bottle of alcohol he'd consumed, she hadn't just killed him.

"Stop her!" Farris bellowed from the exam room.

Soldiers in beds yelled for her to run. The orderlies hurried her along.

With shaking limbs, Abby flew down the stairs, desperate to make it outside. If she could only find Ian.

Choking back a cry, she was met at the bottom step by a barrage of soldiers, Farris' assistant in the lead.

At the top of the stairway, Farris' voice screamed for her arrest.

Trapped like a lost lamb, Abby's world closed in around her.

*"You can't reason with your heart; it has its own laws,*
*and thumps about things which the intellect scorns."*
*~ Mark Twain*

# Seventeen

*I*an stood to leave, lifting his coat from the back of his chair.

The meeting at City Hall had gone longer than he'd anticipated. It wasn't until after Cora and the mayor made their exit that the meeting really got started.

Against most predictions, the Federal General, William T. Sherman, had begun a southward trek from Atlanta with as many as sixty thousand troops. The confederate army had limited forces in place this far south with all roads and railways north of Macon disrupted by Union occupation.

The cities of south and east Georgia had been put on emergency alert. Hopelessly outnumbered, the best they could hope for was to drive his line away from the cities and bring in as many defenseless farmers as would come.

But for tonight, Ian would concentrate on clearing Abby's name.

Farris had not divulged just how she was supposed to be

linked to the questionable break in. Simply having been raised in Ohio was not sufficient evidence to make a formal accusation.

Ian hoped to catch Doc Lambert at Floyd House Hospital before he went back to camp. Hawthorne mentioned that Doc had examined the body of the soldier found behind the warehouses. Anything he'd observed, a bullet retrieved or any identifying articles, could provide crucial information as to this case and possibly even give a hint to the nature of Sherman's advance.

Above all, Ian ached to put his arms around Abby. To reassure her Farris' ploy would not be allowed to go any further.

A commotion erupted outside the room.

"Colonel Saberton! What about the lady spy you were with earlier?" The muffled voice of the newspaper man called through the heavy door.

Ian ground his teeth.

The newspapers had been on a feeding the frenzy for sensationalized stories. All because the panicked public was starving for news declaring their army had the upper hand. He wouldn't let Abby's name be dragged through the mud just to sell a few newspapers.

General Baker opened the door and the newspaper man burst into the room. "Miss McFadden has been charged with aiding the enemy. Colonel, do you have a comment about her arrest?"

Ian froze as if ice water surged through his veins.

He lifted a hand to stay the guards who held the man back. "What arrest?"

As soon as they let him go, the reporter took up his notepad and began to scribble.

Ian barely resisted the urge to knock the pencil to the floor and take the man up by his lapels. "I asked a question. Unless you'd like to be arrested for disrupting official business, I suggest you answer."

"Colonel Saberton is with our specialized forces, Mr. Greely." Hawthorne intervened with concern drawing his gray brows together. "He and his men rarely need to repeat themselves."

Greely ceased his scrawling and looked from Ian to General Hawthorne. "Why do we have a regiment of Specialized Forces in Macon? Is there a whole espionage ring working out of Macon that we don't know about? Was the colonel undercover this afternoon, trying to woo information from the nurse?"

"I'm going to find out what this is about." Ian slung his coat over one shoulder and threw on his hat, pushing past the man on his way out the door.

"She was taken to Fort Oglethorpe—," the reporter called after him.

Farris had her.

Ian picked up his pace down the long corridor of City Hall. One purpose filled every fiber of his being. Get to Abby before Farris made good on his threats.

Unless Farris presented indisputable evidence, he had no grounds for holding her. More than likely, he was drunk, and trying to scare her.

Thankfully, Abby didn't scare easily.

Crowded conditions and lack of basic necessities at Camp Oglethorpe bordered on inhumane. The facilities were not fit to house men, much less a lady.

"Colonel, a word, please." Hawthorne came up behind him.

Ian couldn't hide his consternation at being detained.

Once Abby was behind the twelve-foot walls of the prison camp, it would be infinitely harder to gain her release. He needed to get to her before she was inside the fortress.

"If you hope to see the girl, Colonel, you'd best hear me out." General Hawthorne pushed open a door labeled, CEREMONIAL ROOM. "In here, we can speak in private."

The newspaper man lingered close behind, craning his neck as Ian shut the door.

The general lit the tallest candle in a wide candelabra and then touched the flame to a cigar between his teeth. With a shake of his wrist, he extinguished the matchstick. "I have known Buford Farris for a very long time. He never was a good soldier. Always found reasons to sit on the sidelines." He removed a fleck of tobacco from his tongue with a thumb. "Because of his fondness for alcohol, Farris took a spill from his horse early on. He was removed from the battle grounds to perform guard duty over Macon with very limited personnel. President Davis never thought we'd actually need to be guarded this far south, but here we are."

"All the more reason to get Abby released." Unable to stand and do nothing, Ian moved to the window, looking out in the direction of the prison camp. "With a record like that, it shouldn't be hard to have his false allegations overturned."

"He's horrible soldier, true." General Hawthorne shook his head and blew out a halo of smoke. "But Farris is a brilliant strategist. Don't underestimate him."

Hawthorne, with his white head, hooked nose, and steely gaze reminded Ian of a great eagle he'd seen one winter by the Connecticut river. Astute and aware of his prey.

The general tapped his cigar with one finger on a porcelain dish sitting on the polished library table. "Knowing there are no civilian laws concerning espionage, Farris has managed to eliminate Miss McFadden's right to a trial by jury."

"That's not for Farris to decide." Ian moved closer to where the general stood.

Alarm pressed him to take action, even if it meant storming the gates.

"Oh, but it is. There are no national laws to try—or protect—one caught communicating intelligence to the enemy. Therefore, we refer to international law. Which states in times of war, spies are subject to execution *without* trial. At the discretion of the authorities charging them."

Ian placed both hands on the table and willed himself to take a breath.

Farris was completely irrational when it came to Abby. His hate for her ruled his decisions and dictated his actions. He was not above using fabricated charges to justify her arrest.

Standing, Ian placed a hand on the hilt of the sword hanging at his side.

If what the general said was true, in the eyes of military law, Abby was already declared guilty with no chance to prove her innocence.

General Hawthorne crossed his arms. "In biding his time until he had reasonable cause to charge her, Farris has effectively tied my hands, and that of the mayor, and all local law enforcement for that matter. This is the only allegation he could have brought against her, where he alone dictates her arrest and punishment."

Ian needed to get to Abby.

Farris was devious enough to have her executed before the ink was dry on her arrest papers. He had to be stopped.

With a nod, Ian reached for the door. "Thank you, Sir."

"Saberton, you mustn't let your feelings for Miss McFadden sully your judgement. You can't barge in there demanding her release on a habeas corpus." General Hawthorne met him at the door. "If Farris feels threatened, he will order her immediate execution. And you will have no choice but to stand by and watch."

"That will not happen." Ian ground out. "You and I both know she's innocent. And she's a woman besides. The army would never justify hanging a woman in a prisoner of war camp."

"Farris would be reprimanded, no doubt." The smell of his cigar engulfed the small space between them as Hawthorne placed a hand on Ian's shoulder. "But Abby would still be dead."

The bell tower rang in the ninth hour, and Ian's composure took a beating with every toll.

"I will kill him with my bare hands before I let that happen." Ian seethed with a rage like he had never known.

"And that is why I cannot let you go out to the garrison alone." General Hawthorne extinguished his cigar. "You may accompany me, but you will not take matters into your own hands. Is that understood?"

Moving away from the door, Ian snatched open the confining top button of his collar. "I won't leave there without her."

"You will not leave *with* her unless we persuade Farris to give her up. Short of storming the compound and inspecting every cell until we find her, we will need to somehow secure Farris' cooperation. Otherwise, we will be the ones reprimanded by the council."

Ian didn't trust himself to speak. A bitter taste filled his mouth as he thought about having to placate Farris.

But for Abby's sake he was willing to spit polish the man's shoes if it won her freedom.

"Have you thought about how we are supposed to persuade Farris to give her up?" Ian finally asked.

Thumping the table with the knuckles of his fist, the general suddenly stood up straighter. "I have an idea. But we'll need Cora's help."

Ian turned a skeptical eye toward the general.

The last thing Abby needed was Mrs. Dobbs and her band of militant females.

"No one denies Cora. And he wouldn't dare harm our women."

*"Those who deny freedom to others deserve it
not themselves."*
~ Abraham Lincoln

# Eighteen

Through a thin window next to the ceiling of her small cell, Abby watched dawn fight through a dark blanket of clouds to splay a single ray over the city of Macon. Heavy swirls of mist drifted past, intermittent with the vapor of despair that loomed to her very core.

Every second of the endless night had been spent in prayer. Without Divine assistance, her chances of escaping the tentacles of Farris' revenge was slim to none.

Beyond the stench of misery and disease reeking from every pore of the concrete wall, hundreds of sunken, lackluster eyes had followed her tow through the well-fortified courtyard. Their appearance was more animal than man as they watched her pass with detached interest. As if their sanity had been put aside in order to survive another day.

Abby was no stranger to carnage and disfigurement caused by battle. But this scourge of madness was a different sort of damage that was more disturbing than anything she'd ever encountered under a triage tent.

As though a deeper evil was in operation here. One not satisfied with simply killing the body, but intent on stealing a man's soul.

By the early hours of morning, Abby made a vow that if given the slightest opportunity to escape, she'd accept it as a gift from on high and run as fast as she was able without a backward glance.

With truth as her guard, she'd find a way to escape. Even if it meant leaving her heart behind with the only man who'd ever cared enough to protect it.

"Halt!"

Abby couldn't see the sentry on the high wall outside her window, but his voice pierced the early morning silence setting off a cacophony of barking dogs in the surrounding neighborhoods.

Rising to her feet, she strained to make sense of garbled voices accompanied by a clatter of hoofbeats. If her ears didn't deceive her, the voices were female, one sounding suspiciously like Cora Dobbs'.

It was all Abby could do not to call out to her.

*Please let it be Cora. Help her know I'm here.*

"At ease, private," General Hawthorne commanded when the guard refused to lower his weapon. "We've come to see General Farris."

"My orders are to keep all intruders at bay, Sir." The young private was barely old enough to have fuzz on his lip. Ian had a hard time believing Farris would put a new recruit out front to keep guard.

"We are not intruders, Teddy Dean Junior." Cora leaned

forward from her buggy. "You know exactly who I am. Cora Hawthorne Dobbs. I gave you Sunday School lessons your entire life. Now let us by before I have a word with your mama."

All the ladies were talking at once again.

Ian almost felt sorry for the kid. Backed into a corner, having to decide which was more foreboding, facing the wrath of General Farris, or answering to his mama for being discourteous to Mrs. Cora.

With a defeated head shake, the young soldier let his rifle slide to the ground and called for the gate to be opened.

"Rev." Fitz jerked his chin toward the wall.

Ian's eye was drawn up to the two sentries up on the walkway who still had their guns trained on them.

Ian tightened a hold on his rifle, barrel down but ready to fire if need be.

"Steady, Colonel." General Hawthorne's warning came quiet but clear. "Stay focused on our mission."

Ian hadn't been keen on bringing the women along in the first place.

Fitz had ranted all the way here that the whole idea was ridiculous.

Ian couldn't disagree.

But Hawthorne had insisted. "When the battle gets fierce, you bring out your sharpest weapons."

Part of him had to wonder if Cora Dobbs' brother wasn't as browbeaten by her as the rest of this town.

With Abby's future at stake, nothing but dogged determination and superior wit would see their mission accomplished today. Ian looked over at the six petticoat mercenaries, riding in a fringed buggy beside him. Cora Dobbs, two Lambert women, an ancient woman with magnifying spectacles, the pastor's wife, and a little lady in a huge bonnet that hadn't stopped yapping since they'd first set out.

He could only pray for a miracle.

Camp Oglethorpe was hammered out in huge black letters arching over the double gate. As each gate swung open, they were assaulted by a putrid odor that seemed to come from a murky stream running the length of the west end, obviously used for sewage by man and animal alike. The ladies' yowling was immediate. Lace hankies were brought out to cover their delicate noses.

Once inside the tall, paneled fortress, a separate picket fence made a pen of sorts in the center, filled to capacity with ghostly-thin bodies, filthy and sparsely covered. Some sat with knees up rocking and singing to themselves. Others lay curled and eerily still.

These same men were officers of the Union army. Most had courageously led their men into battle just a few short months ago. Reduced to little more than human waste. Seemingly resigned to starvation and disease with nothing left inside to be defeated.

Fitz let out a slow whistle.

Countless horror stories had been told of Union prisons, just like this one, in Richmond, New York, and Illinois. Evidently, both sides were blinded to humanity by a thirst for victory. Anything was permissible as long as it furthered their cause.

Indignation rose in Ian's chest. Righteous indignation is what the Chancellor would have called it.

Ian hadn't been convinced he could even feel such a thing anymore.

Surveying the disregard for humanity in front of him, he would attest that whatever one chose to call it, he was utterly disgusted and saddened by man's depravity.

Even the ladies fell silent as they left their buggy to follow a sergeant major to the prison's office, which stood only a few feet from the gate.

"I'll inform the general you are here." The hulking man Ian recognized as Farris' aide-de-camp lieutenant gave a stiff bow and exited through another door on the opposite side of the room.

Farris's office was a sharp contrast to the conditions outside its door. An opulent Persian rug lay over a glossy wood floor where two desks sat at an angle with a wall of mahogany bookshelves gracing one entire wall behind them. An expensive crystal decanter set rested atop a Duncan Phyfe sideboard with a tray of pastries set out beside it.

Only one with Farris' callousness would have the audacity to languor in luxury while hundreds of men lay dying of starvation outside his window.

"I knew that old walrus was hateful, but this even more heinous than I could've imagined." Cora Dobbs folded her gloved hands atop the hilt of her parasol. "I don't even want to think about what our poor Abby has had to endure in this awful place."

Elizabeth Lambert covered her mouth with a trembling hand. Eliza Jane put an arm about her mother's shoulders. They both looked as if they wanted to cry.

Ian's blood began to boil.

Fitz spoke up. "If Farris has treated that girl any way less than honorable, I'll personally take it out of his hide. An' there ain't a court in this land that'll convict me for it."

"Let's all remain calm, now." General Hawthorn held up a hand. "Let's not jump to conclusions. We will wait until we see her before we make any rash determinations. At which time, I will be the one making them."

"Georgie, go see what's taking them so long." Cora hitched her skirt and moved to the window. "Somebody better go watch the gate. I wouldn't put it past him to try and sneak her out when we're not looking."

"I took a side door once." The woman with glasses spoke up. "But, the train was still going. I hung on for dear life until the porter swung me back in."

"Mable Lea, what on earth would cause you to do such a thing?" Elizabeth Lambert asked, concern knitting her brow.

"I thought it was the water closet."

Cora turned and set a hand on her hip. "You mean to tell me you stepped off a moving train looking for the necessary room?"

The old woman scrunched her nose trying to find Cora in the room. "Well, it wasn't necessary after that, I assure you."

Eliza Jane snorted.

"Mable Lea, I'm over here." Cora lifted her watch from the chatelaine pinned at her waist. "He has five minutes before I go hunt him down."

Ian was just about to do the same when the door burst open, and Farris stumbled inside. Uniform crumpled with his shirt tail untucked. His thinning hair disheveled, and bloodshot eyes squinting against the sunlight. It was apparent the general had just rolled out of bed.

"General Farris!" Cora balled her white gloved fists and marched over to meet him. "Explain yourself this instant."

"I would have to agree, General. This is most alarming." Hawthorne stuck his hand into an unbuttoned opening in his vest.

Farris' eyes darted from one to another. "The Yankee spy tried to murder me."

"Good for her!" Eliza Jane erupted before her mother and the preacher's wife frowned her into calming down.

"I find that hard to believe." The sound of Ian's heavy boots echoed on the plank floor as he took slow steps to where Farris swayed. The sound appeared to unnerve the man. "Abby rarely leaves matters unfinished. If she truly intended to see you killed, you wouldn't be standing here."

"You tell 'em, Rev." Fitz lifted his foot to rest on the head of a porcelain bulldog next to one of the desks.

"Believe what you will. The McFadden woman will soon get her comeuppance." Farris avoided Ian, skirting around him to take a seat behind his desk. Rubbing his temples, he sent his assistant for dogwood tea. "Dare I ask what brings you all out visiting so early of a morning?"

"It's been reported that you have placed Miss McFadden under arrest." General Hawthorne began. "I would like to see a list of her charges."

"You can just go get her while you're at it." Cora stamped her parasol and came to stand in front of Farris' desk.

The other women fell in right behind her, adding their agreements. "And what's more, we are not leaving here without her."

"I'm not releasing her, ladies, so you are in for a long stay." Farris had trouble focusing. When his aide returned with his tea, he nearly burned himself trying to take a gulp. "Did your informants also tell you she drugged me and tried to escape?"

Ian leaned over the desk, forcing Farris to try and focus on him. "No. But every man on that ward said they heard you attack her. She fled in self-defense." He let his voice rise until Farris cringed.

"Here." Farris pushed a paper to the end of his desk. "See

her charges for yourself."

Ian took up the paper and Cora came to read next one arm, Elizabeth Lambert at the other.

Defendant:
    Miss Abigail McFadden
    Nurse, Floyd House Hospital
    Macon, Bibb County, Georgia

Charge:
    Espionage

Evidence:
    A. Defendant hails from a state involved in the Northern Aggression
    B. Letter found on deceased Union soldier at sight of Union raid included directions to storage at Confederate guarded warehouse signed by Defendant.
    C. Coin pendant in Defendant's possession reported stolen in said Union raid.

Punishment:
    To be hanged by the neck until dead.

"You will not hang Abby!" Cora blurted causing the other ladies to gasp.

General Hawthorne stepped forward and took the warrant. "Sir, this is the South. We do not under any circumstances hang our women."

"I won't personally, but I'll be glad to issue the order to see the deed done." Farris took another drink from his tea and made a face.

It took all the restraint Ian could muster not to snatch the arrogant windbag out of his chair and pin him to the wall.

General Hawthorne must have sensed Ian's struggle. Stepping up to the desk, he put himself between Ian and the desk where Farris sat looking much too smug. "You overlook an important detail, General. According to your warrant, this case is not yours, but falls to Colonel Saberton."

Farris's face paled. The dark bags under his eyes becoming even more visible. "*My* case, *my* prisoner."

"Of course, if you refuse to follow the dictates of the law, it could be your own hanging we attend." Hawthorne pivoted and let Ian regain his place in front to the desk.

The women nodded.

"What are you talking about?" Farris was paranoid in an instant. "I gathered the evidence. I had the defendant arrested. My hard work. Months of having her watched. You'll not take this from me."

"That's right, Georg … General." Cora folded her arms. "When you were making up charges, Buford, you should've made up that she was spying on this den of abomination you're running. That's the only way you'd have any say about it."

Ian folded Abby's warrant and put it in his breast pocket. "The storehouses are my assignment, General. Therefore, Miss McFadden's is *my* case. And she is now *my* prisoner."

"So go get her at once." Cora spoke directly to Farris' aide.

"Immediately, young man!" Elizabeth Lambert stood beside her, pointing to the door.

"You should be ashamed of yourself, General Farris!" Mable Lee whacked the coat rack with her parasol, sending it toppling to the floor.

"She is to be hanged for crimes committed against the Confederacy." Farris appeared anxious as he began to noticeably sweat.

"She'll be put under house arrest at the Lambert home until

her allegations are proven or disproven." Ian settled his hat in place.

One conversation with Doc should take care of that.

The sooner he collected Abby and got the women out safely, the sooner he could send a telegram to the Secretary of War requesting a tribunal inquisition. Hopefully, Ian could clear her name before their set time to meet and the dismissal of her case would just be a formality.

"I'll guarantee you one thing, Farris." Ian turned a hard stare at Camp Oglethorpe's commanding general. "She better not have been mistreated. All findings of today's visit will be included in my report to the Governor."

"And mine as well." General Hawthorne added.

"Me, too." Cora chimed in. "The governor is a personal friend."

Farris dabbed at the sheen on his upper lip. "I don't care if you're all bosom buddies with President Davis, himself. No one is taking my prisoner from here today—or any day. The warrant stands. She hangs at dawn."

"I don't believe I like your tone, General." Elizabeth Lambert pulled her shawl closer around her shoulders. "Have you any idea who you're talking to?"

"What?" Farris looked like he was about to be sick.

"This is Mrs. Cora Hawthorne Dobbs of the Columbia Hawthornes. Her great, great grandfather founded the very ground upon which you stand." She pointed at Ian. "And this young man is Colonel Ian Saberton of the Brechenridge Sabertons. His grandfather helped write the Georgia constitution."

Fitz began to chuckle. "Who thought it was a good idea to bring a bunch of belles to a war conference?"

"You see who got the job done, don't you?" Eliza Jane

folded her arms and lifted her nose at him.

Farris made haste in leaving the room just in time for all to hear him retching outside the door.

All ladies once again took out their scented handkerchiefs to cover their faces.

They heard Farris call for two soldiers to see him to his room. From the window, they could see two soldiers lifting the short man under his arms, half dragging the bulk of him to his quarters.

Ian calmly addressed the general's aide. "Farris no longer has the authority to hold Miss McFadden. If you refuse to release her to me, you would be impeding my investigation. Since I know you wouldn't want to face a court martial, I'll ask you kindly fetch my prisoner."

The large aide looked to General Hawthorne who gave him a nod, then to Eliza Jane who shooed him with her hands.

"Right away, Sir."

*"What would men be without women?*
*Scarce, sir...mighty scarce."*
~ Mark Twain

# Nineteen

*A*bby braced herself as Farris' hulking aide tugged at her arm, pulling her from her cell.

Her eyes burned behind their lids when sunlight hit her full in the face.

Treading across the fetid encampment, she took in the high walls. Noting the heavy cannons positioned at each corner and two soldiers, with rifles resting against their shoulders, patrolling across the top.

No other break in the fortress except a double gate which was heavily guarded and secured with a thick metal bolt. She had but two options. Figure a way to scale the high walls or trick a guard into opening the gate. Neither seemed likely, nor would they be easy.

The hemp cord securing her wrists had been wrenched too tight, chaffing her skin and numbing her fingers. Grateful for an intermittent breeze which gave moments of relief from the suffocating stench, Abby used her arm to move sweat-laden curls that stuck to her face. With her guard's ruthless pace, she needed to focus on the uneven path to keep from falling face first into a river of muck beneath her feet.

Without a word, he motioned for her to take the wooden steps up into an outbuilding that looked like it was more recently built than the rest of the camp.

At the top step she waited for him to open the door.

She knew Farris would be furious at her. Once again, he would blame her for his own humiliation. Being bound as she was, he would have a distinct advantage. From the outside, she noticed two windows. One facing the courtyard and one facing the fortress wall. They were too high to jump from, but not high enough to reach the top of the wall.

The door to Farris' office was pulled open from the inside and Abby's breath left her.

Deep brown eyes of Ian Saberton, the same eyes she'd summoned in the dark over and over again through the night, looked her over from head to foot.

Ian was here. He was real, not imagined. His broad shoulders filled the doorway.

When he reached for her, tears flooded her vision as she suppressed an overwhelming urge to fling herself into the safety of his arms.

But she would not give Farris the satisfaction.

Instead, Abby straightened her back, stepped farther into the room, and prepared to face her accuser.

Suddenly, she was surrounded by Elizabeth and Eliza Jane, Cora and even Miss Mable Lea. Huddling around her, all talking at once. Confused, Abby scanned the room, but Farris was nowhere to be seen. His assistant stood arms akimbo at the door.

Was she dreaming? Abby purposely twisted her wrists to

feel the sting of rough fiber against her skin. Eliza Jane was crying, holding on to Abby like she was afraid to let go. Her hands were bound in front, rendering her helpless to comfort her friend.

"Let's get you out of here." Ian leaned down to speak to her only. She could feel the warmth of his body next to her and, despite her bravado, she couldn't resist leaning into him for a moment to absorb his strength. When his arm came around her shoulder, she finally allowed herself to believe he'd truly come for her.

"You're shaking, Angel." Ian pulled her tighter against himself. "I don't know what he's put you through, but Farris will never get near you again."

Abby could do nothing but nod in answer. She dared not look up at him or risk dissolving into a million tears. The miracle she'd prayed for was standing right here, holding her close. The power of his embrace steadied her as she absorbed the strength of his promise.

Abby spotted Fitz dabbing his eyes with his sleeve.

"You are released into Colonel Saberton's custody, Miss McFadden. An inquiry hearing must be conducted before the charges can be formally dismissed." General Hawthorne herded the ladies toward the door. "But for now, I recommend we continue this discussion elsewhere."

Ian turned her around and with a quick upward slice of his knife, the rope fell from her hands. "You'll ride with me."

Abby watched Farris' aide warily, not understanding why he wasn't stopping her from leaving. She sincerely hoped she hadn't killed the general. The syringe only had 10 mg of morphine in it. But depending on how much alcohol he'd consumed, it may have been enough to create a lethal combination.

Wouldn't she be wanted for his murder if that were the case?

Taking her by the hand, Ian led her down the steps to where the horses were tethered. As the ladies filed into Cora's landau, Ian swung up into his saddle. Reaching down for her, Ian instructed Fitz to help boost her up behind him.

The bolt screeched loudly as it slid back from its hasp and the gates opened slowly on rusty hinges. A more beautiful sound had never been heard.

Pausing, Abby turned to have one last look at the grim faces of the prisoners. Saying a prayer for their miracle too, she slipped her hands around Ian's waist.

Nudging his horse, Ian sent him trotting toward Macon.

With Ian's broad back to shield her from the cold wind, Abby took a deep breath and finally relaxed. Rubbing her cheek against him, she closed her eyes as the steady gait of the horse lulled her into a much-needed sleep.

"I've examined the body. This soldier did not die of a gunshot wound."

Ian watched Doc Lambert walk around the tall wooden table on the third floor of the hospital.

"What would you say killed him then?"

"Do you see this black tissue clear up to his hip?" The doctor showed an area discolored and shriveled. But on closer inspection, Ian saw the skin Doc referred to was farther along in decay. "What are you saying?"

Doc pulled the Yankee jacket open to reveal a hole in the man's chest. "This gunshot wound would have killed him, no doubt. But this man was already dead. Gangrene. As you can see, it had already taken over his organs. I'd say he's been dead over a week."

"So, he didn't die behind the warehouse three days ago." Ian had a good suspicion how he'd gotten there. Now, it was just a matter of proving it.

"No. This man hasn't walked anywhere on his own for weeks. Someone would have had to place him there." Doc pulled a stained sheet over the body.

"Did he have any identification on him?" The double-breasted frock coat with fourteen federal eagle buttons suggested he was an officer. At least a major in rank.

Doc went to a file box and lifted some papers. "I recognized him. I worked on him when he was first sent down with a load of war prisoners from Jonesborough. He was already too far gone to save, so he was taken to the infirmary at Camp Oglethorpe. We needed the beds and Farris had plenty."

Ian took the papers which listed the man as Major Rupert Reynolds with Logan's XV Corps.

"So how did a dying Yankee, under Farris' guard, end up dead behind the storehouses with a bullet hole in his chest?" Ian tapped the paper on the table. "With a letter in his pocket supposedly written by Abby."

"I personally can't answer that. Farris hasn't provided any such letter." Doc shook his head and untied his apron. "I'd wager it never existed."

As evidence against Farris mounted, suspicion against Abby eased. Still, Ian needed to get his hands on that letter. And he wanted the name of the woman who claimed she'd seen Abby with her stolen property.

Farris had taken ill this morning before he'd turned over all of the evidence. Ian would pay him another visit first thing in the morning.

"Thank you, Doctor." Ian shook his hand. "And thank you

for allowing Abby to stay with your family until this is resolved."

"Abby's like a daughter, Colonel." Doc hooked a thumb in his vest pocket. "She regularly tends to my family over and above what's required. It's the very least we can do for her." He stopped at the stairwell. "No matter what perverse satisfaction Farris hopes to gain by all this, I assure you Abby isn't capable of anything he's accused her of."

"Yes, Sir." Ian agreed and donned his hat. "Thank you."

Fitz was waiting for him outside by the horses. "You got a wire from Wheeler."

Ian took the envelope and lifted the telegraph slip. Heaving an exasperated sigh, he crumpled the paper and settled his hat on his head. "Sherman's troops are foraging south. Looks like he intends to take this all the way to Savannah."

"Yep. I read it." Fitz took the reins and hoisted himself into his saddle, leading his horse into an easy walk alongside Ian's. "Yankee raiders were seen near as fifty miles from here."

"I'll take a few men and scout the area between here and Milledgeville. We'll leave at dawn. We can collect any civilians who want to seek refuge. And if we come across a raider or two, we'll bring them in as well."

"What about Miss Abby?" Fitz likely knew the answer to that before he asked.

Ian's priorities had been set for him.

General Wheeler expected the assignment he'd given to Ian to come first. He was bound by orders to see as many Georgians as humanly possible spared from the same fate Atlanta now suffered.

"She stays with the Lamberts and goes about her business as usual." Ian scanned the sky as heavy clouds rolled in from the south covering the noonday sun. "Clearing her name's just a formality. I'll deal with it after we send Sherman's army back up north."

Fitz clicked his tongue at his horse to keep him moving. "You really think Farris is just gonna lay down and give her up just like that?"

The question immediately irritated Ian. Mainly because it was a question he'd asked himself a dozen times today. Truthfully, he knew the answer was that was the real irritation.

"I'm leaving you here to keep an eye on her." As they passed the newest camp set up for refugees near the hospital, Ian looked for Hickory or others from the shanty town.

Mrs. Oberhaus waved with her two small girls playing a game of chase around her skirts.

Abby would feel better knowing they were relocated and safe.

A memory of her gentle, even breathing as she'd fallen asleep at his back that morning made his arms ache to hold her. There was something so innocent about Abby. Not in a way that made her foolish or naïve. She definitely had no problem standing up for herself.

Abby trusted good to overcome evil simply because it was the stronger force. Through all she'd experienced, she never gave up her childlike faith.

He wouldn't risk losing her again.

"Set a couple of guards at the Lamberts." He called over to Fitz. "I want them posted as soon as possible."

Thunder rolled in the distance where storm clouds grew heavy with coming rain. Ian lifted the collar around his neck.

At some point over the past couple of years, he'd lost his ability to believe good could still come in his life. Since the first battle at Shiloh, all he'd stood for had been shaken.

"I just don't get that Blowhard." Fitz popped open a peanut and tossed the nut into his mouth. "He's made it his aim to see Abby pay for his sins. If that don't sound like Lucifer hisself, I don't know what does."

Ian slowed his horse to a stop under a sprawling oak. Fitz's analogy was crude and unconventional. Nonetheless, a truth there begged to be explored. Farris' hatred toward Abby flowed deeper than mere human contempt.

Shaking his head, Ian dismissed his theoretical musings and prodded his horse forward once more. He hadn't thought in terms of Biblical analogies since the last time he'd prepared a sermon. He was a different man now.

Despite his denial, something inside—deep inside—began to stir.

Slowing at the corner of Mulberry and First, Ian gestured toward the river. "Go on back to camp, Fitz. I'll check on Abby and be back to attend evening drills."

"Colonel!" The high shriek caught them both off-guard. "Colonel!" Turning in his saddle he saw Penny Jo running down the street after them. Calming his horse, he swung the animal around to meet her. As he neared, he saw the child was crying.

Ian slid to the ground and handed his reins off to Fitz. On one knee, he pulled the little girl closer. "What is it, Penny Jo?"

"T-That ol' Farris came after her. They tried to grab Abby!" Fury ignited as Ian stood and turned his focus on the Lambert house. "Those bad men that live by Hickory barged right in the house. None of 'em even knocked." A sob took over and Ian could see she was fast becoming inconsolable. "They tried to steal Abby."

"Is she all right?" Ian's voice shook with masked rage.

Penny Jo shook her head and wailed louder. "I don't know. She's not there."

With an arm over her small shoulders, Ian hurried her over to Fitz's horse.

"Fitz, take her home." Ian lifted the child up into the saddle. "Find out all you can from the Lamberts."

Ian walked to his horse and removed a rifle from his saddle holster, checking to make sure it was fully loaded.

"Want me to get a few men to go with you?" Fitz settled Penny Jo in front of him and offered her some peanuts.

"No. Send someone to inform General Hawthorne." With a flip of the chamber, Ian holstered his Colt revolver. "The shanty isn't far, and I don't plan on this taking long."

"She's not at the shanty town." Penny Jo sniffled. "I don't imagine so anyway."

Fitz dumped out the rest of his peanuts and handed her the empty cotton pouch to blow her nose.

Ian turned and patted her knee to help her stay focused. "Penny Jo, what makes you say they weren't headed to the shanty? Did they say where they were taking her?"

"Abby kicked that big bully hard—right where it hurts— cuz he was putting his hands on her trying to tie her up. The other man had a knife, and I think he cut Abby cuz I saw some blood. Mama said it was just brambleberry juice, but I never saw it on the rug before."

Ian's pulse quickened.

"Eliza Jane threw open the door, and Abby took off running fast as she can into those woods over there." Penny Jo suddenly waved at someone. A smile slowly spread across her tear-stained face.

Hickory ran hard toward them. "You found him!"

"He was just sitting there by the tree," she answered. "Mr. Fitz is gonna give me a ride on his horse back to my house."

"Colonel, my Abby's gone." Hickory was breathless and

on the verge of tears. "Mo's real mad that she got away from him. Farris says he's gonna—"

"I'll find her." Ian didn't need hear any more. He needed to find Abby and get her away from Macon. "Listen to me, Hickory, I need your help. Go tell Mama Ivy that Lieutenant Fitz will come by this evening to bring the both of you to the train depot in Gordon. Wait for me there."

Mama Ivy could take care of her if she was hurt. Hoping Hickory was old enough to understand the urgency, Ian lowered his voice. "And tell her to bring her doctoring bag."

The boy's eyes widened but he held his composure. "Yes, sir."

"Farris said they were gonna get some dogs and hunt Abby down." Penny Jo stroked the mane of Fitz's horse as she talked. "Mama sent me to run find you."

Ian had no idea where Abby would go, but with Mo and Farris' other hired hands after her, he prayed she was well enough to stay moving.

As if the heavens agreed, a crack of thunder peeled across the sky before the heavy clouds released a deluge onto the city.

*"If life be a war, it seemed my destiny to conduct
it single-handedly."*
~ *Charlotte Brontë*

# Twenty

Terror swept through Abby.

Thorny brush tore through her skirts as torrents of
rain stung her face, blurring her vision. Still, she dared not
stop. The ferocity of Farris' hatred snapped at her heels like a
rabid dog forcing her to stay a step ahead.

Though she felt no pain to speak of, she kept a hand
pressed on her abdomen. Rain-diluted blood ran through her
fingers. She knew the bleeding needed to be controlled or shock
was sure to set in.

Keeping to the wooded thicket, she kept her feet moving
until her silk slippers skated precariously on a thick patch of
leaves covering the muddied earth. Grabbing onto a low-
hanging vine, she struggled to regain solid footing. Undoubtedly, she would make faster progress if she discarded the soggy
shoes altogether, but slowing her pace for even a second could
prove deadly.

Lifting her face, she tried to detect any sign of the sun

through the pounding rain. Thick, heavy clouds made it impossible to tell what direction she was heading until she was forced to admit she was utterly lost.

The unrelenting surge had her completely turned around. If she could find the river, it would eventually lead her up to Atlanta. Without the sun as a guide, she couldn't tell how long she'd been running. Barely able to keep her eyes open against the constant downpour, she had no choice but to push on.

Exhaustion weighted her legs, cut and bruised from the underbrush. Unable to see the ground in front of her, Abby tripped over a moss-covered rock and landed with a splash in the center of a rushing stream. She gasped as the cold water billowed her skirt.

Below her waistband, her skirt was slashed and a stain of blood darkened the material. Thankfully, she wasn't bleeding enough to suspect a damaged artery. As long as she did nothing to further open the wound, she would be fine to continue on.

A blinding flash lit up the woods, followed by a deafening clap of thunder that shook the ground beneath her, matching the shaking of her limbs. Drenched tendrils streamed down her face.

Ahead, a clearing stretched out just beyond the of cover of lofty trees.

Attempting to climb the slippery bank brought a sudden sharp pain to her middle and Abby cried out in frustration. Fear of being caught offered no time to rest. As soon as her foot stepped onto level ground, Abby began to run.

Another fiery bolt streaked through the sky, illuminating an ambiguous red shape on the horizon against angry, black clouds. With the back of her hand, she pushed aside her sodden strands, blinking to better focus. A red outbuilding was nestled at the other end of the clearing.

No matter what was inside, she needed to escape the pelting rain. Abby lifted her face against the torrential barrage and made a staggering run for the shelter.

Her foot stepped onto a cushion of grass. Thunder rolled ominously from one end of the darkened sky to the other as the rain poured harder in the open. The shield of trees no longer offered protection and she quickened her pace.

As she neared, Abby realized the building was an old barn. One heavy door hung from its rusted hinge and thudded noisily against the wood. A good pull splintered the wood as it splashed in pieces into the mud at her feet.

Abby ducked inside, rubbing at the chill in her arms. Half petrified, half freezing.

Even in the dim light, she could see cobwebs glistening from the ceiling but saw nothing else rustling in the eaves. With chattering teeth, she looked back the way she came in to see if she'd been followed. The rain made it impossible to see anything past sheets of water pouring from the roof of the barn.

Plenty of hay covered the floor. Pails, stools, and a pitchfork lay where they were dropped across two stalls, where a couple of milk cows or maybe even a goat had once occupied this space.

No matter who used to live here, Abby was overjoyed to have a dry place to rest.

Taking up the pitchfork as a precaution, she sank exhausted onto the hay at an inside corner of the stall. Still working to catch her breath, she listened hard for any evidence that she might have been followed.

The pounding of her heart was all she could hear above the roar of the rain.

Twinges of pain had begun to catch in her lower belly,

though the bleeding had abated. Infection was her greatest concern. The puncture would heal with time if the tissue didn't become festered.

Grateful for a dry place to hide, Abby laid her head back against the wall until she caught sight of two glowing red eyes peering at her from the dark loft above. A shard of fright shot through her as she backed farther into the corner. Lifting the pitchfork, she was poised for battle.

The creature didn't move.

A crash of thunder shook the walls and she smothered a scream.

A crusted horseshoe hanging on the wall caught her attention. Slowly, Abby eased over to lift the iron piece from its peg. With careful aim, she flung the horseshoe at the silent spectator.

Again, she lifted the pitchfork, imagining a bobcat ready to pounce.

A fat barn cat padded out to the end of the loft and stretched leisurely. Peering down at the silly dripping human, the feline meowed as if Abby had disturbed a perfectly lazy afternoon.

Abby leaned back against the wall, not sure whether to laugh or cry. Her nerves were stretched taut, and her hand quivered as she released a tight grip on the pitchfork.

She kept an eye on the open barn door. Hearing anything above the pouring rain was next to impossible. Inching closer, she looked out at the clearing in front of her. Sheets of rain moved across the grass as the sky grew even darker. A frigid blast of rain-soaked air drove her back to the corner of a stall.

The cold wind sliced right through her, causing uncontrollable shivers.

A lantern with tinderbox hung on a post in the middle of

the barn and Abby imagined how wonderfully warm a fire would feel right now. Her hair and clothing could dry, and wild creatures would surely stay away from the flame.

The temptation was nearly overwhelming. But in the end, the risk of Farris seeing light from the high window outweighed her desire to be dry and warm.

Settling back down, she tried to listen past the rain for any unusual sounds as she wrung out her hair and the ends of her skirt. After a while, her breathing steadied, and she laid back on the on mound of hay. The pitchfork lay within reach at her feet. With a hand, she warmed the wound in her belly.

Abby listened to the steady thrumming against the wood roof. The smell of rain filled her senses and began to sooth her fears. Her eyes grew heavier with every blink.

If she could make it to Atlanta, she would find safety with the Union Army. The thought of leaving Georgia caused an ache inside her that had nothing to do with the knife wound.

Eventually, her mind wandered to visions of a tall, dark-eyed Colonel.

Elizabeth and Eliza Jane had probably alerted the entire city by now. Had Ian discovered her missing? Abby imagined Ian searching for her high and low. Distraught at the thought of losing her.

The romantic image made her smile.

It wasn't just his broad shoulders or strong jaw that she found appealing, but the way he made her laugh when she didn't want to. The tender way he'd stopped to help an old man pull his cart out of a rut. This was what drew her to him. Little things to most people, but most important to Abby.

Would she ever see him again?

Suddenly, her imagination took her to the middle of a field. Alone, she stood as Ian approached atop a beautiful white charger. It didn't matter why she was alone in the field or that she sensed danger looming all around her. All she cared about was that Ian had found her, and she was no longer lost and scared.

He swung down from his white horse and walked toward her, speaking her name softly, "Abby."

She ran to meet him and, smiling. He held out his arms again, tenderly saying her name, louder this time.

With no hesitation, she took his magnificent face in her hands, and brought his lips down to hers. Abby kissed him with everything she had been holding back. Softly at first, then pouring every ounce of her feelings for him into one lasting kiss.

"Abby." Ian's rich, deep voice was so near it sent shivers through her.

Barely opening her eyes, she looked up into deep sparkling orbs. Her hands still held his face and her lips still puckered.

Instead of being awestruck by their mind-boggling kiss, his eyes crinkled at the corners and he looked ... amused.

Abby's eyes flew wide open.

Letting go of his face, she sat up and grabbed the pitchfork, pointing it at the man who materialized in front of her.

She wasn't in a fragrant field. Nor was the intruder lingering over her a fanciful figment of her imagination.

Ian's deep laughter echoed through the barn and she slowly lowered her weapon.

He reached for her hand. "That was quite a welcome."

Abby's cheeks burned. Reminding herself it had all been a dream, she tried to cover her embarrassment. But her lips still tingled from a kiss that had been blissfully real.

"You're here." A ridiculous thing to say. Of course, he was here. "I mean ... hooray, you're here!"

Ian gave her that lopsided grin. "Hooray," he mocked.

Abby was convinced he must have been an impossible child.

After hours of tracking her, Ian was glad to find her safe. More importantly, he was glad he'd gotten to her before Farris. When he came upon her in the barn and found her sleeping, he'd approached as quietly as possible, doing his best not to startle her.

Abby was mumbling in her sleep, and Ian knelt beside her to make sure she wasn't in pain.

Her sleepy kiss caught him completely off guard.

Considering Abby rarely did anything without putting her whole heart into it, he had to admit her kiss was sweetly passionate. Innocent yet bold.

Much like Abby herself.

"How did you find me?" A charming blush stained her cheeks.

"I followed you." He removed his black slicker, dripping wet from the ride. With nimble fingers, he unfastened the buttons going down the front of his frock coat and shrugged it from his shoulders. Placing it around her, Ian brought the lapels together and pulled her close. "Penny Jo said you were hurt."

"Just a nick." Abby relaxed into the warmth of his coat. "Nothing to be concerned about."

He didn't believe it but wasn't going to push her. Mama Ivy could have a look once they got to Gordon.

"You took quite a spill in the stream. Don't want you catching a chill." He wrapped his scarf around her neck.

"Did you see that? I pray Farris isn't as good at following

as you are."

"I only saw evidence that you'd been there." Ian plucked straw from her hair. "I covered your tracks."

"I'm so thankful you're here." Her gaze shone bright with sincerity. "I couldn't bear the thought of never seeing you again."

Her quiet admission touched a place inside of him he'd closed off a long time ago.

War had calloused him. Duty was best served without emotional attachment. Killing had become second nature in order to survive. Only soldiers with razor-sharp focus and an uncanny will to stay alive walked away from the battlefield to fight another day. Thinking too hard about it meant the difference in living and dying.

Or so he'd told himself.

Gazing now into the serene expression on Abby's face, he questioned everything he'd become. Truth in her eyes drew him in, and made him want to believe in life again. Believe there might still be a plan for him after the last battle is over. Believe in healing and forgiveness.

Suddenly uncomfortable with the direction his thoughts had taken, Ian sat next to Abby and pulled her in next to him. He held her silently until her shivering subsided and he felt her heartbeat began to settle.

The storm calmed as well.

Raindrops pattered against the weathered wood and neither of them moved. Both content to enjoy the moment, not knowing if they'd ever have this chance again.

By the time darkness obscured the barn, Ian went in search of a lamp he'd seen hanging on the center post.

"What if Farris or his men are out there?" Abby stood carefully and moved to the gaping entrance of the old barn.

Ian knelt to scrape flint into a small pile of hay with his pocket knife. After sparking a flame, Ian lifted the glass chimney, lighting the well-used stub of a candle inside the lantern. "There are no windows facing the woods, and the door faces north. If Farris has anyone out in this storm tonight, they'll most likely come from the eastern woodlands. The light won't attract them."

He smothered the remnant fire on the ground with a boot while shifting shadows danced on the walls in the light of the candle.

Ian removed a wool blanket from his bedroll. His horse's winter coat hadn't come in and he needed to be dried. "We can leave as soon as the rain clears."

Loosening the front cinch, he ran the cloth underneath. The gray gelding lifted his ears and swung his head over to peer at Abby.

"Maybe I should go back to Macon." Abby pulled his oversized coat closer around her shoulders and approached the horse. He noticed she kept a hand over her lower belly.

"Farris will come for you again." Ian shook the blanket and used the other side. "I leave tomorrow on assignment, I can't be there to watch over you. Next time, he may succeed in having you killed."

The only way Ian could absolutely guarantee Farris wouldn't get to her again was if she were to take up camp with him and his men where he could keep a constant eye on her. For the sake of her reputation, he wouldn't even suggest it.

Ian rubbed down the horse's back.

New orders had just come in. He was to track Sherman's army and report its location. They would be pulling up camp as early as in the morning. He couldn't risk leaving Abby alone in Macon. General Hawthorne had made it clear, his focus would be on securing Macon against enemy invasion. His troops would have their hands full.

With enemy forces bearing down on the city, Abby would easily be overlooked.

"I'll go north up to Atlanta, but I won't leave Hickory without saying goodbye." Abby smoothed the horse's black mane. "He doesn't need another person abandoning him with no warning or explanation."

Ian knew this was personal for her.

She was that child once, whose loved ones never came home.

"I've arranged for you to see Hickory and Mama Ivy at the train depot in Gordon. You can say goodbye then." The horse stamped a hoof at the barn cat threading itself around Abby's skirts. Ian ran the feline off to keep it from getting trampled. "I'd like Mama Ivy to have a look at your wound."

A frown came over her brow. "Does the train from Gordon go to Atlanta?"

"Yes, unless the Yankees have ripped up the rails." Ian answered, watching her reaction carefully. "Why are you so determined to go to Atlanta?"

"Maybe it's time I go home. To Mansfield." Abby continued to scratch the horse's neck and withers. "If I can make it to Atlanta, arrangements can be made to get me the rest of the way. Where there is no Farris."

"Is that really what you want?" Ian looked over at her.

"Not really." She gave a small shrug. "The church is there. The one that supported my father's mission. I could make an appeal for the children and maybe help build a home for war orphans."

"Division of the nation has divided the churches as well. All are trying to survive on half the income they once had as a whole." Ian hung the blanket to dry over a coarse partition in the stall. "An admirable venture, Angel, but I doubt there will be money to fund it."

Abby didn't answer but went to sit on a little three-legged stool next to the pole. Ian was fascinated by the fiery streaks in her hair each time she moved in the candlelight.

"I know your heart is with Hickory and his friends, but a church organization located in Ohio isn't going to build a home for a bunch of kids down in Georgia."

When her shimmering gaze lifted to him, Ian went to her. Kneeling, he took her hand.

"So it seems they've run out of options just like I have." Her breath caught. "Do you feel how cold and wet it is out there? Hickory is feeling it, too." Her voice had reduced to a whisper. "He has no warm home with a hearth. The best he can hope for is someplace dry to lay his head. He'll go to sleep tonight on the bare earth with no one to place a kiss on his forehead or tell him to have pleasant dreams." A tear rolled down the fine curve of her cheek. "I doubt Hickory even dares to dream anymore."

Abby had a passion much like what Ian imagined her father must've had. She valued truth, felt it deeply, and wasn't afraid to speak it. Like her father, she, too, would have made a fine minister.

Reaching over, he stopped her tear with a finger. He only wished he could solve what had caused them just as easily. "Angel, do you trust me?"

"Of course." She sniffed and gave a reluctant grin. "We're alone in the middle of nowhere with only your horse to chaperone. I'd best be able to trust you."

Ian flashed a wide grin and gently pulled her to her feet in front of him.

Straightening his coat over her much smaller frame, he cupped her shoulders with his hands. "Then let me send you to Brechenridge. Take Hickory with you. My family will welcome you both. General Hawthorne has already contacted the military authorities to call for Farris' arrest. Until then, he won't be able to get to you while I'm gone. You can take the time you need to heal. I'll send a telegraph to Governor Brown in Milledgeville. He can issue you a full pardon."

Ian brought her hand to his lips and left a kiss on her wrist.

"Won't your family find it unusual that you're sending a strange woman to live with them?"

"Strange is a bit harsh." Ian tilted his head with a teasing grin. Sliding an arm around her waist, he brought her close. "Maybe a tad peculiar, but I wouldn't call you strange."

Lowering his head, he erased her pout with a kiss.

When Abby relaxed, he let the soft caress of her lips ease his worries about the days ahead. Time suspended. For a brief moment, there was no conflict, no killing, no suffering.

Just the two of them, surrounded by the heady cadence of rain.

*"Search me, O God, and know my heart: try me, and know my thoughts:
And see if there be any wicked way in me, and lead me in the way everlasting."*
*Psalm 139:23-24*

# Twenty-One

Stepping back, Abby walked away from the warmth of Ian's arms to cool in the open doorway. "The rain has let up." A chill immediately skittered through her body.

Ian came up behind her and rested his forearm on the frame of the door. "We'll wait out the lightning and leave when it's passed."

She had no right to expect he promised anything more than protection. Offering her refuge at Brechenridge was a gracious proposal, but had nothing to do with love or forever.

Abby craved more from Ian than he was prepared to give. He carried a heavy burden inside that prevented him from loving anyone, least of all himself. A wall of indifference. He guarded his heart as fiercely as he guarded his country.

Until he was free from whatever it was that kept him bound, he was unable to share the kind of love she longed for.

The kind her father had for her mother. The kind she'd felt for the briefest moment in the heat of his kiss.

For that reason, Abby had pulled away.

Attraction without commitment was like floating adrift in an unreliable sea of emotion. Without love as an anchor, the draw of deeper waters chanced drowning should the winds change.

Ultimately, they would both be hurt.

"If we leave before dawn, we'll make the noon train for Savannah." Ian spoke softly over her shoulder.

Her troubled thoughts brought a familiar rise of panic that screamed to get away before she got hurt.

Tossing a quick glance up, she saw him studying the sky before looking down at her.

"Why do I get the feeling you're trying to figure out how to run away as soon as I'm not looking?" The quirk in his brow all but dared her to try.

An instant denial sprang to her tongue, but the truth in his question pressed her into silence.

"You run away when you expect rejection. It's how you ended up here, hundreds of miles from home." Ian turned and leaned against the doorframe to face her. "I'm not a threat. I won't abandon you or reject you like the church or foster homes or Malcolm's family did. As soon as this war's over, I'll come back for you. I'll always see that you and Hickory are taken care of."

"I don't need to be taken care of." Abby crossed her arms, leaving a respectable space between them, swallowing the clump in her throat. "I need to be loved."

Ian wrenched back as if she'd slapped him.

As long as he felt at liberty to point out her shortcomings, she decided this was as good a time as any to help him see a few of his own.

"And so do you, Ian Saberton." She frowned when he smiled. "Your typical avoidance of committing to anything other than duty is exasperating."

"Is it now?" Ian strolled over to sit on a bale of hay.

Abby couldn't see his expression in the dim light to know if her direct observation had hurt his feelings.

She suddenly felt contrite.

Her aim had been to help him, but as usual her temper got in the way.

"I didn't mean to accuse you." With a tired sigh, she joined him on the hay, leaning a shoulder against his arm. "I honestly don't understand you." Surely, he wouldn't be offended by the truth.

Now that the rain had stopped, the only sound filling the dank space was the purr of the sneaky cat from a dark corner.

"What would you like to know, Angel?" Ian stretched out his long legs.

Deepening shadows accentuated the masculine angles of his face. For one so perfect on the outside, it pained her to know he was so damaged on the inside. Abby wanted healing and wholeness for him. A reprieve for his hurting soul.

"I know you went to seminary. You mentioned one time that you'd planned to enter the clergy before Georgia's secession."

Abby watched the casual grin fade from his lips. Apparently, she'd struck a nerve.

"What happened, Ian?"

He laid his head back against the rough-hewed wall of the barn and stared up into the rafters. Abby could barely see the muscle working his jaw.

Torment, like she'd seen in the face of hundreds of suffering soldiers, worried his brow.

Instinctively, she reached for his hand.

"I killed a man." His admission was low, without emotion.

After three years of serving in the war, she was pretty sure he'd killed plenty of men.

"In the line of duty?"

Ian shook his head and continued searching the dark rafters. As if sense of it all could be found up there. "No, I never saw him coming. I was the company chaplain straight out of seminary. Was only sworn in for two weeks before they sent me to the battle lines in Tennessee."

Abby could see the memory was painful.

"It happened at Shiloh. Our men were ordered to conduct a surprise attack outside the church there." Though he made an attempt to grin, his expression was humorless. "I came around the corner and Fitz shouted for me to turn around."

He grew quiet again.

Abby laced her fingers around his, wanting to absorb some of the grief she felt in the tightening of his hand.

Such a heavy burden of guilt he'd carried.

"When I turned, I saw a Yankee captain coming at me with his revolver drawn. He shot, but his aim was pathetically off. With no thought other than to stay alive, I swung around and unsheathed my sword, planting it deep in his chest."

Abby closed her eyes.

"I staggered, watched life leave his body, before he slumped over my arm."

Ian had been a man dedicated to saving men. He couldn't justify taking an innocent life. "You were only defending yourself." She rubbed his arm with her other hand. "If you hadn't killed him, he would have killed you."

Ian turned his head toward her. She could barely see his

face. "His name was John Maddox. Six months earlier, we shared courses at Yale." Clenched teeth muffled his argument. "I knew his family, he knew mine. We were like brothers."

Abby took a deep breath, praying for Divine assistance. "Did you set out to murder John?" She held his gaze. "Was hate the motivation in your heart that day?"

"Of course not." Ian sat forward, to rest a forearm across his knee. "But I killed him just the same."

"It's not the same." Abby slid to her knees on the floor in front of him, forcing him to look at her. "You killed a man protecting yourself. You had no choice because he would have killed you first had you not. Murder is a *conscious* choice. When deliberate hate in your heart drives you to take another life. You only reacted."

"John didn't know it was me." Ian stood. "If he had, I'm certain he never would've pulled that trigger."

"He was following orders." Far too many men were maimed or dead for carrying out orders. "Same as you were."

Abby stayed on her knees, looking down at the folded hands in her lap. The wound in her abdomen had begun to throb. "Neither of you set out to murder that day. Murder is an act of hatred. You did not hate John."

Ian walked to the low stall and braced both hands on the top of the wall. "I was an avowed man of God. I had no right taking the life of a good man."

"Neither did King David. He committed a highly thought-out murder. But, God named him a man after His own heart."

Ian said nothing. The shadows were too deep to tell if he'd even heard her.

"Do you know why?" Abby carefully stood to go to him. "David knew he was far from perfect. If he had been, he'd have no need for redemption. No need to trust in the mercy of a good God." She came up against Ian's side and laid her hand on his arm. "King David had a deep desire to follow God with reckless abandon. The same boy who showed unfathomable courage in the face of a giant, became the man who showed even greater valor by learning to admit his own weakness. He knew he wasn't perfect. And knew how desperately he must rely on the God who is."

Ian remained silent and so did Abby. She'd spoken from the depths of her heart. He needed to find forgiveness. And strength to forgive himself.

Lifting her hand, she felt a fresh blood stain spread from the waistband of her skirt.

*"Let men tremble to win the hand of woman, unless
they win along with it
the utmost passion of her heart."*
*~ Nathaniel Hawthorne*

## Twenty-Two

*B*efore daybreak, Ian watched Abby from the doorway of
the old barn. Though the birds chirped high in the trees
signaling the start of a new day, she slept undisturbed.

He looked out over the countryside, watching the first glow
of sunrise spread across the field. Rain left a tranquil haze over
the sated grasslands.

Inside, the lantern hung dark and cold, the candle flame
long extinguished. Their meager shelter was dipped in inky
outlines.

He couldn't say exactly when she'd nodded off, but she'd
slept hard for the past four hours.

Ian had not slept at all.

Abby's innocent questions brought up bitter memories that
had poisoned his soul. After all this time, he could still see
John's face as death overtook him. Eyes rolled back, a snarl of
pain forever caught in his throat. Ian had shouted his name

before the body of his friend fell against him. Pale and lifeless.

That same night, Ian had gone to General Johnston and traded in his Bible for a rifle. No man called by God would strike like a viper without regard to the everlasting consequences of his actions. When Ian resigned as company chaplain, Johnston offered a commission of Major for the Georgia Dragoons.

Last night, Abby's innocent thoughts left his argument in tatters.

He'd spent most of the night grappling with his jaded conscience. Nothing he could do would bring John back from his grave. But by turning his back on his calling and throwing away the fervor he once held for God's work, he'd only hurt himself.

Ian had been mired in self-pity and bitterness long enough.

Only a coward demanded justification for forgiveness. God's forgiveness required no justification. In the wee hours of the morning, the slate had been cleared.

At his commissioning, he'd sworn to support and defend his home, but in a dark corner of this barn, he'd recommitted to uphold a higher calling.

One day, he'd speak to hundreds about the man John was. Not the terrified young soldier that lost his life fighting a battle he was never meant to take on, but the man who had lived well.

Sunlight glittered across the dewy pasture and Abby began to stir. Pushing herself upright, she brought a hand to her abdomen. He needed to get her to Gordon.

"Good morning." Ian unfolded his arms and slipped one over her shoulder as she came to stand next to him.

Even in her morning stupor, she was adorable. The sun caught wild strands of copper amid her honey-colored hair, tousled with hay. Sleepy green eyes stared out at nothing in particular.

"Sorry, I have no coffee to offer. You look like you could use some."

In a drowsy daze, Abby turned and melted into his arms for a hug.

Ian buried his hand in the rain-soft curls at the back of her neck. Knowing today was the last they'd see of each other for a while, he didn't want to let her go.

"Hickory will be waiting." Her dark lashes fluttered as she looked up at him.

"We'll get there in plenty of time." Ian absently stroked her hair before letting his arm slip from her shoulder.

"I'm going to go down to the creek and wash my face before we leave." She smiled and stepped out into the bright sunlight.

It wasn't hard to imagine waking up to find Abby by his side every morning. For the first time in a good long while, Ian was ready to consider a future beyond the confines of war. To believe all God required of him was a willing heart. That he could still be used to champion good in the world.

"Don't wander far. I'll bridle the horse and meet you outside." Fifteen minutes later, Ian leaned against the broad back of his horse, tempted to go in after her.

When Abby finally emerged, her face was rosy from the rain cooled water. Her hair fell over one shoulder, damp and knotted into a thick braid. Morning rays glinted through the trees illuminating her approach. She looked every bit like the angel he'd taken to calling her.

She was much too lovely and delicate to be traveling alone.

As it had most of the night, her hand rested carefully over the wound in her belly.

When they arrived at the station, he'd speak to the porter about putting Hickory and her into a private car. He'd get the man's word to keep an eye on her.

"I have no idea where we are." Abby scanned the trees on the far side of the field as she walked back to where he waited. Rolling her white sleeves down, she buttoned them at the cuff.

"There's a lake about a mile or two west." Ian and his men convinced the owners of this small farm to move to the city to take refuge in Macon a month ago. "Gordon's on the other side."

"Are you able to ride?" Concern for her brought him to her side.

Before she could answer, the faint bay of hunting dogs sounded from a copse of trees behind her.

"We need to get going." Ian lifted her into the saddle and swung up behind her.

Without a moment's delay, he nudged the stallion forward, racing across the field toward the lake.

Abby held her breath as the room began to spin. Mercifully, her feet were not touching the ground. She was certain her legs would no longer hold her up.

Abby bit her lip against the pain.

From the time his horse had skidded to a halt at the train depot, Ian held her close to his chest, taking the stairs two at a time to a room on the second floor of the adjoining hotel.

The swift ride to Gordon was a blur. Certain the jarring stride of the horse had reopened the stab wound, she was almost afraid to look down to see how much blood she had lost.

Over the past couple of years, she'd help treat dozens of

soldiers with puncture wounds. This was not at all how she'd imagined they must feel. Renewed empathy for them filled her.

Abby could hear Ian's heart pounding against her ear.

"Hold on, Angel." Ian kissed her forehead. His voice sounded tense.

"Go on and lay her down on the bed." Abby recognized Mama Ivy's directive. She'd heard her issue the same many times before. "Let's have a look."

Ian gently placed her on a feather bed. "Knife wound thanks to Farris."

Mama Ivy touched Abby's torn skirt, now wet with fresh blood. Lines between her ebony brow deepened with concern. "Hickory done told tol' me all about it."

"Farris put a bounty out on her." Ian drove an agitated hand through the thick hair at his temple. "Every backroads renegade from here to Charlotte is out to collect. Including Mo and his bunch."

Mama Ivy gathered her instruments from her bag.

Caressing her cheek, Ian smoothed a wayward curl from Abby's face.

A searing pain coursed through her abdomen and she bit her lip again to keep from crying out.

Ian gave her hand a hard squeeze.

"Hickory's waitin' out there in the sittin' room with Mr. Fitz, and he's mighty worried. Would you go an' keep him company for a little while, Colonel?" Mama Ivy took up a needle and syringe. "You leave Abby to me. She'll be jes fine."

Abby turned her head to watch Ian leave. She stared at the door while Mama Ivy prepared to close the wound.

"It ain't too very deep, honey. But its startin' to look a little angry. I'll rub in some herbs and mustard to scare off infection. We'll get you sewed up, an' you'll be good as new." She lifted the syringe. "This here'll help with the pain."

Abby reached out for the older woman's hand. "Did the knife damage the womb?" The question had burned in the corner of her mind the instant she'd felt the knife puncture her lower belly. "Will I be able to bear children?"

*"He was part of my dream, of course ... but then I was part of his dream, too."*
*~ Lewis Carroll*

# Twenty-Three

$\mathcal{H}$e'd done all he could for Abby. She was in God's hands now and Ian asked Him to guide Mama Ivy's hands also.

As soon as he joined Hickory and Fitz in the larger room just outside the door, the boy ran over to meet him. "Is my Abby gonna be all right?"

Fitz came up behind him. "The kid's fit to be tied with worry."

"Hickory, I'm counting on you to help. We need to get Abby to Savannah." Ian kept his tone light for the benefit of the child. "She isn't safe in Macon as long as Farris is there."

Wide-eyed, the boy slowly nodded.

"That windbag ain't gonna be there for long." Fitz added with a smirk. "Not with all he's tried to pull."

"I need you to do a man's job." Ian bent down to the boy's level. "Go with Abby to Savannah. Mrs. Tori will meet you at the station and see that you two get to Brechenridge. You'll need to introduce the two of them. Can you take care of that for me?"

"Yes, Sir. But is she gonna be all right?" Without moving his head, Hickory's eyes flew to the door where Abby and Mama Ivy were. "Is she gonna die?"

"Why, o' course not!" Fitz pulled off his hat and swiped his forehead with a sleeve before slapping it back in place. "A little ol' scratch like that won't keep a gal like Abby down."

Ian had to get the boy's mind off that room. "Did you ask Mrs. Lambert to send along some of Abby's things?"

"Mama Ivy brought Abby's bag. It's downstairs with mine." Hickory walked to the door and placed his ear against it. Obviously, he was going to need more of a distraction than small talk.

"Fitz, I need you and Hickory to find the telegraph office and send a wire." Ian removed a coin from his pocket. "You can get yourself some penny candy."

When Hickory refused to move, it was apparent he wasn't keen on leaving Abby.

"She won't be long, so you'd best hurry. I promise I won't let her run off without you. We'll wait for you right here." Ian grinned when Hickory finally accepted the coin. "Pick a couple out for Abby, too."

Ian lifted a gold watch from his jacket. Ten forty-five.

"The train to Savannah leaves at noon." Ian handed more coins to Fitz. "Have my mother and Tori meet the train at six twenty-nine. Mark it "urgent"."

Ian was anxious to get Abby out of Gordon before Farris's men caught up with them.

"Colonel?"

Ian looked down at the solemn little boy.

"Are you gonna have to help Abby get to heaven, too?"

A full thirty minutes later, Hickory rounded the bannister onto the second floor of the hotel where Ian waited with mounting concern. Mama Ivy was still in with Abby. Their time to make the noon train was stretching thin.

He'd spoken with the porter and made arrangements for a private car. The trip was not a long one, but Ian wanted to see that she was comfortable for the ride.

"I sent the telegram like you said." Fitz came up the stairs with a stick of penny candy in his own mouth. "Are we headed up to Milledgeville from here to have a talk with the governor?"

"I am." Ian absently nodded, tempted to knock on the door to see if Mama Ivy needed anything. "I need you back in Macon."

"Surely, you don't mean to send me back to that coop of hens all alone. With all of 'em wantin' news about Miss Abby?" Fitz complained behind him. "I'd rather face down a battalion of Bluebellies than be set upon by that bunch of biddies."

"Colonel." Mama Ivy opened the door. "You can come in now."

Fitz slid the worn hat from his head and nodded a greeting.

"I didn't have the heart to sew her up without giving somethin' for the pain. I suspect she'll be a mite sleepy for the trip."

Hickory came to stand beside Ian. "The colonel says I'm going on the trip, too."

"Abby wouldn't have it any other way." Ian put a hand on the boy's back. "Did you know she refused to go to Brechenridge without you?"

"Really? She said that? That she wasn't gonna go without me?"

"Wouldn't hear of it." Ian answered with a half grin.

His bright-eyed smile was a welcome sight. "I'll sure miss you, Mama Ivy. But Abby needs me."

Mama Ivy opened the door wider to allow them both to come in.

"You'll have your own bed and as long as we hold off the Yankees, a table with food on it every evening."

Hickory's smile faded, replaced by a look of awe. "No foolin'? Living *inside* a house?"

Ian approached the bed where Abby was half awake. "How's my Angel?"

When Abby didn't immediately answer, he noticed a tear slip from the corner of her eye.

Hackles of unease rose on the back of his neck.

"What is it?" He directed his question to Mama Ivy.

"Go on over and sit beside Miss Abby awhile." Mama Ivy spoke to Hickory. "Don't be talkin' her leg off, jes' hold her hand real quiet-like, hear?"

The boy was quick to obey.

Ian didn't like the way Mama Ivy avoided his question.

Motioning for him to follow her to the other side of the room, she lowered her voice. "You'll need to send a letter with Hickory to your mama. Have her get a doctor to come out and check on Miss Abby. She don't need no infection."

Ian heard every word but nothing in her request warranted the troubled look on her face. "Infection is your only concern? Other than that she'll be fine?"

Mama Ivy folded a small towel and placed it in her bag, avoiding his question until Ian put a hand on her elbow. "Please, what are you not saying?"

With a shake of her grayed head, Mama Ivy frowned. "It wouldn't be fittin' if for me to be tellin' Miss Abby's affairs.

You two ain't married."

His attention was drawn to Abby, so pale and still on the bed.

Life had been full before the war. If anyone asked, Ian would have boasted he had the best of everything. Nothing more he could have possibly desired. A loving family, a promising profession, elite education from one of the most prestigious universities in the country.

Then, in Shiloh he was blind-sided by his own mortality. He'd spent the past three years questioning whether he even had a right to be alive.

Due to the love and compassion of Abigail McFadden, and her exasperating persistence, he had renewed purpose. Not the empty goals he'd once held, but impossible aspirations that could only be accomplished by God's grace.

And with Abby by his side.

"We will be betrothed." Ian spoke his thoughts aloud before he could stop himself. "As soon as it can be arranged."

Mama Ivy set a hand at her waist. "Did you ask her about that?" Her tone suggested she highly doubted it.

"It's been implied." Ian answered honestly. "As soon as I'm free to go to Savannah, we will be married."

Mama Ivy's attention bounced from Ian, to Abby, then back again. "Well, I suppose if you all is betrothed ...."

Ian took in a deep breath, preparing himself for whatever it was she might have to say. As long as Abby had a good chance of surviving, anything else was a matter of taking time to heal.

"Miss Abby took a nasty strike. The cut wasn't deep, 'bout this much or so." She held her fingers about an inch apart. "But she don't have 'nuff fat on her to buffer. The knife nicked her womb. Left a scar on it. I put some cactus jelly on it to ward off infection. Long as she don't come down with fever, she'll likely pull through jes' fine."

"This is good news, right?" Ian perked up.

Mama Ivy heaved a sigh. "That's why she needs to be seein' a doctor. Could be, her womb won't fill out like it's s'pposed to should she ever find herself with child. Or could be she'll carry a babe with no cause for worry at all."

Abby's greatest desire was to be a mother and have a family. If what Mama Ivy said was true, there was a chance she'd never carry a child of her own.

He refused to consider that Farris might have gotten revenge after all.

~

"Hush, Child. Rest, now." The soothing sound of Mama Ivy's voice penetrated Abby's foggy mind.

"Time to go, Angel." Ian spoke softly against her ear, as she felt herself being lifted into strong arms. She couldn't quite remember where they were going.

"Careful, Colonel." Mama Ivy spoke beside her. Abby tried to shift, but a burning pain hit her, and she relaxed back into Ian's arms.

"I'm going with you, Abby. I promise to take good care of you." She heard Hickory's voice and smiled.

A burst of sunshine caught her off guard, and she buried her face in Ian's chest as her stomach took a lurch.

How long had it been since she'd had anything to eat.

"You two are ridin' in style." Was that Fitz? Abby opened her eyes to try and see him.

The blare of a train whistle brought a bit more clarity.

They had been heading to a train station.

Ian climbed the treadboard leading up to the door of a train car. Once inside he sat her carefully on the bench and laid a blanket across her lap.

"I hope you know I'm going to miss you, Colonel." Her mind had not cleared enough to care whether her declaration sounded too bold or not.

Ian dropped to one knee next to her. "I'm glad to see you're more awake." He clasped her hand and brought it up to his lips.

Abby gave him a weak smile.

"Hopefully, it won't be long before I can come for you." Ian tenderly smoothed her hair.

Abby tried to sit up straighter, but a bandage was wrapped around her middle, and the muscles were sore and tight.

She recognized the dress she had on as one of Eliza Jane's favorites. Mama Ivy must have brought it for her.

Ian quieted her with a hand to her shoulder. "Be still before you pull Mama Ivy's needlework."

Abby didn't want to meet his family looking like she belonged on a sick bed.

The porter entered with a tray of food and Abby's stomach groaned in response.

Hickory came in to sit next to her. He had on a crisp white shirt with britches instead of overalls. His feet jiggled in a new pair of shoes. And a stylish gray cap was placed his head.

The Lamberts must have seen to it he had new clothes for the trip.

"Are you in pain?" Ian frowned.

"No." Not like she had been this morning anyway. "But, I would like something to eat."

Hickory hopped down and fetched a plate of cheese and crackers from the platter of food.

Abby knew he was probably hungry, too, so she encouraged him to get a plate for himself.

Lieutenant Fitz entered the car with Abby's bag and another bag she supposed was for Hickory.

Ian accepted a small pillow from the Porter. "Hickory, make sure she rests if she gets tired."

The child grinned and nodded, his cheeks full of grapes.

"I've heard she can be stubborn as a mule so keep an eye on her." Ian flashed a brilliant smile.

She'd roll her eyes if it wouldn't make her head hurt worse.

"I have a very important letter." He tucked an envelope in Hickory's shirt pocket. "I'm trusting you to deliver it to my mother when you arrive."

"Yes, sir!" Hickory saluted and ran over to share a snack with Fitz.

Ian sat on the bench beside her. "Abby, remember when you said you didn't need to be taken care of? That you needed to be loved?"

"Yes." Abby dipped her chin, slightly embarrassed.

Ian held out his hand and she placed hers inside. "Agree to marry me and I promise you'll be the most loved woman in Georgia."

Abby's jaw dropped and she was certain she hadn't heard right.

"The letter Hickory's holding is a letter of introduction to my family—as my betrothed."

Abby's eyes were wide as he removed a folded parchment with a gold seal. "These are gold bonds for your doctor care. I want you to go get yourself some new dresses, too. With all the finery that goes with it." Adding one more envelope he placed them both in her hand. "This is a letter of credit from the Savannah Bank and Trust in my name. It's yours to use at your discretion. This will take care of any other needs you and Hickory may have."

Now Abby was sure she was hallucinating. Trying to comprehend everything Ian just offered her made her head swim.

"Will you agree to be my wife?"

Ian was asking her to wait for him. He'd said he would come for her and they would be married. The sincerity in his eyes told her she had no reason to doubt him.

Abby already knew the depths of her feelings for him, so her answer was a whispered, "yes."

His arm came around her, and she laid her head on his shoulder. He gave the top of her head a kiss.

As thrilled as she was to accept his proposal, she longed to hear that love for her was what inspired him to make such an elaborate offer.

Two short whistles sounded outside the train followed by the porter's call. "Savannah, all aboard!"

With one last kiss, she became almost desperate to keep him with her. She couldn't think about him not returning with all the uncertainties of war.

"Aww, geez, why'd you have to go and kiss her?" Hickory screwed his lips to the side and looked disgusted. "Does that make you married now?"

"Not yet." Abby smiled in spite of the tears clouding her eyes.

"Soon." Ian tucked the envelopes inside her bag and prepared to leave.

She grasped a handful of his sleeve as he started to go.

His hand covered hers. "What is it, Angel?"

"Be safe, Ian."

"I'll do my best." His smile never failed to make her heart skip a beat.

"Just so you know, I do love you." She wanted her feelings for him to be clear.

"I believe you mentioned it."

"When?" Had she rambled on under the effects of pain medication?

"Once when I found you dreaming in a barn."

A final kiss to her forehead and he was gone.

*"How fresh the smell of the washed earth and leaves,*
*and how sweet the still small voice of the storm."*
*~ John Muir*

## Twenty-Four

 reat plumes of black smoke belched from a stack above
them, marring their view of gnarled tree branches dripping
with dried moss. As the evening sun lowered, brown swamp-
lands spread below as far as the eye could see.

Artist's renditions she'd seen of Savannah looked nothing
like this dreary marsh yawning out on either side of the high
tracks. According to Hickory, the colorful beauty she expected
wouldn't appear until they crossed over Little Ogeechee River
into the city. A city of vast contrasts. Like the diverse array of
people who lived here.

Abby pulled the blanket higher on her lap, smiling at Hickory who had two crackers in each hand. As they'd watched the
scenery go by, he became more excited with each telling of the
days when he and Sallie had lived near Savannah.

Abby only hoped Ian's family would be gracious to this
precious boy with a quick smile. Thinking about Cora's
reaction to Hickory and his friends, gave her pause until she

considered Hickory was here at Ian's invitation. If his family was as considerate as he was to the child, she had no reason to worry.

As the train rolled into the station, Abby set Eliza Jane's bonnet on her head, and tied the wide purple ribbon under her chin.

"Last stop! Savannah!" The porter poked his head in to make the announcement.

The pain in her belly had subsided, but nervous flutters there were even more bothersome.

Hickory's carrot-colored hair was in wild disarray. It took them a minute to find his cap which had fallen down behind the bench.

Shrieking brakes brought the train to a jarring stop. The door to their train car was opened. Occupants from other passenger cars began to stream down the steps carrying carpet bags and valises. Excited conversation erupted all around as Abby carefully stepped through the doorway.

Holding Hickory's hand, she took the narrow steps carefully. Lamplighters made their rounds as the sun vanished, and the cobblestone streets were bathed in shades of twilight.

As soon as her slippered foot touched the platform, she heard a voice calling out her name.

Peering around the countless people passing by, she didn't immediately see anyone who appeared to be summoning her. A man, pushing a cargo wagon, cleared the area directly in front of her and two strikingly elegant ladies came walking toward her with pleasant smiles on their faces.

Abby's knees threatened to give out from beneath her as she leaned heavily on Hickory's arm.

"That's Miss Tori." His voice was quiet as he kept a firm hold on her. "She's just a plain ol' human bean like you and me."

To Hickory she may be an old bean, but there was nothing plain about either of them.

"Abigail, it's wonderful to finally meet you, dear." The taller woman who favored Ian caught her in a tender embrace. Her cream-colored walking dress with matching short jacket was trimmed in expensive black braid and was the height of fashion. A black feathered hat demurely framed one side of her face. "Ian wired us that you two were coming. We must get you settled in. I have a carriage waiting at the street."

"Thank you. You're very kind." Abby replied, touched by her thoughtfulness.

"Hello again, Barnaby." The other lady, in lavender taffeta, spoke to Hickory. But when Abby looked over to see if he was offended at being dubbed the wrong name, she found him blushing from head to toe, giggling with the silliest grin on his face.

Apparently, the lady was not as "plain" as he'd remembered.

"I'm Dottie Saberton." Mrs. Saberton then turned to the other lady. "This is my daughter-in-law, Mrs. Nicholas Saberton."

"Please, call me Tori." She spoke with a clipped accent that made her sound all the more sophisticated.

"Abigail McFadden," she answered. "Everyone calls me Abby."

"And this handsome young man must be Hickory." Mrs. Saberton shook his hand. "I must thank you for escorting Abby to Savannah." Mrs. Saberton gave a smile that was achingly familiar. "I've heard about how brave you are."

"Let's get you home, dear." Mrs. Saberton motioned for a large man standing down at a polished barouche. "Don't try to walk. Amos will carry you."

Before Abby could argue, the man made his way up to where they were, and scooped her up like she was a rag doll.

"Be careful with her, Amos. Ian would not appreciate us breaking her on her first day in Savannah."

The younger Mrs. Saberton opened the door of the open carriage and Abby was placed on the seat facing ahead. A white fur lap blanket was handed to her for additional warmth.

Hickory climbed in beside her, followed by the two stylish Mrs. Sabertons.

November held a definite chill and the air was wonderfully fragrant as they drove down a boulevard housing a bakery and several eateries. The aroma of gingerbread, fresh from the oven, lifted Hickory's nose higher in the breeze.

"Something smells good." He looked back as they passed the bakery. "I'm kinda hungry, Abby." He half-whispered next to her.

She couldn't imagine it. He'd eaten all the way from Gordon. He must be growing.

"We must make some cookies ourselves sometime. Would you like that?" Tori gave him a fond smile.

"Could we?" He gave her a bright smile.

"I don't see why not." When she tilted her head, Abby noticed she had vivid blue eyes. "Tonight, I believe Cook has prepared fried chicken and cornbread dressing. Do you suppose you might like that?"

"Yes, ma'am!" Hickory looked elated.

"And I specifically requested she bake a blueberry pie for our dessert." Tori added with a wink.

"Blueberry pie?" Hickory fell back in his seat and laughed.

"Yes, but this time, we shall use forks." She laughed along with him.

The two of them obviously shared private memories. Abby loved the easy rapport between the them and hoped, one day, to hear all about how'd they'd come to meet.

Hickory's hand dropped to the shirt pocket at his chest and his face suddenly became serious. "I almost forgot. Colonel Saberton asked me to give this to you, ma'am."

With long slender fingers, Dottie Saberton opened the sealed envelope and removed the handwritten letter. Though she read silently, at one point she lifted a brow and looked across at Abby with a trace of a smile. "Congratulations," was all she said.

"Thank you." Abby wasn't sure how she was supposed to reply.

Ian meant so much more to her than he could have conveyed in a short letter.

Refolding the paper, Mrs. Saberton turned to Tori. "Ian and Abigail—"

"Abby." She corrected, then realized she had rudely interrupted. "I apologize. Please, call me Abby."

"And you may call me Dottie." She didn't appear offended in the least. "Ian and Abby are to be married as soon as he's free to come home." Reaching over, she took Abby's hand with sincere affection. "Welcome to the family, dear."

When tears clouded her dark eyes, Abby became more and more curious as to what Ian had written in his letter.

"Really?" Hickory asked a little less enthusiastically. Abby could tell he needed a bit of reassurance that he would not be losing her friendship.

She put an arm around him and gave his shoulder a squeeze. "Only if you come along, too. You can't get rid of me that easily."

"How exciting! Two Saberton weddings to look forward

to." Tori grinned widely.

"Two?" Abby smiled back.

"Zachery is Ian's youngest brother. He and Aurora are betrothed as well."

"You'll meet Aurora when we get home to Brechenridge. She and her mother have come to stay until things settle down." Mrs. Saberton offered Hickory a tea biscuit from her bag. As the mother of three strapping boys, she must have come prepared for the constant hunger.

Abby had been alone for so long, she almost didn't remember how to be part of a large family. She always knew she was part of a large extended family, but after her mother's death, Abby felt like an outsider. One or two of her mother's relatives had treated her kindly over the years, but none ever felt the need to take her in.

Her foster home provided a place to live, but that was about the extent of it.

Ian was offering her so much more. She hoped to spend a lifetime showing her appreciation.

Rolling in under a canopy of autumn leaves, Abby caught her first glimpse of Brechenridge under the light of a crescent moon. The grand estate looked more like an elegant hotel. She counted ten palatial columns curving around the white bricked front. Two sets of floor to ceiling windows flanked the heavy wood front door.

Hickory appeared just as awestruck as he sat forward in his seat to take in the view.

Tori looked over at him with a fond smile, then caught Abby's eye. "I'm sure you're ready to get settled." She folded her gloved hands neatly in her lap. "Ian's telegram told briefly of your attack. The whole ordeal must have been horrifying."

Mrs. Saberton draped a throw over her skirt. "That general

has much to answer for."

"If Ian hadn't found me, I don't know what I'd have done." Abby answered honestly.

"That's why we gotta hide her in Savannah." Hickory agreed with a nod. "Or else if Farris catches her, he's liable to hang her for a Yankee spy!"

Both women sitting across from her looked astonished as they glanced from her to each other.

Out of the mouth of babes …

*Prepare at once for enemy invasion!*

The courier delivered General Wheeler's letter a half hour ago. Union General William Sherman had begun to surge south with up to a hundred thousand troops. Only a flailing Confederate presence was left south of the Federal line, and Macon was the next logical target.

Ian stood over the dining table at Dobbs' house with Macon's three commanding officers, scrutinizing area maps and trying to predict Sherman's next move.

"All artillery from the armory has been transported northeast to Columbia." General Hawthorne drew a line on the map with his finger. "Saberton, your men have refugee camps in place along the river. We have more field available up here should any of our neighbors from surrounding farms and plantations to the east decide to come in."

"More than likely the Federals will make another attempt at freeing their officers from Camp Oglethorpe." Walter Dobbs dabbed at the sheen on his brow despite the cold wind blowing outside the window. "Especially since Colonel Saberton and his men deposited their General Stoneman there. If they succeed in turning loose twenty-three hundred officers, crazed with hunger and looking to destroy all things Confederate ... Well, the good citizens of Macon won't be safe in their own homes."

They weren't safe now in their own homes.

Ian had been in Macon for nearly four months trying to prepare the city for this day, but even the mayor preferred to tread in a sea of denial.

"It will take a concentrated effort to protect our citizens now." Hawthorne spoke Ian's own concern. "Removing Farris from Camp Oglethorpe is the first step to securing the area. Thankfully, as soon as he gets here we can put an end to his military career and appoint another to take his place." The general checked his time piece and snapped it shut. "Where is he? He was supposed to be here an hour ago."

"Are you certain Governor Brown petitioned the Secretary of War to remove General Farris from command?" Walter dabbed at his upper lip. Seemingly oblivious to the hard looks he got from the Confederate officers standing around him. "I have never seen the actual telegraph that says his court martial has been approved. I suppose you have that with you, George? The general will most certainly demand to see it before he is arrested."

"Walter, how can you still be intimidated by the man?" His brother-in-law wanted to know. "Cora can't stand him. She's tried to get him transferred from here for months. We owe it to Colonel Saberton for alerting the governor concerning the wolf among us."

Ian didn't need gratitude. Watching Farris march off in shackles would be satisfaction enough.

Major General Baker of the Georgia Militia clapped him on the back. "Good work, Colonel. Your diligence in exposing Farris will benefit us all."

"Yes, indeed." Hawthorne also straightened from the table.

"Your letter to Governor Brown was key in this."

"I'm not ready to let the guard down." Ian wandered to the tall window, looking out over the bustling street. "Not until Farris shows up and is actually apprehended."

A small division of Hood's infantrymen stood waiting outside. They would escort Farris in chains to a wagon bound for the court house in Milledgeville. He'd go before the tribunal there, and if found guilty, would likely face a firing squad.

"We have no leeway for less than honorable soldiers." Hawthorne said firmly. "In the days to come, each man will be called upon to defend our homeland with every bit of fight they have left."

"Now that Sherman is preparing to further infiltrate our jurisdiction, it's up to us to drive him back to Atlanta. From there clear back to Washington!" The general over the civilian militia sounded much like the multitude of gallant secessionists that had voted to escalate their grievances which started this madness in the first place.

More bravado than good judgement. More pride than common sense. Ian had seen enough of it on both sides. The pompous rhetoric never failed to make him disgust him.

Neither side had the lion's share of honorable intentions. Both had an abundant population of good, honest, hard-working men that now lay dead or maimed for a fight that was never theirs to begin with.

Ian laid the majority of blame at the feet of Congress, who'd failed to debate and settle the differences with no political or monetary gain. New laws were what was needed to change the tides.

Once week from today, the Union would vote for their choice of president. Lincoln or McClellan. McClellan made big promises to negotiate a peace treaty with the Confederacy if he was elected. While Lincoln continued to count on the Union outlasting the South and forcing their hand.

Ian prayed whoever won the election, the man use wisdom.

"Wouldn't you agree, Colonel?" Dobbs asked.

*Probably not.*

Ian turned from the window, reluctantly admitting to himself his lack of sleep had taken a toll on his disposition.

"General Baker was saying it would be a travesty to see your family's champion horse stock fall into the hands of Yankee thieves when so many of our men are reduced to riding bare-boned nags."

"My mother has seen to the safe removal of her horses. She's only kept a scant few for personal use."

Nicholas had most of them corralled at Fort Sumpter. The others had been sold to Edward Haverwood and shipped to England.

A disturbance out front signaled Farris had probably arrived.

Ian vaulted down the hall and out the front door just in time to see Farris cuffed at the wrists and ankles. "Dobbs! What is the meaning of this?"

Ian rested a hand on the hilt of his sword.

Walter Dobbs and the other two generals joined him on the porch.

"General Farris, the governor has insisted you be brought to Milledgeville for trial." Dobbs called out. "This is a state's matter, not city. Therefore, I have no say."

"Public service is not for the fainthearted, Walter. Stand aside." General Hawthorne, the highest-ranking officer in attendance, stepped forward and motioned to the two men on either side of Farris. "This man has proven to be dangerous. I expect you to keep your weapons drawn. Should he make any attempt to escape, shoot him."

Ian's brow rose.

Farris had plenty of enemies, but few were willing to stand up to him publicly. His respect for Hawthorne rose even higher than it had been before.

A crowd quickly gathered around the Dobbs's white picket fence, talking all at once and craning their necks to catch a glimpse of the portentous general hobbled and bound like the prisoners he despised.

"Looks like your bounty on Abby's head was just cancelled, Farris. Those northern bank shares you've been hording are now forfeited." Ian's voice rose over the commotion. "Making false accusations never pays."

Farris shrieked like an angry crow. "You're all fools! Now she's led Sherman and his troops right to your doorstep."

The chatter of those gathered around grew to a fevered pitch while Ian watched the reporter from the Macon newspaper taking frantic notes.

*"Both sides forget that we are all Americans. I forsee that our country will pass through a terrible ordeal, a necessary expiation, perhaps, for our national sins."*
*~ Robert E. Lee*

# Twenty-Five

"Good Lord, have mercy! A Yankee spy?" Charlotte Haverwood nearly choked.

Her daughter, Aurora, came up beside her and took the newspaper from her hand, trying to shush the woman with pinkish hair.

Abby glanced up from the book she was reading. Dread seeped through her veins as every other set of eyes in the room lifted in question.

"Mama's deathly afraid of Yankees." She spoke to the room as a whole, though her blue gaze cut toward Abby more than once with an apologetic smile. "She seems to think one is waiting to grab us behind every bush. Although, I can't say she's ever really met one, except you, Abby. We all know you wouldn't hurt a fly."

Mrs. Haverwood was Tori's aunt. From all Abby had seen, she was highly nervous.

"Is there something in the newspaper we should see, Charlotte?" Dottie sat writing a letter at her polished mahogany desk.

"No, no." Charlotte Haverwood gave her head a quick shake, causing her short ringlets to bounce. "Nothing of interest. Surely nothing about a Yankee spy on the loose from Macon." She jerked her head toward Abby a couple of times when Dottie looked over at her.

Abby watched the stout little woman closely, convinced she must have read something about Farris' claims against her.

"Would you mind if I have a look?" Abby rose from her chair.

While working at the hospital, she'd rarely had the chance to read. But since coming to Brechenridge a week ago, she'd read everything she could get her hands on. Every day, she scoured the paper hoping for news as to how Macon was faring.

A wire from Cora Dobbs three days ago instructing Abby to stay in Savannah until further notice was the only correspondence she'd received.

At this point, the unspoken view shared by the women at Brechenridge, who each had men they loved serving in the heat of conflict, was no news was infinitely better than bad news.

Rumors had come in that General William Sherman was on the move with several thousand men, heading south. Some said he was heading to Florida to secure the gulf waterways. Some said he would turn due east to take the capitals of Georgia and South Carolina. And still others predicted he would head southeast to Savannah where one of the Confederacy's most valuable supply ports was located.

The single thing they all agreed upon was that his first stop was likely Macon.

When Abby reached for the newspaper Mrs. Haverwood rolled it up and held it in front of her as if it were a rapier staving off an evil dragon.

Abby backed up, both hands raised in surrender.

"Charlotte what's come over you?" Dottie came around her desk. "Behave yourself."

The sound of the front door echoed in the large foyer just outside the parlor. Tori entered first, followed by Hickory and her three year-old daughter, Rachelle.

She stopped short as she took in the odd view of Abby being held at bay by her aunt's newspaper.

"Charades?" Tori asked, removing her fur-lined shawl.

"I wanna play." Rachelle clapped.

"Me, too." Hickory unwrapped his new red scarf from around his neck.

Abby shook her head no.

Dottie moved between Mrs. Haverwood and Abby, retrieving the newspaper from the woman's hand as she passed. Scooting aside a tray with sweets and silver carafe, she smoothed the newsprint out flat on a side table.

Abby came up to look over her shoulder with a hand on her hip.

*A Spy on the Loose?*
*Bibb County, Georgia.*
*As both Generals and Colonel Ian Saberton looked on,*
*General Buford Farris was led away*
*from the Dobbs house in*
*chains to stand trial in Milledgeville.*
*His parting avowal to seek retribution against*
*Colonel Saberton*
*was witnessed by the gathered citizens of Macon.*
*"I know you helped her escape and I will see you*

*both hang!"*
*With further investigation, this reporter discovered*
*the identity*
*of General Farris's named Union spy is none other than*
*Floyd House Hospital's beloved nurse,*
*Miss Abigail McFadden of Lancaster, Ohio,*
*last seen boarding a train in Gordon.*

With a concerned frown, Mrs. Saberton turned to Abby. "Is this the man who has been harassing you?"

Abby's heart sank.

At least he hadn't posted a likeness or reported where her train in Gordon had been bound. She couldn't stay here if it meant putting the Saberton women in danger from well-meaning vigilantes out to rid Savannah of a known Yankee spy.

But, what proof could she offer that she wasn't exactly what Farris accused her of? Simply being from the North was enough for some to refuse to ever hear the truth.

"General Farris is insane." That was all Abby could think to say about him.

"Have a seat and tell us how he's come to this ridiculous conclusion." Dottie walked Abby back to her chair.

Abby honestly didn't know where to begin. In times past, she'd found it best to ignore Farris' raving accusations. And always before, no one took his comments seriously. Most knew her and, more importantly, knew him.

But looking around at the expectant expressions of women who'd taken her in, she decided nothing but the entire story would do.

"When I first came to Macon two years ago, I was looking for a boy I had been governess to. He'd run off to join the

Union army though he was barely fourteen. His mother was inconsolable. I knew she blamed me for not watching Malcolm closely enough. Even accused me of perpetuating his decision to go. Eventually, I was asked to leave."

Mrs. Haverwood, seemingly recovered, sat forward in her seat, waving her fan.

Abby continued. "I followed the army through Kentucky until I found a camp of men who said they knew Malcolm. He had been stricken with smallpox and taken to a hospital in Atlanta. When I got there, I found he had been transferred down to Macon, so I took the next train."

"I applied for work at the hospital, just as I had all along the way. Doc Lambert interviewed me and was gracious enough to let me see Malcolm's records. He had been treated, but because of his young age, Doc had not sent him to the prison camp. Rather, he had personally seen to it that Malcolm was taken back to Cincinnati by escort and returned to his mother on condition he never return to the army."

Dottie encouraged her to go on.

"I'd only missed him by four months." Abby sighed, remembering the relief in knowing he was safe and at home. "But, by that time, I'd run out of funds. I had no travel pass to get back across the lines. Doc Lambert offered me a job at the hospital as a nurse but the only one who could sign a travel voucher in Macon was General Farris, who was then the Commanding Officer."

"My first encounter with General Farris was the day I met Hickory. Do you remember that?" Abby smiled at him when he nodded. He'd stopped playing with his Jacob's ladder to listen to her account.

"Hickory was living at the shantytown and had come to the hospital hoping to get some medicine for one of the girls who worked at a brothel in town."

Mrs. Haverwood gasped, but apparently decided to forgo a fainting spell lest she miss any of the story.

"I delivered the mercury salts myself. It's much too potent to entrust to a child."

"When she got there, ol' Farris was beating on Sallie." Hickory spoke up. "Abby sure got riled up that day. She took a pot and busted it over his back. And she kept on swingin' it til she had the general backed clear out the door in his long johns. Everyone laughed that a skinny girl like her could get the best of a army general." Hickory grinned.

"Abby threw that medicine bottle out at ol' Farris and said he needed it worse than Sallie did 'cuz it was likely he's the one spreading that sickness around at Dove's in the first place."

Abby closed her eyes briefly while the other ladies snickered. She'd forgotten that part.

"Ol' Farris stood out in the street while folks came from every side of the street to have a look at him standing out there in his red drawers with his medicine bottle in his hand."

"Oh, my!" Though it was forty degrees outside, Mrs. Haverwood's fan waved furiously.

Somehow Hickory's version of it sounded much tawdrier than it had felt in the moment. Abby smoothed her skirt. "Yes, well, over the next few months, it became apparent that General Farris was one to hold quite a grudge."

Dottie Saberton leaned a hip against her desk while Tori took a chair next to her.

"Hickory, would you mind taking Rachelle out to see if cook needs any help with those cookies she's making?" Tori asked and the two children bounded out of the room. "Go on, Abby."

"Anyway, I discovered that not only did General Farris

frequent the brothel regularly, but he actually owned the establishment and took most of the profits. The women who worked there were indebted to him and had no choice but to continue working to survive."

"Farris has a fondness for bourbon." Abby added quietly. "And often makes a fool of himself by evening time. He started having me followed and spread a ridiculous rumor I am a Yankee spy. His full intent was to see me hanged."

"So you think all of this is some sort of ploy for revenge?" Dottie Saberton walked over to have another look at the newspaper.

"That's my guess." Abby shrugged. "I'm relieved the governor's directive finally came through. I pray they lock him away and this whole mess can be forgotten."

"Except that the integrity of your name has just been questioned in every newspaper in the South." Tori lifted her chin and went to stand beside Dottie. "We shall have a retraction printed and insist they print it in every newspaper that published the original story. That very reporter should be held accountable for neglecting to tell the entire truth."

Dottie agreed. "I'll wire the newspaper in Macon personally. The editor there is a fair man. He wouldn't want his name associated with a bunch of sensational drivel. Especially if it's been proven untrue." She went to Abby and took her hand. "We made a promise to my son to look after the woman he loves. I fully intend to keep it."

"We'll see to it that horrendous man never has cause to come near her in his filthy red drawers ever again." Mrs. Haverwood rocked back and forth on the divan to come to her feet. Once upright, she straightened the Bonnie Blue flag she had pinned in her hair. "You have that paper print a full apology to our sweet Abby. Tell them she's no Yankee spy or

Yankee anything else. She's reformed. I suspect we'll have her singing Dixie by evening."

Abby couldn't help but laugh.

The support of these women was humbling and empowering all at once.

She made a vow then and there. No no matter what the next few days held, she'd earn the trust they had shown her in that moment.

Turning, Dottie's words still echoed in her mind.

"Look after the woman he loves."

*Be strong. Act promptly. Fear not.*

The latest telegram from Richmond was succinct, but between its three short lines lay the precarious fate of every Georgian.

Since General Joe Wheeler had come down to prepare his celebrated cavalrymen, messages with similar urgency had steadily arrived from higher commands until the Yankees cut the telegraph lines sometime in the night.

Ian's commander was determined to burn every bridge and block every road from here to Atlanta in effort to obstruct Sherman's dogged pursuit.

With diminishing troops, the Confederate presence in Tennessee, Alabama, and Northern Georgia wasn't capable of taking much of a stand. The battle lines were pushed farther south by the hour.

The best they could hope for was to beat the Yankees to the provisions nestled inside individual farmhouses and plantations dotting the rolling countryside.

Food, valuables, and livestock could provide much needed fortification to Sherman's men. At the same time, if they were successful in pillaging for vital necessities, it would leave hundreds of citizens with nothing. Depleted government rations because of blocked waterways and destroyed railroads, could possibly deliver the final, crushing blow to the Confederate's quaking stand.

Ian swept off his hat and knelt beside a cold stream. After cupping a long drink, he splashed cold water over his face. His division had ridden all day, and scouted most of the night to get a location on the raiding forces.

Having headed them off at Griffin, burning every bridge, Ian's men blocked the roads with sandbags—whatever it took to bar easy passage. In spite of it all, he knew their efforts would only stall what was fast becoming an organized assault on the Georgia landscape. Ian's cavalry could trip them up, but Sherman's men would merely change course, and find another route into the heart of this fertile land.

With no opposition to speak of at either side or flanking him, Sherman was cutting a swatch virtually uncontested.

General Wheeler had gone on to Macon to help fortify the city, but the Union Cavalry was close behind. Allowing for a quick drink, Ian had no choice but push man and beast to keep going.

Macon's officers had to be made aware of an impending assault.

Stepping up into his stirrup, Ian swung a leg over his saddle and motioned for his men to move forward. With a quick nudge, he sent his horse racing down the road toward Macon.

*"War is cruelty. There is no use trying to reform it. The crueler it is, the sooner it will be over."*
*~ William Tecumseh Sherman*

# Twenty-Six

*Macon, Georgia*
*22 November, 1864*

A rare dusting of snow covered the streets as a who's who of the Confederate Army converged on the city of Macon. Ten thousand additional soldiers poured in to bolster the city's defenses while their Generals met with Governor Brown and the Secretary of State.

Ian's horse cantered down the main thoroughfare now void of civilians. Businesses were closed as all men from oldest to youngest had been recruited to take up arms and join the Home Guard.

After the recent skirmish at Griswoldsville, Ian had seen firsthand the enormity of Sherman's rogue procession. Split into two wings, they cut a swatch down the middle of the state leaving nothing useful in their wake.

Compared to the South's haggard remnant, the Rebels were outnumbered by at least five to one. Now that they'd located

Sherman's army, however, plans could be made to counter him.

Lieutenant General Richard Taylor waited for him in front of the train depot. "For once, my train was early." He smiled and retrieved his leather bag. "It's good to see you, my friend."

Ian swung down from his saddle and gladly took the officer's outstretched hand.

Son of the Union's late president, Zachery Taylor, Richard had been a Louisiana senator before the secession and a good friend of Ian's older brother, Nicholas.

Ian figured since he was also Jefferson Davis's brother-in-law, he was here to represent the Confederate President without putting him in the direct line of fire.

"Colonel?" They walked into town, with Ian's horse following at a leisurely pace. "Last time I saw you, you were wearing a Chaplain's pin."

Ian lifted his face into the cold flakes, welcoming the chance to clear his mind. "Seems like a lifetime ago."

Neither of them said anything for a block or two.

Heaviness weighted them from all they'd seen and experienced. Gone were the days of easy banter over a long game of chess. When they'd each been so certain they had all the answers to life and the golden ring of success was theirs for the taking.

"I was sorry to hear about John." Richard finally broke the silence, choosing to look ahead rather than at Ian.

"He was a good man."

"He was indeed." Richard clasped the collar of his coat closer around his neck. "But then, so are you."

There was a time not so long ago that his affirmation would have made Ian's blood run cold. Before Abby, he would have railed at the thought that he could ever be thought of as a good man again. He'd have argued the point to his death.

Thanks to Abby, the bitterness was gone.

"And you as well." Ian turned to his friend with a friendly grin.

Passing by Harbor House, Ian explained the generous support Macon's women provided here. The tantalizing aroma of fresh baked bread and black coffee met them as they passed the doorway. Even in icy temperatures, the place was a constant hub of activity with a steady stream of hungry soldiers and refugees to attend to.

As they rounded the corner of Mulberry Street, it wasn't hard to figure which house was their destination. The Dobbs' home had a solid lineup of tethered horses out front beyond the wrought iron gate.

Several men in long overcoats and scarfs hung around the porch trying to get a good look inside from one of the two long windows set in front. Ian recognized them as reporters from various agencies. Hawthorne had set guards at each door and window to remind them they were not welcome at this meeting.

Time and again the army's tactics had been foiled by the tattle-tale nature of the free press. Without regard to the danger and loss of life their careless reporting caused, these men had one objective. Sniff out a story and sell as many newspapers as possible.

When one of the men spotted Lieutenant General Richard Taylor coming up the walk, he scrambled to get to him. The others quickly followed suit.

"Sir, there's talk that the Yankee Army is twelve miles east of town. Do you see this setting up to be the biggest battle so far?"

Another man pushed to the front. "General, I hear Sherman has Milledgeville in his sights. Do you have plans to send a battalion over to defend the capital?"

Richard sent a questioning glance over to Ian with no response. Quickening their pace up the brick steps, both were even more intent on getting inside.

A tall guard opened the front door and hastily shut it after them.

Removing their hats, they joined the others in the dining room.

Richard went directly to the blazing fire burning in the hearth to warm his hands.

"It couldn't be helped." Governor Brown shook his balding head while pulling at his long white beard. "We need the manpower. Convicts are strong and have been kept healthy. Most know how to handle a gun."

"Yes, but there are those who would just as soon aim it at a friend as they would a foe." General Hawthorne countered. "Farris in particular has lost his perspective. He's become too volatile to trust with this kind of responsibility."

Dread knotted Ian's stomach. Surely, they weren't considering letting Farris walk free.

"Colonel Saberton, here, can verify what I've said to be true. Farris tried to kill his fiancé on more than one occasion."

"And where is your fiancé now, Ian?" The governor wanted to know. "Tucked safely away out of harm, I hope."

"What is this about?" Ian didn't bother to remove his wet overcoat. He walked to the table where generals, their aides, and other dignitaries occupied every available seat. Half empty glasses sat before them while a few puffed on their pipes and cigars.

Hawthorne, the governor, and General Baker, head of the Georgia Militia, were standing at the head of the table with a large hand-drawn map spread out in front of them.

"I see no other way, Colonel." General Baker was the first to speak up as he looked apologetically at Ian. "We need troops to counter this brazen assault on Georgia. Without men to fight 'em off, we're no better than dabblin' ducks."

"You can bet if we don't put a stop to them here in Macon, they'll march straight through to Savannah." The governor pounded his fist on his other hand for effect.

"What does this have to do with Farris?" Ian didn't need scare tactics. He was only interested in seeing that Abby was safe.

"Our esteemed governor has proposed that we empty the penitentiary in Milledgeville in search for recruits. He is willing to offer full pardon to any willing to join Baker's militia."

Ian turned and swallowed hard at a burst of rage that flamed in his chest. Farris was no good to them on a battlefield but had proven he'd go to any lengths to get to Abby.

Getting himself court marshalled for insubordination wouldn't help anyone.

"I don't see how we have a choice. Short of signing up our women, we need able bodies to stand between the Yanks and our homes." Baker responded with a nod to the agreements he received all around the table.

"Wheeler, have you been able to locate the Federal columns heading for Macon?" Governor Brown was apparently ready to move past the subject of Farris's release.

In Ian's mind, the matter wasn't settled by a long shot. As long as Farris drew a free breath, he was a threat to Abby. But with so many high ranking officers champing at the bit to send their troops out to block Sherman's path, he'd leave it alone for now.

He'd speak to Joe Brown personally as soon as this meeting

was over.

Until then, he needed to get a telegram out to warn Abby. Farris may go looking for her in Savannah, but he'd never get past the river at Brechenridge.

"Saberton's band just returned at dawn. They've screened the Blue for two days." Ian's commander, General Wheeler, stood in the corner with his gloved hand stuffed into the unbuttoned opening of his coat. A maroon plume tacked to the side of his hat had become his signature guise. Fighting Joe Wheeler was short in stature but a giant in the eyes of his men. "Sherman's taking his own sweet time, letting the threat of his coming stir up panic in folks once they realize he's not being met with much resistance from their own army. He's giving his men free rein to ravish and destroy, steal and burn." Wheeler came to the table and leaned a fist on the corner. "This battle has not been waged against an opposing field army but against our private citizens. Most are widows and women holding down their homes while their men are off fighting for the glorious cause. They're rendered defenseless and subjected to unspeakable brutalities."

Murmurs of outrage filtered throughout the room.

With arms crossed, Ian rested a shoulder against a heavy cabinet at the back wall.

Wheeler enjoyed stirring up a hornet's nest. Before it was over, he'd have them all convinced his unit was the only one capable of putting a stop to Sherman's march. This was why Wheeler's Cavalrymen had become legendary within the corps.

"What's more, I don't believe he's intending on coming to Macon." Wheeler gave a knock to the table.

Shouts of disagreement caused General Hawthorne to raise both hands. "Gentlemen, please."

Lieutenant General Richard Taylor looked amused as he

glanced at Ian and shook his head, walking away from his spot in front of the fire.

"General Wheeler, I suppose you have a basis for that statement?" General Hawthorne asked.

"I must agree with General Wheeler." Richard spoke up, pouring himself a cup of coffee from the silver pot on the table. "If he was coming this way, you'd have seen him last night. He'd have come before Ian and his men could report back on his whereabouts."

"You give the man entirely too much credit, sir." Although Governor Brown kept his tone light, his gazed darted from one commander to another as if looking for someone to dispute his claims.

No one did.

"My gut feeling says he's taking this fight to the capital at Milledgeville. If he can lay claim to the capital, the people of Georgia will consider themselves all but captured." Wheeler put a match to his cigar, puffing a couple of times while his prediction sank in. "From there he has enough men with him to split into two or maybe even four separate columns. They could inflict a wide corridor of destruction from which we might never recover."

"What good would it do to terrorize innocent women and children rather than have it played out on the battlefield between soldiers?" The Secretary of State wanted to know. "There are rules to warfare to be followed."

The others agreed, though not as adamantly as they had before.

"Our soldiers live for the day they can come home and get back to normal. If he takes that away, ravishing their lands and crushing their families, that could effectively destroy their will to continue fighting." Wheeler smashed his cigar into a china saucer. "Without the will to fight, we are defeated."

His point was well-taken as the commanders sobered noticeably.

"What do you propose then, Wheeler?" Baker straightened, his dander obviously raised. "We can't just stand by and let him do his worst. But our forces from the north have been blocked in getting down here to offer aid."

Just then an odd whistle wailed above before a deafening explosion shook the house all around them. Glass shattered from the front and every man in the room leapt to his feet.

Once in the entry, they all stood gaping at a large smoking cannonball imbedded in the hall floor. A hole was torn into the parlor wall and one of the four stately white columns out front had a round bite out of it.

"Oooh!" Walter Dobbs dabbed at his upper lip with his monogrammed handkerchief. "Cora's not going to like this one bit.

*"I think I have learned that the best way to lift one's*
*self up is to help someone else. "*
~ *Booker T. Washington*

# Twenty-Seven

*I*n happier times, a trip into Savannah would have been a
pure delight. Abby had never seen a more beautiful city
with its perfect squares and grand residences tucked behind
arching branches of centuries-old trees.

Instead, a melancholy had settled over the city. Cold rain
fell in a steady drizzle contributing to the somber feel.

Abby and the Saberton ladies had planned to shop for a
few incidentals before Abby had her final appointment with the
doctor. He had come out to Brechenridge twice. Once to
remove the stitches and another to check for infection.

Understanding the importance of what Abby desperately
needed to know, he'd asked her to come to his office in the city
for a more complete examination.

Once in Savannah, however, the women found the shop-
ping district completely shut down. Lovely creations were
displayed in darkened windows with no shopkeepers in sight.
The eateries were closed as well, leaving the streets abandoned

and desolate.

Mrs. Saberton commented about once elegant people who now dug holes in their backyards to hide valuables and important documents. Disappearing into their homes to prepare for the worst.

Soldiers patrolled the streets warning the ladies that it would be best if they got back to their homes and stayed until the danger passed. On their drive into town along the river road, they couldn't help but notice activity on the winding Savannah River was stilled. Ferries had been dismantled and Argyle Island evacuated.

Although, Dottie had been quick to point out the people of Savannah were not faint of heart. Most had chosen to stay and face whatever may come. According to the latest newspapers, the enemy was heading straight for them like a mammoth hurricane churning ever closer. Their only recourse was to watch ... and wait.

The dreary day took an immediate turn as soon as Abby met with the doctor.

After examining her wound, he declared it had healed nicely. No significant scarring. No signs of infection. The cut had barely nicked the uterus itself, and ran horizontal rather than vertical. The possibility of her carrying a pregnancy to term, was no less than any other healthy young woman her age.

Abby's hopes for a family of her own had not been taken from her.

What had Ian known before he'd left her that day? Had Mama Ivy told him of the possibility that she might never have children? Had he made the decision to marry her anyway? The possibility had her weeping as she walked from the examination room.

Rushing to her side, Dottie and Tori assumed the news had

been detrimental and held her tight. Their empathy toward her only made the tears flow harder.

They were halfway back to Brechenridge before she was able to explain that she'd simply been overcome by happy tears.

Oddly, she'd made her mind up before going in to see the doctor that no matter what his prognosis, she wanted Hickory to be hers. Legally adopted, bearing the proud name of Saberton. Whether he ever had any brothers or sisters sprouting from her womb, in her heart Abby knew he belonged with them.

She'd pondered it for days now and couldn't wait to discuss it with Ian.

The smell of something delicious greeted them at the magnificent carved wood doorway of the Saberton home, beckoning them inside.

Fires glowed in every hearth, and children's laughter wafted down the hallway. For the first time since she'd arrived, Abby let herself imagine having a family here.

"Just in time." Aurora came through the swinging door that led to the kitchens in the back of the house. "Dinner is served."

Flour smeared across the bridge of her nose as she wiped her hands on an apron. "I hope you don't mind, Mrs. Dottie, I couldn't resist. Cook was showing me all the wonderful recipes in your cookbooks and the next thing you know, I was standing over a pot of chicken stew with dumplings."

"I certainly don't mind. It smells scrumptious." Dottie Saberton removed her fur-lined cloak and unbuttoned her gloves at the wrists. "We are chilled to the bone and didn't get to have lunch. Warm stew and buttered bread sounds heavenly."

"Cook also showed us how to make gingerbread men. Hickory and Rachelle have been helping me while Mama has her nap." Aurora sighed heavily. "What with Christmas coming and all, we could use a little cheer."

The same look of sadness on Aurora's face would come over Eliza Jane when she was missing Will. Abby now knew how they felt. Christmas had always been a lonely time, but without Ian the holiday would seem unbearable.

"I suppose we could all use a bit of cheer." Tori's features were marred by gloom as well. Removing her hat, she went toward the kitchen in search of her little one.

"Mrs. Dottie, what will we do if the Yankees come take Brechenridge?" Aurora's question took both Dottie and Abby off guard. "Christmas would be especially sad with no place to call home."

"We'll get by, just like we always have." Dottie patted Aurora's arm.

It had been a long while since Abby called any place home.

These past couple of weeks with Ian's family, she'd experienced a grounding of sorts. Late night talks with various ones, hearing the proud history of Saberton ancestors. Listening as they told of the sacrifices Dottie and Samuel had made to lead by example, encouraging those who were slave owners to find better ways to work the land and turn a profit. They'd made huge strides before Samuel was killed in the Mexican War.

To these ladies, Abby was one of them. They were the women who loved the Saberton men. And for the first time since losing her parents, Abby had a sense that was somewhere that she truly belonged.

"Come help us decorate, Abby." Hickory poked his head from the kitchen door. "We've been having so much fun." Without waiting for a response, he was gone again.

"I'll set out some bowls and we can eat in the main kitchen." Dottie followed him through the swinging doors.

Abby hung back, as one by one the others disappeared down the hall.

Unwrapping her worn woolen shawl from around her shoulders, she thought about how the ladies in Macon had often teased her about her lack of cooking skills. It was the truth. She was an awful cook.

Now with the real possibility of one day having a family of her own, she should probably examine her "lacks" more closely.

Her mother had been a remarkable seamstress. She'd handmade all of Abby's clothes with only a needle and thread.

Abby sewed her quilt square to her skirt.

Her mother, like Aurora, had played several musical instruments. One of Abby's fondest memories was listening to her lead the mission in hymns on Sundays.

Abby only mouthed the words at church, pretending to sing because she could never quite find the right note.

What did she truthfully have to offer as a wife? No man deserved to be bound to a woman who might poison him every time she tried to cook a meal.

Especially not a man as wonderful as Ian. He'd given her the world—his world.

Abby looked around at the opulent home he'd grown up in. She could imagine fine dinner parties given in his honor someday with his loving family at his side. A big family. Seventeen children at least. All with his roguish good looks and big brown eyes.

How soon after marrying her would he realize she simply had nothing else to contribute to their perfect life other than a head full of good intentions and a heart full of love?

Would that be enough? Could love alone ever be enough?

Abby squelched a familiar urge to run.

"What has you troubled, dear?"

Abby realized Dottie Saberton watched quietly from the kitchen door.

"Must be the weather." Abby turned, letting out a sigh. "My thoughts run rampant sometimes until they become completely irrational."

"Your thoughts?" Mrs. Saberton approached her and laid a gentle hand on her arm. "Or your fears?"

"Fear I suppose." Abby confessed with a shrug. "If fear is realizing you're a completely inadequate helpmate for the most magnificent man in the world."

"You mustn't be so hard on yourself." Mrs. Saberton rubbed her arm. "You've already helped Ian more than you know."

Abby shook her head. "I don't cook, or sew or sing or ..."

"Neither do I." Dottie poured a cup of coffee from the sidebar and handed it to Abby before pouring one for herself. "But there are strengths inside of you that you've only begun to discover. You always have something to offer. You just need to look for it and don't be surprised if it doesn't look at all like you think it should."

Dottie turned up the sconces brightening the room as Abby took a warm sip, thinking over what she'd said. Being a governess had resulted in failure, so teaching obviously wasn't her strength.

"You were telling us about your early years. They were quite literally destroyed by ashes. But we've been promised beauty for ashes."

Abby watched her light the candelabra at the center of the large table. "Yes, but when things start looking like they'll end up in ashes again, I tend to run. How can beauty come from so many failures." Abby shocked herself at having expressed her deepest fears aloud.

"Have you failed, Abby, or have you been failed?" Dottie crossed her arms.

"Both I suppose." Abby rested her arms on the back of a chair. "At six, I ran away from the first two homes they sent me to." Abby was ashamed to admit it. "The first man beat me with a razor strap on my first night there. The second had an older boy who terrified me."

Dottie didn't say anything, just shook her head.

"I was finally placed with a prominent family in the community that had six children already. They were kind and upright. And, though they were not affectionate toward me, they did provide well for my education. I was very blessed to have them."

"What made you run from Ohio?"

Abby had never thought of it like that. In a way, she'd run from the disgrace of having lost the first job she'd ever had. Her foster mother had gone out of her way to arrange the position for her. Of course, she'd hoped to find Malcolm and return him to his home where all would be forgiven. But, once she found out he'd been returned, with no help from her, she'd simply started over somewhere else.

"I was dismissed from my position as governess when I lost one of the children."

"I can see where that might be frowned upon." Mrs. Saberton laughed which lightened Abby's mood. "But didn't you say since arriving in Macon, you've found a love for helping birth healthy babies into the world?"

Abby smiled. "Thanks to Doc Lambert's guidance, I've become comfortable with the process. So much so, Doc said my knack for attending births is almost instinctive."

"A high compliment, indeed." Dottie took a drink of her coffee.

"For whatever reason, the Lord has seen fit to grant me favor with the people of Macon. Those who have plenty, as well as with those who have nothing." Abby wasn't sure why that thought had come to mind, but she had to admit some might see it as a strength. "I'd hoped to help bridge the chasm between them someday."

"So, you see? There are many, many ways the Lord may choose to use you to help your family. And anyone else He puts in your path. Cooking and sewing are only one of many strengths. Find yours. Do what only you can do. Then, do it well."

Dottie gave her a warm hug before Aurora poked her head in from the kitchen. "Come on, you two. Your dumplings are getting cold."

# Twenty-Eight

Scents of cinnamon, nutmeg, ginger, and vanilla filled the warm kitchen giving the house a holiday feel. Abby and Tori sat at the long table where Rachelle bobbled on her mother's knee eating a gingerbread man.

Aurora was on oven duty, making sure the wood fire stayed hot while Dottie and Mrs. Charlotte chatted over the worktable.

"I read the Yankee president, Mr. Lincoln, declared tomorrow to be a Day of Thanksgiving." With pinkie fingers up, Mrs. Charlotte pressed a cookie cutter into dark dough rolled out on the table. "I don't know what he has to be thankful for. Doesn't he know there's a war goin' on?"

"He declared every last Thursday in November to be a Thanksgiving Day." Aurora removed a pan of cookies and replaced it in the oven with another.

"What can you expect from a bunch of Yankee Doodles? How does that silly song go, Aurora?" Mrs. Charlotte abandoned her station to go see what she could sample from the pans set out to cool. "They stuck a feather in their hat something ... something ... cup of noodles." She waved a wooden spoon like she was leading an orchestra. "I believe I'll have Jean Pierre make me a hat like that."

Abby couldn't help but laugh. Mrs. Charlotte was as love-able as she was sassy. Give Eliza Jane about fifty years and she'd be much the same.

"Wish I was old enough to go whip their tails." Hickory lifted his battered spoon like it was a sword. "I'd show those Yankees a thing or two."

"You mustn't say such things, Hickory." Tori set Rachelle down to go help Dottie roll out the dough. "Too many of our men are off fighting as it is. I'd like to keep you here with us a bit longer."

"Well, I've had about all I can stand of this war nonsense." Mrs. Charlotte ate a candy button from a gingerbread man. "It's high time someone call a truce."

"Ow!" Aurora touched a hot pan then shook her hand. "I haven't gotten a letter from Zach in four months."

"Mrs. Saberton, Constable's at the door to see you, ma'am." Amos announced from the doorway.

"Send him back, Amos." Dottie lifted the last man shaped-cookie onto a sheet.

"...never in a million years." Constable G.W. McCallister ambled into the kitchen mumbling to himself. "Ladies." He removed his hat and greeted them with a bob of his head.

"What brings you out this evening, G.W.?" Dottie poured a cup of coffee and brought it to the peace officer who appeared slightly shaken.

Abby noticed he watched her with a leery eye.

"No, thank you, Dottie." Again, his gaze cut to Abby.

"She's not a Federal spy." Tori set a hand on her waist. Her British clip was a tad more pronounced. It was obvious she didn't particularly care for the man. "And she rarely bites unless she's provoked."

Rachelle laughed when Hickory did.

"I'm making the rounds and wanted to be sure you all got the word, too." He pulled a folded newspaper from his hip pocket. "The bluelegs are comin' this way."

"What? Yankees here?" Mrs. Charlotte was suddenly in a dither. "They wouldn't dare!"

"Their General Sherman has broken communication with his superiors. He's conducting an illegal ransack right down the middle of Georgia. Pillaging, burning, stealing everything in sight. No one's safe."

His heavy jowls shook like an old hound dog when he spoke.

"We got word, he and his men are destroying the capital in Milledgeville as we speak. They'll burn it clear to the ground just like they did Atlanta. Word has it, he's bound for Savannah next. Left orders that nothing and no one is to be spared."

Mrs. Charlotte slumped into a chair.

"Come, children. Let's get you cleaned up." Tori wisely removed the frightened children from the room.

Constable McCallister flicked open the newspaper and read aloud. "General Sherman was quoted as saying, 'War is cruelty. There is no use trying to reform it. The crueler it is, the sooner it will be over.' He's made it clear he intends to punish any who oppose him, and he won't stop until he's completely desolated our homeland. He ends with saying, 'he's gonna make Georgia howl.'"

"Let me go. I'll show him." Hickory burst into the kitchen with fire in his eyes from where he had been listening at the door. So much like Malcolm that Abby was stunned.

Without delay, she went to the boy and ordered him to sit.

"Now, you listen to me, Hickory." She pulled a chair over to look him straight in the eyes. "You are not going anywhere.

Do you understand me? I couldn't bear to lose you. My heart would break in two."

Hickory's fervor noticeably cooled as he took in what she was saying. "It would?"

"You're all the family I have for now."

He grew serious. "Abby, you think we are a family, you and me?"

"I'd like to think we are. If we promise to always love and care for each other, I'd say that's what family does."

"Everyone here is family," Dottie added.

"I promise." Hickory nodded slowly. "And I won't go fight the Yankees if you don't want me to."

Abby pulled him close. "I appreciate that. I love you too much to lose you, Hickory."

"No one ever said that before." She heard him say against her shoulder.

Abby heard the constable still rambling about the mass destruction the dreaded Yankees would likely cause. "Mayor and me, we're taking a boat and heading upriver. My suggestion is, you pack up what you can take with you and get on out of town. Once they get here, no man, woman, boy or girl will be safe from—."

"Thank you G.W.. Amos will show you out." Dottie Saberton dismissed the constable, and he quickly obliged.

"Think on what I'm tellin' you, Mrs. Saberton. A house full of purty ladies ..." He shook his jowls and walked out the door.

"Besides, Hickory, we need you here." Tori came over to smooth his curls. "If you were to go, who would defend us should the soldiers show up on our doorstep?"

Lifting his head, he gave her a determined smile. "Yes, ma'am."

"Rachelle, you might as well come in here, too." Tori called to the door.

The girl slowly entered the room. "Can I sleep with you tonight, mama?"

The constable's warning had only managed to frighten everyone. He'd given no real suggestion as to how they should prepare other than to run.

Oddly, that option didn't appeal to Abby in the least.

"I wish Zach were here." Aurora whispered.

Tori removed a cookie from Rachelle's small hand. "And Nicholas. Lord, keep him safe wherever he is tonight."

"We'll pray for them all." Dottie swept the scraps into a bucket. "And pray mercy for our dear Georgia."

"Such travesty." Too afraid to faint, Mrs. Charlotte peered over her hankie. "What will become of us?"

Their festive gathering from moments before had dissolved into a collective puddle of nerves.

Abby couldn't stand by and do nothing.

Dottie had said, "Find your strength, do what only you can do and do it well."

Her parents had done nothing. They'd burned with the rest of the mission. How many times had she wished they would have fought back? Used any means at their disposal to spare their own lives and the lives of those they loved.

Well, Abby did have the means to do something. And she had every intention of using it. If she were killed for her effort, then so be it. Standing by, helplessly waiting for the inevitable, was not in her.

"Mrs. Saberton, I must ask a favor." Kissing Hickory's cheek, Abby stood.

"What is it, Abby?" Ian's mother stopped wiping down the worktable, giving her full attention.

"I need the use of a strong horse."

"Tonight?" Mrs. Saberton lowered her towel.

"As soon as possible." Abby untied the apron from her waist and rolled down her sleeves.

"Abby, what are you planning to do?" Aurora came to her side with concern on her face.

"You can hardly stop an army all by yourself." Tori added at her other side.

"Maybe she's gonna go get Mrs. Cora. *She* could stop an army all by herself!" Hickory offered with conviction.

"What have you in mind?" Dottie motioned for Amos to come into the kitchen.

Abby had made up her mind and was eager to get going. "The constable said General Sherman and his men were in Milledgeville today. Tomorrow has been declared a day of thanksgiving by the President of the Union. That means it's a mandated holiday for their troops, so they will still be there tomorrow. Whatever else General Sherman may be, he is not one to openly defy his president's wishes."

Mrs. Saberton spoke quietly to Amos who nodded and left out the back.

"Abby! You can't be thinking of going straight into that pit of vipers." Mrs. Charlotte wrung her hands. "Dottie, do something."

"That's exactly what I plan to do." Abby came around the table in front of them, smoothing a wisp of hair from her brow. "I am from the North. A citizen of the Union. They will accept me into their camp and take me straight to see their general."

"I had considered going myself." Mrs. Saberton put her arm around Abby's waist. "But I'll agree you definitely have the advantage."

More than they knew.

"But Milledgeville's a good day's ride." Aurora took out the last batch of cookies. "And it's frigid cold out there."

"If I recall, the train to Milledgeville leaves tonight." Dottie started for the door. "As long as the rails haven't been destroyed, we could possibly make it all the way before noon tomorrow. If the rails are not there, we'll go as far as we can. I can check our horses into a stockcar in case we need them."

The women all began talking at once.

"Did you say we?" Abby hurried to the door to intercept Mrs. Saberton. "I can't put you in that kind of danger."

"Well, I'm not letting you go by yourself." Dottie accepted a railroad flyer from Amos. "Let's see. The train leaves for Milledgeville at eleven twenty-nine." Lifting a timepiece pinned at her waist, she nodded. "That gives us two and a half hours to get to the depot. It'll take an hour to get there from here."

Ian would never forgive her if anything happened to his mother because of a reckless chance Abby felt she must take. She'd considered stealing away in the night, borrowing a horse from the stables, but decided it was best to be upfront and ask permission.

Hopefully, she wouldn't regret that decision.

Mrs. Saberton looked at Abby through clear brown eyes. "Abby, Samuel was at West Point with William Sherman. My husband was well thought of there. I'm hoping the general will agree to see us when he hears that I am Samuel's widow."

"But you don't understand, I—"

"No, I'm not naïve enough to think I can persuade him to end this brutal rampage all together. But I'm hoping we can at least convince him to make some concessions where Savannah is concerned."

"Dottie, you mean to say you're going to meet with that

devil, too?" Mrs. Charlotte was beside herself. "Whatever will we do?"

"Pray for us, Charlotte. We'll need all the prayer you can muster." Dottie removed her apron and tossed it over a chair.

"Well, at least put on a traveling gown first." Charlotte Haverwood tsked. "He'll never let you in looking like that."

Abby's brows drew together. The little woman was as variable as the wind.

"Tori, take Abby upstairs and do something with her hair." She waved her hand toward Abby as if she were planning a garden party. "Those Yankees won't know what to do with such elegance and style."

"Come with me." Tori ushered her out to the staircase. "Just keep moving and whatever you do, don't let her put you in a hat."

Exactly one hour later, Abby stood at the top of the stairs wearing the most elegant green traveling ensemble she'd ever laid eyes on. Trimmed in dark blue ribbon that perfectly matched the cuff sleeves and leather gloves, the dress belonged to Aurora and had easily cost two years' worth of hospital wages.

Mrs. Charlotte dropped her lace fan to the floor with a clatter as soon as she saw Abby coming down the stairs. "Is this the same girl?"

"I can't get over how pretty you are, Abby." Aurora had been staring at it ever since Tori had inserted the last pin into the upswept curls. "You wear that color of dress much better than I do."

Abby was having a hard time believing it herself.

"Here's your reticule." Tori lifted Abby's hand and hung a fringed bag from her wrist. "I've included a few essentials, including a slingshot. You never know when you'll need a slingshot."

Slingshot?

"I'd like it if you'd wear these as well." Mrs. Saberton descending the grand staircase in an exquisite burgundy suit. As she approached, Abby saw that she held a flat velvet box.

"They belonged to Ian's grandmother, the Duchess of Brechenridge. They are to be a gift to his wife." As she opened the box, Abby's eyes grew large.

A pair of diamond and emerald drop earrings lay nestled inside. "They are merely a loan until the time comes when Ian can give them himself."

Abby barely recognized herself when she passed a large mirror set in an intricately carved coat rack. All of the beautiful trappings and frippery made her feel like a *grande dame* of the ball.

"And there's a pocket in your petticoat in case you need it." Aurora lifted the outer skirt and showed a slit in the side of Abby's petticoat. "Mama said the Parisians invented them to keep the keys to their lover's apartments."

"So, I've been told anyhow." Mrs. Charlotte had retrieved her fan and gave it a respectable flutter. "Before Jean Pierre hopped on a ship back to Europe, he used to tell the most scandalous stories."

"Wait for me." Hickory bounded down the stairs with Rachelle at his heels. He had a hunting rifle tucked under his arm that was as tall as he was.

"Where on earth did you find a gun?" Tori wanted to know.

"Over the fireplace in the room with all the books." Thankfully, he made it to the last step without shooting a hole in the ceiling.

"It isn't loaded." Mrs. Saberton swung her heavy sable

cloak around her shoulders and lifted the hood over her auburn hair. "But I'm afraid you won't be coming with us, Hickory."

"I promised the colonel I'd take care of you." With a dejected slump, he sank to the bottom step.

Abby went to him. "I need you to stay here and protect the rest of our family. Only for a day or two. I promise to come right back."

"Yes, ma'am." He was clearly unhappy with the plan but too courteous to argue with her. "But will you tell that Yankee something for me?"

Abby smiled. "Of course. Whatever you'd like."

He beckoned her to come down closer so he could whisper in her ear.

Abby had to laugh at his audacious message.

"I'll tell him." She gave him a hug.

"We need to get going, Abby. We don't want to miss the train." Mrs. Saberton held out a dark blue cloak for her with a matching muff.

Unified by a common purpose, the two ladies from opposite sides of the Mason-Dixon, stepped into the cold night, determined to save their home.

*"It isn't what we say or think that defines us, but what we do."*
*~ Jane Austen*

# Twenty-Nine

The Yankee flag flew high over Georgia's capital building.

Ian laid flush on a craggy bluff overlooking Milledgeville. He and a few of his best men had been sent to monitor Sherman's movements when it had become apparent that Macon would not be Sherman's next conquest.

Smoke rose amid the cold fog as the penitentiary burned on one side of town while hungry flames lapped at the three-storied Lunatic Asylum on the other.

Lifting his field glasses, Ian watched with restraint as Sherman's men set out to destroy the capitol city in a fit of drunken revelry.

The main body of Federal forces had ridden in yesterday parading through the streets like a mob of lawless raiders. Bands played while Federal troops rummaged freely, destroying what they could and setting everything else ablaze.

Two days ago, Wheeler and the home militia had taken a

hard loss at Griswoldville. The sheer number of troops that had been set against them made it a lopsided fight from the beginning.

Governor Brown had released the state prisoners last Sunday and sent Farris into battle at Griswoldville. Nearly twelve hundred Confederates had been left dead on that frosted field. Ian couldn't help but wonder if he'd been one of them.

Yesterday, Sherman had finally ridden into Milledgeville with General Slocum and a full Corps behind them. Slocum took over the Milledgeville Hotel, and Sherman took up residence in the Governor's mansion.

All night, Ian and his men witnessed the Yankees demolish Capital Square, pitching furniture and paintings of State dignitaries from every window. Volumes of ledgers and legislator records lay in carpets of smeared parchment in the muddy streets. Thousands of Confederate dollars blew in the frigid breeze, catching on the barren limbs of sycamore trees.

"Ain't no soldiering going on down there." Fitz sat up with forearms resting on his knees. "Them bluelegs ain't no better than a pack of feral hogs." He tossed a pebble down at a young Federal lookout below who flicked it off without looking up at the ten men in gray occupying the ridge above him.

"Mind your post, Lieutenant." Ian snapped just above a whisper. "As soon as they make a move in any direction, we'll head back to Macon. In the meantime, eat some hardtack. Keep your hands and mouth quiet."

His mood was as icy as the bitter wind.

Somewhere along the way, the Federals had decided to discard every acceptable rule of warfare and strike out against civilian homes full of helpless women and children. This conflict was between men who'd agreed to fight it out on a field of battle. Not *carte blanche* for an authorized army of tyrants to do as they please, steal whatever they want, and desecrate at will.

What he'd witnessed today could only be described as anarchy. Harassment and lawlessness of the highest order. While the generals were conspicuously absent, seemingly uncaring, their men ravaged everything they could put their hands to.

Including St. Stephen's Cathedral.

Outrage gripped Ian. Followed by intense sorrow when pews and statues from the sacred place of worship were carelessly tossed into the street. Fuel for a raging bonfire set in the square.

Somewhere he'd read Sherman was quoted as saying, "War is hell."

Today he'd proven his own words.

He and his army were representing the devil himself.

The overnight train had been blessedly empty. Only one other couple had boarded with Abby and Dottie at Savannah. When the couple changed trains at Millan, a tattered pack of ex-convicts from a prison in Athens came aboard. Quiet and subdued, they were on their way to join the State Militia in Macon in exchange for their freedom. Thankfully, they kept to themselves.

By the time they reached McIntyre at four in the morning, word met them that the next stop at Gordon was overrun with Yankees. A weary troop of Confederates waiting to take the train to Macon decided it best to make the journey by foot to avoid conflict. Most of the men already on board got off to join them.

Dottie gave them the bit of food she'd packed in a basket.

When she saw some of the soldiers wore no shoes in the bitter cold, she sent them off with scraps of her sable cloak wrapped around their feet.

Abby was immensely humbled.

She'd not seen that level of compassion since she was a child. Her own mother would have done the same for the Cayuse Indians.

Between McIntyre and Gordon, they had the passenger car to themselves. As the night progressed, the two women settled into comfortable conversation. Ian's mother was well-versed and had an innate wisdom that Abby admired.

Time had come for Abby to confide everything to Ian's mother.

A defining moment of truth, which would either solidify their bond or sever it forever.

By six o'clock AM, the train was commandeered by Federal soldiers at the Gordon depot, twenty miles out of Milledgeville.

Impervious to the threat of danger, Abby and Dottie devised a plan. Together, they would find and confront the man who held Georgia's fate in his despotic hands. Between the two of them, they agreed not to budge one iota until they had his consent to spare her oldest city.

An Alabama cavalry captain intervened on their behalf when a skirmish broke out amongst them for claim of the Saberton horses and saddles.

Abby announced they were on their way to speak to General Sherman and needed their horses to get there. When asked if the general was expecting them, Dottie replied that the general was in no position to be turning away callers, considering he was the uninvited guest to this party.

Whether from curiosity to see what the women were up to, or simply a gallant gesture from a Southern gentleman, the captain stepped forward and insisted on escorting them the rest of the way to Milledgeville himself. Being a Southerner who had stayed loyal to the Union, he wasn't in friendly territory.

He recruited his aide, a snide young corporal who clearly had no use for rebels, to accompany them to the confederate capitol.

Abby's allegiance would forever lay with the Union cause. Just the same, she wouldn't waste a breath defending herself to the brash Yankee soldiers flocking around their rail car. A good majority of them were restless and agitated like caged animals, waiting to pounce on anything worth taking. These men had been given permission to wreak havoc on enemy homeland.

The intensity of their disdain for common decency made Abby's skin crawl.

With the captain's help, they were able to retrieve their horses. An hour later, the four topped a vast tree-lined hill where a view of Milledgeville appeared beyond the Oconee in the valley below.

Pulling up on the reins of her chestnut mare, Abby took in the sight.

A bridge over the river, stood half charred and smoldering. A long procession of conveyances snaked along the river road where the city's inhabitants waited for a single ferry to escape hundreds of blue coats that occupied their streets.

What looked like thousands more Union soldiers were camped on the outskirts surrounded by hundreds of covered wagons. If she were guessing, she'd say some were filled with provisions, the rest were for bring back their spoils.

"I can honestly say I've never seen anything so disheartening." Dottie Saberton rode up beside her. "Those poor people."

"Best to keep moving, ladies." The captain urged.

"The line for the ferry will take some time." Abby pointed out.

"Those folks are not going into town." The other soldier drew ahead of them. "They're trying to get out." He sounded a bit too pleased about it, almost smug.

The two women shared a glance before pressing forward.

As predicted, they were the only ones waiting for a westbound ferry.

Ahead of them lay a misty field where fortifications appeared long abandoned. Cold cannons sat useless in the fog.

Along the road, they passed people of every color wandering in a lost daze. Some with babies on their hips, some assisting the elderly and infirmed, all seemed to be traveling with nothing but the clothes on their backs.

Nearing the city, Abby grew even more determined to do all she could to prevent this same kind of devastation from happening in Savannah. There was certainly no guarantee the general would consider her proposal, but she was not leaving here without at least having him hear her out.

Smoke burned their eyes and throats as they neared the capital square. Groups of soldiers huddled around fires built in the streets. Some lay sprawled out with empty bottles still in their hands.

Abby accepted the captain's assistance to the ground in front of wide steps leading up to the palatial mansion. The velvet hood pooled around her shoulders. Lifting it carefully, she covered her elegantly coiffed hair.

Dottie came around her horse and handed the reins to the captain. "I expect our horses to be waiting for us here when we get back."

The soldier offered no smile just a matter-of-fact nod.

The Alabama captain held up his hand at the foot of the mansion's wide porch steps. "Wait here, ma'am. I'll speak to the general and ask if he'll see you."

"If you don't mind, I'll see to this myself." Abby brushed past him. "We've traveled too far to be put off."

Lifting her green skirt, Abby hurried up the steps with Dottie right beside her. Two guards, one on either side of the wooden portal, stepped in front of the door. "You can't go in there."

"We've come to see General Sherman." Abby took another step forward.

"He's busy." One of the soldiers smirked.

"I can see that." Dottie looked over the debris filled street before turning her attention back to the guards. "You may announce us if you'd like. Otherwise, we will announce ourselves."

The younger soldier swallowed hard, not exactly sure what to do with two belligerent females. The older, more seasoned officer, called down to the Alabama captain. "What's this about?"

"They have an appointment with the general," came the answer. Though it wasn't entirely the truth, neither of them felt inclined to correct him. Maybe later, *after* they'd had their meeting."

"You got some kind of letter to prove it?"

Before either of them could answer, the door was hauled open and a hard scowl of the Union commander met them in the doorway. "What's the commotion, O'Riley?"

"A couple of belles say they have an appointment to see you, Sir."

With a cigar between his teeth, General William T. Sherman, squinted against the morning sun looking at Dottie for a good long while without speaking.

To her credit she held his gaze, never wavering once.

"Do I know you, Ma'am?" He removed the cigar, flicking a roll of ash from its tip.

"We've met." Dottie took a step toward him. "May we come in?"

The guard went to stop her but the commanding general waved him off.

Both ladies stepped inside the governor's mansion.

Abby was immediately struck by the sparse furnishings in the empty foyer.

"Please, refresh my memory." William Sherman could be gracious when he chose to be.

"You attended West Point with my late husband. We met at a cotillion his senior year." Dottie had given her cape and muff to the soldiers at McIntyre. But her suit of burgundy was still crisp and fit her lovely figure to perfection.

"Dottie Maxwell." His voice was raspy.

Abby wondered if it was the cigars or if he was ill.

"Dottie Saberton," she amended.

"I'd offer you a chair, but it seems your governor didn't leave us any." He held out an arm to invite them into the expansive parlor where an inviting fire blazed in the hearth.

"Thank heavens for that." Dottie entered the room and looked over the barren walls. "From all I've seen, his cherished possessions would end up in a pile of cinders if he had." Her lilting drawl echoed in the empty room.

Abby kept her head lowered under her hood as she passed the general.

He stopped her just before she got through the doorway.

"And who have we here?"

On a long breath, she lifted her chin and peered into his jet-black eyes.

"Hello, Uncle Cump."

*"Let us, then, be what we are, and speak what
we think,
and in all things keep ourselves loyal to truth."*
~ *Henry Wadsworth Longfellow*

## Thirty

*I*an bolted down the bluff's steep curve, skidding over
rock and brush to where the horses were tied in a grove
of cypress.

He'd spotted Abby and his mother as soon as they had
entered the square. Under guard, they'd been taken to Sherman.

What were they doing in Milledgeville?

They'd never have left Brechenridge unless the plantation
had come under siege. To think his mother and Abby, in her
delicate condition, had been taken prisoner was unconsciona-
ble.

"Hold up there, Rev!" Out of breath, Fitz caught just as
Ian wheeled his horse toward the center of town. "What's your
all-fired hurry?"

"They have Abby." Ian shouted, stark dread gripped his
throat. Kicking his mount into a full run, he raced down the

river road, his heart thundering in his ears.

Channeling his fear into rage, Ian laid low over his horse's back and spurred the animal beyond its limits. God help the Yankee who tried to stop him.

Entering the city through a back alley, Ian tore off his hat, frock coat, and jacket, stuffing them into saddle bags. His brown riding pants and tall boots were less conspicuous topped with just his plain white shirt. Holster and sword in place, Ian led his horse from the alley out onto the street.

Stepping over drunken soldiers, he kept his attention ahead, making no attempt to engage anyone in his path. On several occasions, he had been a guest of the governor prior to succession, he knew his way to the mansion, but could only guess at the side street which would service a domestic entry.

Hordes of soldiers reclined in the roads and in private yards. Open fires dotted the streets, where meat roasted on crude spits while half used carcasses were tossed aside to rot in manicured rose bushes.

The governor's mansion wasn't hard to locate. Easily the grandest estate set in the center of the city. Ian left his horse tied to a tall lamp post and slipped through the fence. An entrance facing a turnaround drive looked to be where delivery wagons would likely be directed.

The door was bolted.

Standing back, he surveyed the back of the house. A window off of the second floor balcony was cracked. Ian could see it was enough that the cold wind ruffled the draperies. Climbing the white trellis, he scaled the balcony. With the wooden butt of his pistol, he gave the fractured glass a hard tap. A large piece broke off into his hand. Reaching in, he unlatched the window and climbed inside.

The room was a library. Books were scattered from empty

shelves, and family keepsakes were strewn across the floor.

Ian cautiously opened the door, to peer down the hall. All lamps were dark and cold. No movement brought him to venture deeper into the house.

Ian kept to the shadows, listening for activity at every doorway. He followed the hallway to a round balcony overlooking the marble foyer. A gold-leaf dome loomed overhead.

Still no sight of the Federals.

With back to the wall, Ian took the stairs slowly down to the main level. Voices drifted up to meet him. He recognized his mother's muffled tone. The closer he got, the less she sounded afraid but more like she was agitated.

Ian watched shadows pass in front of the sidelight windows on either side of the front door. With his revolver drawn, he scanned the area past the foyer for any more soldiers milling around inside. The corridors were still. No light burned in any room that he could see.

Even if Sherman was holed up in the enormous mansion alone, surely he would have aides and messengers coming in and out.

A man spoke close to the door, and Ian pressed against the wainscoted wall.

"Abby, you look so much like your mother, Julianne. It's as if my sister has returned to me." The Yankee moved away from the doorway. "She got the greater portion of our father's red hair."

Stunned, Ian wasn't sure he'd heard right.

"I miss her, too. Very much." The quiet answer was unmistakably Abby's voice.

Ian couldn't take in a decent breath. His gut wrenched like he'd just taken a hard blow.

In all the times they'd talked, she hadn't thought this was important enough to mention?

∼

Abby occupied one of the two unmatched chairs positioned in front of a black marble fireplace. Dottie sat across from her in the other. The general pulled a highbacked dining chair from the corner. Otherwise, there was no other furniture in the room.

After a few minutes, warmth from the fire finally began to chase the chill from her bones. Abby could feel him watching them both and deliberately avoided his steely gaze.

She'd only met her uncle once that she could remember. He'd come to visit not long after her parents died. She'd received intermittent letters from him over the years and imagined he probably corresponded with many other members of his family as he was always a wealth of news.

The man in the letters was attentive enough, but always seemed to be a lost soul looking for connection.

It was no secret that William Tecumseh Sherman had struggled with great sadness in his life. The newspapers had written for weeks about his reported breakdown after one of the earlier battles up north. But just as characteristically, he picked himself back up and was celebrated for returning to the battle lines.

He had written to her about how he'd been sent to live with neighbors as a child after the death of his father. And how Abby's mother, older by two years, had been farmed out to live at the preacher's house. The two of them had managed to stay close in spite of the separation.

When Julianne Sherman married Silas McFadden and left for the west to brave the vast Indian mission field, her brother had pleaded with her not to go. When her death was reported, he took the news exceptionally hard.

On several occasions before the war between the states broke out, he'd invited Abby to his home in Louisiana but her obligations as governess kept her in Mansfield.

A part of her always regretted she'd never taken the time to know her mother's younger brother. He was no better than a stranger to her. The stories she'd read in the Southern newspapers lately, made him out to be the worst sort of monster.

As with everything else, Abby supposed the truth lay somewhere in between.

"I had quite a fascination at that cotillion as I remember." General Sherman addressed Dottie and didn't mince words. He never had. Rolling a cigar between his lips, he took a long puff.

"You were a young cadet. Fanciful and a bit full of yourself." Dottie removed her gloves and placed them in her lap. "Much too intense for one so young."

Abby smiled. Dottie didn't hold back either.

"Your wit charmed every military man in attendance." Again, a certain despondency flooded his craggy features. "All sugar and champagne, you were. With just enough salt to keep things interesting."

"That was a very long time ago." Dottie gave him a half smile.

"Samuel was the envy of all that year." The general's callous demeanor was back in place. "A shame he was killed. He would have made a formidable opponent, no doubt."

"He has three sons who are just that." Her eyebrow rose a tad. "All officers for the Confederacy."

The air was thick with a sudden hush that fell between them.

Abby decided to intervene. The reason for their visit was

too important to let their hostilities get out of hand.

"Samuel Saberton's middle son and I are to be married." Abby turned in her chair to better see him. "As soon as this conflict is resolved."

His reaction was less than she'd hoped for. The look he shot her could frost the windows.

A surge of irritation rose in her chest. She was cold and tired and desperate to help save Ian's home. Frivolous chit chat was getting them nowhere.

"Uncle Cump, we've come to negotiate a deal." Abby stood and walked to where he sat. Without thinking she laid a gloved hand on his shoulder. "The Macon and St. Louis newspapers agree that you and your gorilla forces intend to annihilate everything between here and Savannah."

Removing the cigar from his mouth, his scowl turned to a serious frown. "Is that what they said?"

"I believe she means your guerilla forces. Although ..." Dottie cocked her head and left it at that.

"The news agencies overstep their principles." Sherman came to his feet and his chair hit the floor with a clatter. "The movement of my army has one purpose—to see this blasted rebellion ended. I do not intend to justify my actions to the newspapers, nor do I intend to discuss it any further with you ladies."

"In case you haven't noticed, General, this war does not just affect the men out on your battlefields." Dottie stood and slowly placed herself in front of him. "Countless women and children are caught in the crosshairs."

Abby admired her calm.

"A war instigated by your rebels I might point out." His gritty voice raised as he looked down at her.

Dottie nodded, then pinned him with a direct look. "That

is highly debatable. But, since we haven't the time to hash it over, let me just say this." Moving closer to Abby, they presented a united front. "If you continue this path you've chosen, allowing for no concessions, history will only remember that it was the Federals who did the robbing and pillaging, ravishing and whoremongering—overstepping their principles as you say."

Abby rushed ahead to take up the gauntlet. "And it will forever be remembered that in the name of freedom, private citizens, the women and children, were the ones who suffered the most in your march for freedom."

Examining the cigar he held between his fingers, he finally glanced over to acknowledge their argument. "My perspective remains as it has since the first shots were fired countryman against countryman. If a necessary evil hastens an end to an even greater evil, then let history be hanged."

"Don't you see?" Abby hitched her skirt and followed him as he moved to the window. "You have an opportunity to show that good can overcome *all* evils."

"Good must have teeth to win wars."

His countenance was weary, and her heart went out to him.

"Uncle Cump, for the past three years I have nursed men on both sides who have been shattered in battle." He continued to observe the melee going on in the street. "One night, not long ago, a Union sergeant captured at Donaldsonville came in. He had the most incredible story to tell."

Sherman kept his attention fixed outside.

"He said Atlanta had fallen. But that the great general, William T. Sherman, had been moved with compassion for her frightened and disillusioned citizens."

His gaze cut down to her.

"That you provided clothing, food, and blankets to those

displaced from their homes. The soldier even described you as a Merciful Conqueror."

General Sherman lifted a hand to touch his niece's cheek, but refrained. "A conqueror just the same."

Dottie approached him from the other side. "So it would seem." She gave a pointed look out the window to the destruction of Georgia's capital. "However, we have come to ask that you conquer elsewhere and leave our home in Savannah intact."

Turning from his niece, Sherman narrowed his eye at Dottie.

"In the event our opposing forces are not able to put a stop to this defilement, we've come to ask that you spare Savannah as graciously as you did Atlanta." She shrugged and folded her arms.

For the first time he gave a genuine smile. "The true motive of this visit is revealed."

Dottie remained unruffled. "I'm prepared to offer you a fine mansion on St. James square to use as your headquarters and that beautiful black thoroughbred you see out there on the street to keep as my gift. In addition to your army rations, we will see that you and your men have ample provisions for your stay. You may enter the city unopposed as long as you and your men respect the dignity of our citizen's homes. Cause no personal harm to any individual or their livestock."

"So far, I've not had much opposition to speak of. Why should I agree to your terms if we can take the city without incident?" He strolled over to the mantle and tossed his cigar into the fire.

"Because if you don't agree to our terms, you will not take Savannah without incident." Abby had to make him see the wisdom in the offer. "Fort McAllister is on high alert. The ports are heavily guarded by Confederate Navy, and they have troops in position to give a fight to the end. More bloodshed and more innocent lives lost."

He stared down at waning embers.

Abby bit the inside of her bottom lip.

Her mother had always said a prayer for her brother, who she called Tecumseh. Just like the Shawnee chief he was named for, he was both savage and gentle. Abby prayed his thirst for victory would not overrule his compassion for those who were left defeated.

Finally, he turned and straightened. "I'm afraid I underestimated you ladies. You are better negotiators than either Secretary of War."

Dottie gave him a most gracious smile. "So you'll agree?"

"On the condition that you are able to deliver all that you've promised."

"I suppose you will have to trust me just as I'm forced to trust you." Dottie went to him and held out her hand.

When he didn't readily accept her gesture of goodwill, Abby stepped in. "President Lincoln has said Savannah is one of his favorite coastal towns. Won't he be pleased when you spare it from ruin?"

A course grin lifted his mouth. "Touché, little one."

He shook Dottie's hand. "Your wit is even sharper with age."

"Thank you, general." She retrieved her gloves. "Now if you would be so kind as to allow the captain out there to escort us back to the train station, we will not presume to waste any more of your time."

He gave a formal nod and held out his hand to allow their departure.

"In the time I've spent in Georgia, Uncle Cump, I've discovered a thing or two about these people of the South." Abby allowed him to help her on with her borrowed velvet cape. "With the exception of one evil man, they've accepted me into their homes and treated me with utmost kindness."

The crooked tilt of Dottie's smile made Abby miss Ian all the more.

"I've found that both good and evil exists on every side."

He chose not to answer her.

Though she'd never agree with the atrocities that brought rebel forces to arms, Abby hoped her uncle would at least consider the motives and actions of his own army in this fray.

"Before I forget, I promised to relay a message to you from a copper-headed nine year-old." Abby held tight to her reticule where Hickory's slingshot lay. "He wants you to know you are sorely mistaken."

Sherman walked beside her with his hands behind his back. "Indeed?"

"I believe his exact words were, 'you may tromp over every inch of Georgia's red dirt, but you ain't never gonna hear her howl.'"

"Amen." Dottie agreed with a shake of her head.

In spite of himself, General William Tecumseh Sherman actually chuckled. Probably more at her gall for actually relaying it than at Hickory's daring declaration.

As Abby reached for the handle of the glossy pocket door, a loud shot split the air, echoing through the empty room.

Her hand drew back as if she had triggered it.

Sherman threw open the doors as bluecoats poured through the entrance. Weapons drawn, they swooped upon the staircase like a volt of vultures after a kill.

"Stand aside!" Their commander gave the order and one by one they backed down the stairs.

Without thought, Abby took Dottie's hand as they waited to witness the fate of a hapless intruder who'd dared to invade the Yankee headquarters.

As the last soldier retreated, Abby drew a sharp breath when Ian's face came into view.

With the back of his hand, he swiped at a trickle of blood beside his mouth.

"Ian!" Dottie cried out.

Abby was rooted, unable to move.

Her heart sank to her feet at the dark accusation in his gaze.

*"T'was grace that brought us safe thus far, and grace*
*will lead us home."*
*~ John Newton, Amazing Grace*

# Thirty-One

"Identify yourself, soldier." The Yankee general strode to the middle of the foyer where his men were spoiling for a fight behind him.

Ian's attention was transfixed on the woman standing at the bottom of the stairs.

Abby never looked more beautiful.

With all he'd just heard, however, she felt like a beautiful stranger. Ian couldn't help but wonder if he'd ever really known her at all.

"Colonel Ian Saberton." His voice was low as he tore his eyes from Abby to provide the expected information. "Georgia 4th Cavalry, Confederate States Army."

Curses arose among the gathering of soldiers.

"When I returned, I came upon him lurking on the stairs, Sir." An arrogant captain, apparently Sherman's Aide-de-camp, stepped forward to give his account. "It was my shot you heard. Sadly, my mark was off by mere inches."

"You'd best be thankful you're a poor shot." Dottie Saberton joined Abby, glaring at the young captain.

"State your business, Colonel." Sherman ignored the snickering of his men.

"While observing your troops' movement into Milledgeville, I identified my mother and Miss McFadden entering this residence. Naturally, I followed."

The truth would either set him free or have him hanged.

"This is the man I plan to marry." Abby stated, lifting her chin. The readable plea in her eyes begged for understanding.

He wanted to go to her and demand to know why she'd chosen not to mention her ties to the slayer, William Sherman.

Instead, he stayed where he was. Any movement toward the commander could be misconstrued as aggression. With this many Yankees itching to get at him, he'd be shot in an instant.

"Where is your regiment?" The general issued another gruff inquiry.

"Not here." Ian's answer was deliberately vague. Let him do his own scouting and figure it out himself.

"The way he's dressed I'd say he's special units, Sir." The captain jumped in, evidently needing to sound important. "Perhaps an enemy spy."

"He's no more a spy than I am." Abby rolled her eyes. "General Farris tried to have me executed, but Ian risked everything to defend me."

Sherman turned to her, frowning. "You failed to mention that when expounding on the good and evil of the rebels."

There was plenty she had failed to mention.

"Back to your posts!" Sherman barked the order and men scattered. "You as well, Captain."

The upstart gave Abby a toothy grin and sauntered back down the hall eating an apple.

"Colonel, you may come down here."

His summons irked Ian.

But since he was in no position to defy the Yankee command, he grabbed his gun from where it had fallen on the step behind him and made his way down the staircase.

"General Sherman, meet my son, Colonel Ian Saberton." Dottie pulled on her gloves. "Ian, this man intends to take Savannah."

Ian's head snapped up.

"And we will not oppose him." Abby tied the ribbon of her cloak under her chin. "Be sure to tell your commanders."

They'd both gone mad.

As tempting as it was to stay and engage in war talk with a power-hungry Yankee and two delusional females, Ian was more concerned about putting distance between himself and this hotbed of Yankees.

Sherman had every right to have him arrested and held a prisoner. That would not end well. He had no intention of leaving Abby and his mother to their own defenses.

"Colonel, against all practical wisdom, I must rely on you to see these most exceptional ladies back to your camp." Sherman gave Abby a fond embrace, then turned to Dottie and took her hand.

Ian wasn't sure he'd heard right. Had Sherman just invited him to walk out unscathed?

Glancing over at the Federal commander, Ian didn't care for the way he was devouring his mother with his eyes.

"We'd best be going then." Offering Abby his arm, Ian took his mother's elbow and directed her away from Sherman.

He would take them to Macon. General Hawthorne could arrange an escort to see them back to Brechenridge. "My horse is around back."

The women said their goodbyes while Ian went before them to clear a path through the hundreds of troops gathered to have a look at them.

Ian helped Abby up into her saddle. She was a vision in green. Her expressive eyes caught the winter sun and took on a glow that lit her whole face.

He ached to take her into his arms. But he refused. He wanted answers first. There could never be secrets between them. Abby had to know he'd never judge her based on anything other than who *she* was. It didn't matter who her uncle was.

Another Federal officer helped Dottie mount, and she thanked him by name as if they were old friends.

Would he ever know all there was to know about women? Just when he thought he had them figured out, they did an about face and he was scrambling to make sense of them again.

What he needed was to have a good talk with Nicholas.

Surely after four years of marriage, his brother had Tori all figured out by now.

Abby was exhausted.

With a frigid northeastern wind at her back, she huddled down into a satin-trimmed quilt her uncle had placed over her shoulders for the journey back to Macon. Fairly certain the beautiful throw belonged to Georgia's governor, Abby made a mental note to have Cora see that it was returned.

Her hands felt like ice beneath her lambskin gloves.

A glance over at Dottie, similarly nestled under a pink chenille bedspread, suggested the older woman might have fallen asleep in her saddle. Even with her eyes closed, she was still one of the most stunning women Abby had ever known.

Not so much in looks alone, though she was undeniably attractive, the confident manner in which she conducted herself had everyone she met eating from her hand. Even a hardened Yankee with a no-mercy reputation.

Dottie had tempered her uncle without an ounce of trepidation. What a fine man Samuel Saberton must have been to have won her heart.

Abby lifted her head to see past the men surrounding her to where Ian led his unit up front. Her heart grew weary waiting for him to fall back to talk to her. As it was, he'd barely spoken a word.

So many times she'd wanted to tell him about her mother's family.

She had hesitated at first, afraid he might use the information against her. But by the time she was certain he would never do anything to harm her, her uncle had declared an overt attack on Ian's home state. She'd thought to meet with General Sherman and dissuade him from taking the Saberton family home, considering they were to be her own family someday.

Just as she had told Dottie, she'd fully intended to tell Ian about her idea but not until after she was certain the daring plan would succeed.

Never in a million years had she thought he would intercept their meeting right in the middle of enemy territory. He could have been killed.

Abby pulled the blanket closer around her as the thought chilled her to her toes.

They had much to discuss. Apparently, however, Ian was not prepared to have that discussion in front of his men. Abby would give him that. What they needed to say was better said between the two of them. Alone.

Two hours after leaving Milledgeville, they arrived on the

outskirts of Macon. From what she could tell, most of the Union troops had already moved south, bypassing Macon altogether.

Turning onto First Street, Abby immediately noticed the city was inundated with refugees. Easily twice as many as when she'd left. Tents occupied every available space and supply wagons rattled along with children in worn coats running in the street beside them.

A large plat of tents housed cots teeming with wounded soldiers. The hospitals must have exceeded capacity, forcing incoming patients to be treated on the cold street.

Ian brought the unit to a halt in front of Harbor House.

The yard was brimming with new faces. She'd never seen so many soldiers here. Some in tattered uniform and some in plain working clothes. All cold and waiting for the lady with a coffee pot to come by and fill their cups.

At Ian's dismissal, his men were free to join them.

Fitz helped Dottie dismount while Ian reached up for Abby. She yielded to his strong hands, sliding from her saddle.

"Where have all these men come from?" She kept hold of Ian's arms simply because she missed the feel of them around her.

"The State Militia was called in. Two more divisions were brought over from Alabama." His answer was quiet. He didn't seem in a hurry to release her and she warmed under his passionate gaze. "I missed you."

Suddenly talking was the last thing on her mind. Standing on her toes, she took the lapels of his coat and pulled his lips to hers, letting her heart speak for itself. A familiar draw pulled them closer, and Ian tightened his hold.

Oh, how she'd missed him, too. This man who had ridden into Macon one day and brought clarity where she'd only known turmoil. Offering love after a lifetime of loneliness.

Abby slowly brought both heels back to the ground.

"Why didn't you tell me?" Ian laid an arm across his saddle behind her.

"I couldn't risk losing you." She whispered as raw and honestly as she knew how. "I tend to lose the ones I love." She tried to look away, but Ian caught her chin with his finger. Her clouded gaze lifted to his. "They never come back."

"I'm not going anywhere." His promise was as strong and sure as his embrace. "You'll just have to trust me on that."

She caressed his forearm, unable to speak past the lump in her throat.

When she hesitated, she saw the muscle work in his jaw. "Abby, whatever comes our way, we face it together. No secrets. No running. Trust me. As long as I'm able, I'm never going to leave you."

Abby believed him. This man who held her heart would never willingly walk away.

She answered from her heart. "I love you, Colonel Saberton."

"And I love you, Angel." His kiss proved the truth in his words.

"Rev, the boys are ready to hit camp." Fitz came around the horse and stopped short. "Pardon me, Ma'am. I didn't see you two was tryin' to warm up."

"I'd say they've had enough warming up for now." Without her covering, Dottie rubbed her arms against the cold. "Where can we find some coffee for ourselves?"

"Oh, Abby! Colonel!" Every head turned to watch Cora Dobbs and her usual flock of ladies patter down the porch steps of Harbor House.

Ian dropped his arm to allow Abby to go over and greet

them.

"Mrs. Saberton, I presume?" Cora smoothed the work wrinkles from her brown taffeta gown and ran a hand over her upswept hair. "You must agree to stay with the mayor and myself while you visit."

"Thank you." Dottie cut her gaze to Abby. "Mrs. ...?"

"Mrs. Dottie Saberton, meet Mrs. Walter Dobbs." Abby supplied. "Mayor's wife."

"Ah." Dottie flashed a gracious smile, but Cora was jolted from behind when a fight broke out between several of the men in the yard.

Abby pulled Dottie out of harm's way as women all around them, picked up their skirts and ran for cover.

Soldiers formed a circle, picking sides and egging on the offenders. Ian and Lieutenant Fitz immediately sprang into action, entering the fray to break up the brawl.

Too many weapons in the hands of soldiers eager for a fight could easily escalate into an uncontrolled mob.

"I say we grab a hose pump and start spraying 'em down." Cora was ever full of ideas.

"Count me in." Dottie agreed.

Abby shook dust from her borrowed skirt. She knew a thing or two about breaking up fights between men acting like a bunch of unruly boys. Many a wounded soldier taunted others into a scuffle, to alleviate boredom and frustration, she supposed. Once separated, a sympathetic ear was usually all they needed. Someone to assure them they were not forgotten and promise all wounds would eventually heal.

A body of onlookers gathered in a tight circle, making it impossible to push through. Abby tried another way. Over the long porch and down the steps into the side yard where she could get a better view.

Stepping from the last wooden step next to a fragrant magnolia tree, her breath left her as she was slammed backward into rough brick of the chimney hidden behind the bushes.

Before she could make sense of her predicament, she came up against the barrel of a rifle aimed straight at her chest.

Squelching a scream, Abby raised her hands to show she wasn't armed. If Macon was under Union attack, she would insist on being taken to the commanding general at once.

A demented laugh caused her to look down the long iron barrel to the lunatic who held it.

Farris.

*"She was powerful, not because she wasn't scared*
*but because she went on so strongly despite the fear."*
*~ Atticus*

# Thirty-Two

The war stripped many of their sanity.

Those, like Farris, who used innocent suffering for their personal gain were the most deranged of all.

Abby took a step back.

"You should've left well enough alone, Miss McFadden. The Dove's Nest was mine." Farris jabbed the muzzle of his rifle into her shoulder. "You owe me much. And you will pay." His guttural threat was hard to decipher. Swaying, he reeked of whiskey. "I was locked away to rot because of your lies."

He gave another sharp prod that that sent a wave of pain down her arm. Visible vapors of his soured breath assailed her in the frigid air. A gag gripped her throat.

Easing out from under the shade of high bushes, she hoped to be seen by someone who could bring help. Bumping into the splintering side of a cellar door, her hopes were dashed.

"Sallie turned the rest of them against me. Holding out behind my back. Keeping *my* money. And you were behind it all."

He poked harder into her bruised flesh.

"Abby!" From the corner of her eye, she watched Dottie come around the side of the house. Her heavy skirts whirled at her feet as she made an abrupt stop.

"Stay where you are." Farris demanded. The hard glint in his eyes remained focused on Abby. "This time I will take care of you myself. No one will interfere."

Abby could see Dottie whisper something quietly to a man standing beside her. In her sideview, Abby watched the man slip away into the jumbled mass of soldiers. An inkling of hope coursed through her. Surely he'd been sent to fetch Ian. She closed her eyes, listening hard for the sound of Ian's voice above the rumble of commotion.

"... both dead." Farris muttered.

Opening her eyes, she saw him staring at her, but Abby had the feeling his mind had wandered off again.

"Yankees charging up the hill. Slaughtered boys like worthless pigs."

Tamping down panic that threatened to choke her, she watched his finger brush the trigger of his weapon.

She had to stay calm.

This was not her first time to elude Farris. She'd dodged his threats and nauseating advances for two years. As long as she kept her head, she could evade this demented rant as well.

Over Farris' shoulder, Abby could see a crowd gathering. Dottie had worked her way around to alert a couple of soldiers who stood with unholstered pistols. Even if they were to try and take Farris from behind, he would no doubt get a shot off first.

Abby had no choice but make an attempt to run.

Twisting her shoulder, she fiercely pushed the barrel of his gun toward the ground to escape a direct hit. The sudden action threw Farris off balance. His rifle discharged flatly into the dirt.

Gathering her skirts, she dashed around back of Harbor House, bent low behind a line of holly bushes. A large carriage house and the summer kitchen stood separated by a cobblestone path. Praying Farris would be apprehended, she focused on remaining out of sight until she could be certain.

First, she veered toward the carriage house. The tall doors were closed, and to her utter dismay, tightly locked. A quick glance over her shoulder told her Farris was not in pursuit.

Frantically, she pulled at the only side door to the building. Locked.

Across the path, she spotted one of the women exiting a door to the larder. Her arms were laden with food as she headed back out toward the kitchen, but she'd left a spare piece of wood to prevent the door from closing all the way.

"She's in the back!"

Abby looked back to see Mo yelling from the porch rails and gesturing her way. Several men she recognized from the shanty streamed around the corner, kicking up dirt as they came after her.

She dashed toward the open storeroom.

Pitching the piece of wood out of the way, she jerked the door closed behind her. Farris' men pounded on the other side just as she threw the small latch in place.

Her heartbeat thudded in her ears. The simple hasp couldn't possibly hold against their incessant pummeling. With only the light from a single long window, Abby searched the larder for something heavy to move in front of the door—just in case.

Three large barrels stood in a corner with table clothes and napkins folded neatly on top.

Surely, they would hold the men back.

Abby tried desperately to move the barrel closest to the door, but the heavy container refused to budge. Removing her gloves, she gave it another try, coming from another angle. Whatever was in that one weighed a ton.

The door creaked under their heavy battering.

Abby got behind a small, pine-hewed cupboard and pushed hard. First with her arms, then with her hip. Slowly, she scooted the piece to cover the door.

The small room was enclosed on all sides. Herbs and vegetables filled baskets lining whitewashed shelves hanging on red brick walls. Shanks of ham and cured bacon hung from hooks in the back.

The pounding stopped.

Abby paced back and forth across the room. She didn't dare open the door. Trying to see through the only window was impossible with a maze of herbs hung there to dry.

An exchange of gunfire erupted outside causing her to crouch low out of pure instinct. Followed by a heated discussion just on the other side of the door, evidence that Farris' men were not giving up a chance to collect on her death.

Surely Ian had been located by now. Was it him shooting at Farris' men? Had he been hit in return?

The sound of shattering glass sent shards of alarm over her already tattered nerves.

A ball of flame sailed into the storeroom, forcing her back into the shadows.

Bunches of herbs that had been hung in the window ignited like kindling, dripping to the wood floor below. A pungent stench of kerosene burned her throat as the flaming dart consumed the woven baskets lining the floor.

Black smoke began to fill the room.

Acrid fumes stung her eyes and she made a desperate attempt to reach the door but the cabinet she'd placed there earlier blocked her path.

As the fire grew, so did her panic until stark fear nearly paralyzed her.

Fire had taken her family. Visions of her mother's last moments trapped inside that burning fortress had tormented her as long as she could remember. A terror so profound, she never spoke of it.

*Please, Lord, don't let me suffer the same fate.*

Abby crouched to the floor where the air was easier to take in.

Crawling on her knees, she blindly searched for the broken window.

*Please, Father in heaven …*

Bumping into the barrels, she reached for the folded napkins to cover her mouth and nose.

Unable to catch a decent breath, she prayed she wouldn't lose consciousness and be consumed by the growing flames.

Snatching another scrapping soldier by the scruff of the collar, Ian flung him to the side of the road where Fitz and eight other officers were corralling their unruly men.

By the looks of empty bottles in the road, someone had thought it was a good idea to hand out cheap whiskey. The haggard soldiers went without such indulgences for months and imbibed much too freely.

At first, Ian attributed the misguided gesture to a citizen trying to provide comfort to the military men milling about Harbor House. But as he got deeper into the fray, he came up against more of the rabble from shanty town who appeared to be stirring up hostilities.

Then, he'd spotted Mo. Immediately, he began to search for Abby.

It made no sense for Farris' men to come down and openly start a brawl unless they were creating a diversion from the real reason they were here.

The most profitable reason Ian could think of was the bounty Farris had out on Abby.

"Ian!" His attention was drawn to the yard of Harbor House where his mother waved frantically.

Ian stepped over a discarded rebel jacket wadded up in the dirt, taking long strides to where the ladies were huddled.

"That general is here! The one that despises Abby so." Dottie grabbed him by the arm as soon as he was within reach. "He had a muzzle on her, and she was frightened half to death."

"Where is she now?" Every muscle tensed at the thought of Farris getting his hands on Abby. The man was crazed and had nothing left to lose. He'd obviously wasted no time in escaping his assigned post and returned to Macon.

"He was in a drunken rant, and Abby caught him by surprise." Dottie fairly ran next to him in effort to keep up with his determined pace.

Ian came to an abrupt halt when a black plume of smoke rose from the back of Harbor House just as a scream rent the air.

Apprehension surged through him as he burst into a full run.

Rounding the corner of the main house, he saw Elizabeth Lambert desperately tugging at the door of an out building off the kitchen. Beside herself, she screamed something about

Abby.

A thin stream of smoke poured from a single broken window. He couldn't risk breaking in the door, outside air would only serve to fuel the flame. He'd have to go through the broken window and fight the fire from inside.

Ian threw off his jacket and wound it around his arm to clear the jagged edges of the broken window. Stepping inside the smoke-filled storehouse, he breathed into the crook of his elbow, squinting as he searched for movement.

"Abby!" He shouted, delving deeper into the haze.

The far end of the room was ignited. The fire popped and sizzled, shooting orange cinders down to the wooden floor.

Somewhere to his left, he heard coughing. Following the sound, Ian made out a form crouched near the door. The green of Abby's dress glinted in the flickering light.

"Hang on, Angel." His boot came up against a barrel in his haste to get to her. Tossing it out of the way, he dove to her side.

He found Abby on her knees, fighting to take in a breath.

"Are you hurt?" Ian could barely see her face. At the shake of her head, he stood and pulled her to her feet. Slipping her arm around his neck, he scooped her into his arms. "Let's get you out of here."

Carefully, he retraced his steps, holding his breath until his chest burned. Low flames crept toward the shattered window. If the stores of cooking oil ignited, their only way out would be sealed by an inferno.

"The door is blocked." Abby trembled in his arms and he clenched her closer against himself. "W-We can't get out."

Ian knew she was terrified of fire. The smell of smoke stirred achingly raw memories, a cruel reminder of her parent's death.

Farris couldn't possibly have known it.

Whether he had, or simply had an innate sense of evil that drove him in matters concerning Abby, he was responsible for the hot tears Ian felt against his chest.

There was a time to turn the other cheek and there was a time for evil to be dealt with.

Farris and his men had hurt Abby for the last time.

A thin stream of light led him to the broken-out window. Ian wasted no time getting her out through the fragmented opening to taste a breath of cool, fresh air.

Laying her on a patch of winter grass, Ian turned, scouring the area for any sign of Farris.

Men with axes chopped at the wooden door to the storehouse while a few of Ian's soldiers filled buckets full of water.

Abby coughed as Elizabeth urged her to take a drink. She was shaken, but unharmed. If he hadn't found her ...

Movement beside a tall bush near the carriage house immediately caught his attention. Farris staggered and tried to run as soon as he noticed he'd been spotted. His cowardly attempt to escape only served to infuriate Ian more.

Unholstering his gun, he took measured steps toward the man who'd done all he could to torment everyone he came in contact with. A wretch of humanity, with no discernable conscience or remorse.

If faltering justice wouldn't put an end to the man's constant torment of Abby, Ian would take care of it himself.

Closing the gap between himself and Farris, Ian raised his revolver to take aim.

"Ian, no!" Abby rasped behind him.

Without looking around, he could tell activity in the yard quieted. "Stay back, Abby. This man's deserted his post." Ian pulled back the hammer with his thumb. The sound of the click of the lock filled the courtyard. "He threatened a female civilian, and defied an officer's direct command." Gritting his teeth, he kept his aim. "My orders are to shoot on sight."

"You're not defending yourself, Ian. This time it's a choice." Abby stood at his back and though she spoke softly, the weight of what she said slammed into him with brute force. "You are acting out of hate. If you chose to kill him, this time it's murder."

Farris narrowed his bleary gaze at her but held his tongue.

Ian's finger itched to pull the trigger. He deserved to die. According to the articles of war, Ian had every right to fire.

But he was bound to a higher law.

Abby was right. He despised this man for all he'd done. But killing him would ultimately be Ian's own ruin. He'd lived in absolute torment for three years.

With a flick of his wrist, he pointed the end of his revolver to the sky and released the hammer.

He wouldn't go back.

Abby stepped forward to put a hand on his arm and lay her head against his back. "There's been enough death."

"He'll still stand trial. And eventually get his due." Ian's gaze remained on Farris until he signaled for two of his men to apprehend him. "I'm sure Hawthorne can find a place for him at Camp Oglethorpe until then."

*"A noble type of good. Heroic womanhood."*
*~ Henry Wadsworth Longfellow*

# Thirty-Three

~ ❧ ~

Abby sat in a rocking chair on the front porch of Harbor House.

A colorful quilt warmed her shoulders and a steaming cup of cocoa warmed her hands. The ladies fussed shamelessly over her. Much more than the ordeal warranted.

"I'm glad to see you're getting color back in your cheeks." Dottie smiled as she came up the brick steps. "I've secured a carriage. We can leave in the morning."

"You will stay with us tonight." Elizabeth Lambert offered her a warm cup. "You both need rest."

"Posh! They're staying with us." Cora was obviously riled. All the fighting seemed to have put her on the offensive, ready to lead a charge.

"Our house has a doctor living there, in case Abby needs one." Elizabeth patted Abby's knee. "Besides, Eliza Jane will want to hear all about this betrothal we've heard about."

"I won't argue, Elizabeth, that's very kind of you." Abby's throat still burned, but other than feeling exhausted, she was content. Being here with Ian, even for a short time, had made it abundantly clear she wanted to spend the rest of her life with him. No matter what happened with the country, she no longer dreaded the future.

"What sort of general has the audacity to run his own brothel to service his men? Taking what little pay they receive?" Dottie took a careful sip.

"Buford Farris, that's who." Cora provided. "I don't know why they ever let that old walrus out of jail.

"Fitz has him under guard. He'll be cashiered and locked away as soon as Hawthorne arrives." Ian climbed the front steps. Removing his hat, he ran a hand over his thick hair before settling it back over his brow.

"Has the general been summoned?" Elizabeth offered him coffee which he politely declined.

"General Hawthorne," Cora spoke to Ian's mother. "He's my brother."

"I see." Dottie winked at Abby.

A young soldier came around from the back of the house. "Colonel, sir, the fire has been extinguished. The storehouse was saved, but most of the provisions ain't fit to eat."

"Send the bill to Farris." Cora clapped a hand on her hip. "And he can pay to replenish it, too."

"Well, you'd best empty his pockets before he goes to jail, or we'll never see a penny of it." Elizabeth joined Cora at the end of the porch looking out across the road to where Fitz escorted Farris to a wagon.

Ian took Abby's hand. Without a word, she was bolstered by his strength.

"He'll be limping back to jail is what he'll be doing." Cora came back from where she had taken a quick assessment of what was going on out front. "When they took his rifle, the drunken fool shot himself in the foot. Pretty certain a toe or two is missing."

Abby sat forward with a look of consternation marring her brow. "Does he need a doctor?"

"He's not hurt. Only a hole in his boot. Cora, will be tellin' everyone he shot his whole leg off before this is over with." Elizabeth took Dottie's and Abby's cups and went inside the house.

Cora smirked in answer, neither confirming nor denying the accusation.

"The men are restless. Must be the feel of winter coming on." Ian surveyed the heavy clouds. "We lost several to the cold last winter. The memory's still fresh." He leaned down to speak next to Abby's ear before placing a kiss at her temple. "I need to see that Farris is transported. I'll be back."

"Duty first, Colonel." With a tender hand, she cupped his face next hers. "Don't worry about me. Your place is with your men."

Abby knew as long as she was in Macon, she was a distraction. Ian was torn and with all he had bearing down on his shoulders, his full attention should be dedicated to his mission—and to the men who depended on him.

"The Yankees are coming." Cora followed him down the porch steps. "Our troops have more important battles to forge, than to fool with Farris and his bunch of hooligans."

Abby noticed that Ian didn't bother informing Cora that the Yankees had most likely bypassed Macon altogether. She had so been looking forward to deploying her Ladies Militia.

Abby left the rocking chair to join Dottie down in the yard. The sooner they made their way to the Lamberts, the sooner Ian could focus on his task at hand. Besides, she did want to see Eliza Jane and the baby. So much she wanted to tell her.

"Looks like the main ruckus has run its course." Dottie observed beside her. For the most part, commanding officers appeared to have regained control. A few of Farris' men were shackled and waiting for transport in a work wagon at the road where Fitz stood writing on a small piece of paper.

It disturbed her that Mo was not counted among them.

"Fitz!" Ian called to his lieutenant.

"Yes, sir." Fitz tucked his paper and pencil in the pocket of his jacket and hurried to answer his commander. "Miss Abby, you all right?"

"She will be." Ian lifted the collar of his jacket against the cold. "Where's Farris?"

Fitz lifted his chin toward a sprawling elm by the road. "The State Militia boys have him under guard over yonder."

"Personally guard him until Hawthorne gets here. Don't let him out of your sight."

"Yes, sir!" Fitz obeyed the command with a broad smile.

"Where do all these men belong?" Dottie looked one side of the yard to the other.

"And where is their commander?"

"Most are new recruits from the Georgia State Militia. Volunteers from the backwoods. General Baker has his hands full with them." Ian started back toward Harbor House. "As soon as Hawthorne's troops arrive, my men can go back to camp and Baker can better settle his men down."

"What started the fight? Do you know?" He looked a bit surprised when Abby followed to walk along with him and Dottie.

Despite regulations preventing public displays of affection, he slid an arm around her shoulders and pulled her to his side to keep her warm.

He tipped his head at three ruffians sitting with hands

bound in the center of the wagon. "Seems Mo and Farris' men from Dove's Nest were the ones stirring up the trouble."

Abby observed them for a minute, then turned to Ian. "You think Farris planned all of this as a distraction?"

"Not all of it," Ian snatched up an army issued weapon left unattended in the dirt. "My guess is he sent them in to cause a diversion to occupy us long enough to get to you. Which he did."

She gave Ian a tired smile, taming her hair which had long escaped its pins. She was certain she looked more hoiden than lady with her hair loose and flowing down her back, nearly to her waist. One sleeve of her green dress was ripped at the shoulder and only one glove remained on her hand.

"You're beautiful just the way you are." Ian read her thoughts.

"Indeed, she is." Dottie agreed.

Abby's heart swelled. She wasn't used to being complimented so freely.

A disturbance caught their attention near the elm where Farris was being held. Another fight had two sets of men tumbling to the dirt.

"Surely not again." Dottie crossed her arms as a cold wind blew against their skirts.

A looked of annoyance crossed Ian's brow at the prospect of having break up another fight.

"Looks like Mo is one of the men throwing fists." Abby pointed out, oddly relieved to know of his whereabouts.

"If he thinks he can distract Fitz long enough to free Farris, he doesn't know him well." Ian started toward the fracas when a clatter sounded from up at the house.

"Attention!" Cora stood at the top step of Harbor House porch, banging a copper pan with a wooden spoon. "Stop this nonsense immediately. Go clack heads at your own camp. You're destroying the shrubbery."

Not one of the men fighting gave her a second glance as the rose bushes took a beating.

"Very well, this calls for action." With two handfuls of her skirt, Cora marched down to where a kid soldier sat gaping at the spectacle going on in front of him. Before he saw it coming, she snatched the bugle from a rope at his side.

"Ladies! To arms!" With a hand cupped next to her mouth, she rallied her troops. "Defend our domain!"

Squawking out an off-key tune on the bugle, Cora's reveille sounded like a cow caught in the fence.

Women appeared out of nowhere. As they drew closer, Ian watched the proper Mrs. Elizabeth Lambert, wallop a fighting pair of men with a corn broom, breaking the handle in two across their backs.

Fitz and two other men standing guard roared with laughter, open appreciation on their faces.

"You'd think he'd learn to control his tongue with ladies present." Abby noted dryly at Fitz's exuberant oath.

Another woman lifted a broomstick to sufficiently end another disagreement.

"I could certainly use one of those brooms." Merriment in Dottie's eyes made Abby smile.

Turning at the sound of screeching, they witnessed a barrage of peaches blast from the second story windows of Harbor House, bombarding the brawling men and effectively putting an end to fist fighting in the rose bushes.

Abby looked up and was shocked to see Mama Ivy leading that charge.

Mo and two of Farris' men, lifted elbows to cover their faces, yelping like wounded pups with every direct hit. The bombardment continued until they finally gave up, lifting their hands and begging for mercy.

A chorus of cheers went up as the ladies effectively cleared the yard of Farris' rabble.

Excitement fluttered among them while Cora stood at the head of the porch, taking in their victory as valiantly as any general having served a crushing defeat.

Cora Dobbs and her Georgia Ladies Auxiliary Militia of Macon finally had their day.

Fitz swabbed peach juice from the side of his head. "Dad blast it! *This* is why you don't bring no women to a squabble." Disgusted, he picked up one of the discarded peaches and was about to hurl it in frustration when he stopped. Hefting the fruit in his hand he dug inside and brought out a rock the size of a walnut where the pit had been.

"And *that*, Lieutenant, is why you do." Cora called down to him from the porch.

Soldiers broke out in laughter all around him until Ian gave the order to round up Farris and his men.

"He's liable to puke all over us." Fitz protested, but did as he was commanded anyway.

Dottie moved to the porch and Abby heard her congratulating Cora on the successful peach maneuver.

Smoothing a wisp of hair from her eyes, Abby watched them load Farris onto the flatbed.

"He won't hurt you again." Ian came up beside her.

"I know." She tried to smile. "As much as I want to despise him for everything he's done, I only feel pity. His own depravity was his greatest enemy. And ultimately his defeat."

"He won't escape Camp Oglethorpe. I'll be glad to know you're safe at Brechenridge with no possibility of his getting to you." Ian lifted her chin and lightly kissed her.

"God, in His infinite mercy has granted the greatest desire of my heart."

"Oh?" Ian set her arm inside the crook of his own and they began to walk. "And what might that be?"

"He gave me a man who loves me the way my father loved my mother. There's no higher honor in my opinion."

"A high honor, indeed." He grinned. "And one I look forward to living up to."

She leaned into the warmth of him. "I hope you always feel that way."

"I'll always cherish you, Angel. Every obstinate, impetuous, irrational, ounce of you."

"Irrational, really?"

Ian only laughed when she tried to move away from him.

Dottie and Cora came up beside them, joined by Elizabeth and Mama Ivy.

"You two best behave." Cora raised a brow. "You'll set the tongues to wagging."

"Let them wag, Cora." Dottie held out a gloved hand as a soft sprinkling of snow began to fall. "They are young and in love. We could all do with a little more love this Christmas."

At the head of the street, General Hawthorne appeared with two columns of men riding behind him. As he approached, soldiers and militia men alike quieted down.

Dusting hats on their thighs they looked contrite and prepared to return to camp.

A lift of the general's hand brought his unit to a halt. "What's been going on here, Colonel?"

Ian stepped forward with a casual salute. "General Farris directed a skirmish between the men, Sir. Then held Miss McFadden at gunpoint and tried to burn down the lauder."

"With her in it!" Cora added.

The general's concern was evident on his face. "Were you hurt, Miss McFadden?"

"Not too terribly, Sir." Abby's hair fluttered around her shoulders.

General Hawthorne turned to the soldier on a horse next to his own. "Captain, take this man in. See that guards are posted outside his cell."

The soldier moved to do his bidding.

"Good work, Colonel Saberton." General Hawthorne shifted in his saddle.

"I had help, Sir." Ian's mouth quirked into a grin. "The Ladies Militia took matters in hand and deserve a medal for going above and beyond the call of duty."

Hawthorne laughed heartily. "Well then, Ladies, I commend you." He lifted a salute and all other men followed suit in show of their respect.

Standing with their various kitchen weaponry, the ladies beamed, exceedingly pleased with themselves.

Cora, as usual, chose to speak for them all. "Thank you, General. We will take our medals and wear them with honor."

"Troops, fall in!" General Baker prepared his haggard militia to march down to their encampment.

General Hawthorne signaled his men to change direction. With a salute to Ian, he kicked his horse forward to head up their escort to Camp Oglethorpe.

Cora turned to Dottie rubbing the cold from her hands. "From the first day I found out Colonel Ian Saberton was assigned to Macon, I knew he was exactly what our city needed. We were set on keeping him from the start."

"He is brilliant, I must agree. He inherited a love of knowledge from his father." Dottie threw a teasing grin at her son. "But those devilish good looks come from my side."

A twitter of agreement swept over the ladies standing nearby.

"Fitz, return the men to camp." Ian issued the directive to mount up, but not before Abby caught sight of his deepened color. "You ladies best settle in. The evening promises to be a cold one."

Elizabeth brought up the hood of her satin cape to cover her head. "If you'll come with me, Mrs. Saberton, I'll show you to our carriage."

"Will we see you in the morning before we leave for Brechenridge?" Dottie pulled Ian down to press her face against his.

"We'll ride with you as far as Gordon." He gave her a fond embrace. "You'll board the train there unless the rails are damaged. The carriage driver can take you the rest of the way south through Roundtree if need be."

"We'll wait in the carriage, Abby." In passing, Elizabeth gave Ian a pointed look. "Don't be long."

Ian chuckled and drew Abby's arm threw his. "If I had my way, I'd keep you here with me." His hand covered hers. "But, with Christmas coming, it's time to get you two home where you belong."

"I belong wherever you are." Leaning heavily into him, Abby suddenly felt exhausted. She'd put in quite a day.

"Once this is over, we'll go wherever you chose." He stilled, suddenly solemn. "You need to go rest. Your carriage leaves at first daylight."

He was awfully adept at giving orders. Tilting her head, she decided to help him work on that.

"There it is." As usual, Ian's grin caused her heart to skip a beat.

"What?" Abby looked around her to see what he was referring to.

"The same green sparkle that first caught my attention." He lifted her hand to his lips, his focus unwavering. "'twill forever beckon me to follow ye, lass."

Abby adored it when his Southern drawl took on a bit o' her father's Irish.

Mimicking his tone, she gave him a saucy smile. "If it wouldn't make tongues wag, Colonel Saberton, I'd kiss you right here in the street, I would."

Ian stopped and pulled her into his arms, a sly grin tugging his lips. "Do it anyway."

"Is that an order?"

"Consider it a standing order."

# *Epilogue*

*Brechenridge Estate*
*Christmas Morning, 1864*

" $\mathcal{I}$ t's Christmas, Hickory!" Rachelle jumped up and down with excitement in front of a tall fir tree filling the entire corner. "Look in the back. We might find more presents!"

With candles lit and strands of berries and popcorn criss-crossing the fragrant tree, the house had a festive feel despite reports of Sherman presenting the city of Savannah as a gift to his President this morning.

As agreed, no opposition prevented his take over. Neither was Savannah destroyed in the taking.

"I'll let you hold my doll, if I can play with that whirly thing." Rachelle's dark curls were caught up in a satin bow at the back of her head which matched her new Christmas dress. She looked like a little porcelain doll herself.

They all laughed when Hickory made a face.

A couple of toys and several opened packages were scattered beneath the tree, all indications that Dottie and the other women had been putting aside gifts all year.

Christmas day had dawned with heavy clouds and an icy

nip in the air, as each one of them said a prayer for the men they loved. With such a precarious turn of the tides, the new year held many uncertainties.

Aurora was seated at the Steinway grand piano, playing Christmas carols while her mother looked on. Both were noticeably quieter than usual.

Dottie and Tori sipped wassail as the savory aroma of stuffed goose filtered through the house from the kitchen.

Unexpectedly, the hinges of the large wood door groaned as heavy boots sounded on the marble floor of the foyer.

"It's the Yankees!" Mrs. Charlotte exclaimed, crawling under the piano and knocking her Christmas hat askew.

"Colonel!" Hickory's eyes lit up as soon as Ian stepped through the door.

Completely surprised, Abby met him with a hug as he greeted Hickory.

Fitz stepped in behind him, and pulled the hat from his head.

"How did you get here?" Dottie was also on her feet.

"We came down from Athens." Ian held her so tight it brought tears to her eyes. "General Wheeler approved my leave for a couple of days before we move camp to Columbus on Wednesday."

Hickory tugged on the arm of his coat. "You think maybe we could play chess while you're here? Mrs. Dottie got me a board with a king and everything. I've been practicing with Rachelle, but she's not very good."

"We'll play a game or two right after dinner." Ian ruffled the boy's hair, causing a small giggle from Rachelle. "I'm starved."

"Somethin' sure smells good in here." Fitz bent and offered his hand to Mrs. Charlotte. With a bit of coaxing, she came out of hiding. Smoothing her red plaid dress, she righted the miniature Christmas tree atop her head.

"That, there, is what I call a fittin' get-up for the Yuletide, ma'am." Fitz winked with a click of his tongue.

Charlotte Haverwood tapped his arm with her fan before flapping it open with a titter.

Abby was thankful she'd let Tori talk her into wearing her hair up. And, now, Aurora's cream-colored dress she wore didn't feel quite as overdressed as it had moments before.

"Merry Christmas." Ian offered her his arm, with a kiss against her temple.

"Merry Christmas." Accepting his offer, Abby smiled up at him and almost forgot to breathe when his gaze fell to her lips.

The children brushed past them as Dottie came back into the parlor with a tray full of steaming mugs. The pungent smell of wassail filled the room.

Fitz gladly accepted a mug and sat on a settee near the warm blaze.

The children took cookies and milk from another tray Tori brought in, and joined Fitz by the fire.

"Now this feels a little more like Christmas." Dottie smiled as she served Ian from the tray.

With obvious effort, he tore his attention from Abby to take a warm cup.

"Did you know Cook's makin' us a whole goose for dinner?" Hickory asked with a white mustache glistening on his lip. "A real Christmas dinner. Like the rich folks have."

"Only one cookie for now." Tori stopped Rachelle from taking another. "Dinner is just about ready. You'll want to have room for Bread Pudding."

"Colonel?" A somber expression on Hickory's face caught Abby's attention.

Ian crouched beside the boy. "What is it, Hickory?"

"You just came from Macon, right?"

"I did." Ian nodded.

"Abby's been talking to me about the baby. The one Eliza Jane calls Samantha. How she's my flesh and blood and I got no right to wish she wasn't born." Hickory's quiet admission made them all turn his way. "Sallie woulda wanted me to be nicer to her."

"I believe Abby has given you sound advice." Ian's eyes watched the boy draw swirls on his milk glass with a finger, keeping his eyes averted.

"She's my baby sister. I wish I could give her some of my presents."

"The last time I saw Eliza Jane, she had an armload of presents for her. When Eliza Jane's husband comes home, they have decided to keep Samantha as part of their family." Ian provided. "I think maybe you should write her a letter or two. The Lamberts would be glad to read them to her. Maybe you could draw her a picture."

Tori put a hand on Hickory's shoulder. "That's right. And one day when she's older, she can come visit you to see for herself what a wonderful young man you are. Rachelle enjoys playing with you very much."

Hickory smiled. "And I could show her how to play chess, too."

Their thoughtfulness toward him warmed Abby's heart.

"I believe dinner is ready." Dottie said from the doorway.

Looking around at the eager faces of the folks who would hopefully be family one day soon, Abby took in Fitz's nod toward Ian.

"Actually, I have something I'd like to say first." Ian went to Abby's side, clasping her hand in his own.

Mrs. Charlotte hushed Aurora who sighed from the piano bench.

Lifting her hand to his lips, he removed a gold circlet from his breast pocket.

All Abby could hear was her own pulse pounding in her ears.

Two or three quiet whispers were heard around the room, but Abby just stared at him, wide-eyed and unmoving.

"Abby, do you remember when I asked you to trust me?"

She slowly nodded.

"Well, do you trust me enough share your life with me?"

Her eyes clouded over as she nodded again.

"I love you, Abby, and I want to know that you'll be mine when I come home to stay."

She moistened her lips.

He placed the circlet on her fourth finger. "Every time I see this, it will remind me that *you* are my greatest treasure."

Ian brushed his lips against hers. "Let's get married tonight."

"You can't get married tonight. It's just not done." Mrs. Charlotte shook her head, causing her tight ringlets to bob. "No wedding? No reception? And it's the sabbath and Christmas Day besides."

"He done stopped by the parson's on the way in. Him and his wife's gonna be here 'bout seven." Fitz rubbed his hands together. "So let's eat."

Blinking back tears, Abby could barely take it all in. Here, with her hand in Ian's, she knew there was only one answer to his question. "I'd be honored."

Cheers sounded from all around them. Ian pulling Abby into an enthusiastic embrace.

"My gift for you isn't nearly as exciting." Abby bent to

recover a small package from under the tree wrapped in plain brown paper and twine.

"You gave me your promise to be my wife. I couldn't ask for anything better." Ian untied the string. Unfolding the paper, he lifted her painstaking attempt at a knitted scarf. One end hung awkwardly wider than the other.

Looking at it now, Abby skewed her lips and gave Ian an apologetic shake of her head. "You can always use it to dry your horse."

Ian draped the wool over his shoulder. "I'll do no such thing. It's just my style. Besides, green's my favorite color."

Ian's spontaneous kiss surprised her and got an appreciative response from the others.

"I brought another gift for you, too. Call it a wedding gift." Ian reached behind her to accept a flat velvet box from Dottie.

Abby knew the box held his grandmother's costly earrings.

Lifting the lid, she was again awed by the sparkle laying inside. "Thank you, Ian, they're exquisite."

"Look inside. There's more." He urged with a smile.

Tucked into the top of the case, was a folded paper.

As she read, her mind began to spin. The document looked like a deed, but she couldn't guess what this had to do with her.

"I bought you ninety-two acres in Bibb County from Walter Dobbs."

Her gaze flew up to search his.

His eyes sparkled with sincerity. "Outside of Macon. It's a good piece of land. Flat with plenty of space for kids to play. Even room for a garden on the west side. Mama Ivy said she'd be happy to come grow a few vegetables for us. Mrs. Oberhaus agreed to come live there, too. I figured we'll need a cook and there'll be plenty of mending. She knows it won't pay much, but it's free room and board for her and her girls."

"What are you saying?" Abby had to remind herself to breathe.

"I bought the land and applied for a charter to build your children's home. The Julianne S. McFadden Home for Orphaned Children."

Abby was utterly speechless.

Hickory came to stand next to her, caught up in the excitement that suddenly filled the room. "Is that where I'm gonna live?" His innocent question was almost more than Abby's heart could take.

Ian lifted the boy to stand on a lamp table, closer to eyelevel. "I was blessed with a very good father, Hickory."

Hickory dropped his whirly-gig to focus on what Ian was saying.

"My father made it his lot in life to see that my brothers and I grew up to be decent, responsible men."

Hickory scratched the side of his cheek.

"I'd like to be that for you." Ian waited for the boy to take in what he was saying. Finally, a slow nod came in acknowledgement. "I got a telegram a couple of days ago from some important people in this state. It said I've been appointed your permanent legal guardian."

At Abby's gasp, Ian reached over to squeeze her hand.

"That means I will be your father. And as soon as I can get Abby to marry me, you can come live with us both as our son. So we can love you and help you grow up to be a good man someday."

"You mean I get to be a real Saberton? Can folks call me that?" His excitement tore a sob from Abby's lips.

"Hickory Barnaby Saberton. Has a rather nice ring to it,

don't you think?" Tori smiled.

Hickory put one arm around Ian's neck and the other around Abby's.

"Abby? Would you be my mama?" Hickory's question caused her to laugh through blurred vision. She put her arm around his small waist and kissed his sweet face. "Of course."

"The prettiest one in town." Ian asserted.

"Uh huh!" Hickory agreed before jumping down and motioning for Rachelle to follow. "Come on, cousin. Let's get some food."

The two ran off down the hall and their laughter was music to Abby's ears.

The others followed as the delicious smells of Christmas dinner beckoned them.

Ian was only here for a couple of days, but that was long enough for Abby to make him officially hers. "On Christmas Day, I become your wife." She said it aloud, more for her own benefit than his. She still had a hard time believing all she'd been given today.

"My lady will have a Christmas wedding." Ian took one last sip and set his cup down before pulling Abby into a hug.

As if they weren't the only two in the room he spoke close to her ear. "Have I mentioned that I've loved you since the first time you launched a bucketful of water at me?" Ian looked down at her and grinned. "And that I plan on loving you 'til I'm old and gray, still dodging your Irish temper?"

His deep chuckle resonated through her as he teased a loose curl that escaped her Christmas updo.

"Best not tempt fate, Colonel." Abby gave a small jab to his rib with a finger.

Pressing into his hug, she laid her head against his chest and was overwhelmed by the love she had for him.

"Angel?" An afterthought caused him to pull back, and she saw concern furrow his brow.

"Yes?" Abby rubbed his arm hoping to ease whatever had him worried.

"If Mrs. Oberhaus should ever leave us ... it's probably best if we get Eliza Jane to do the cooking." He lifted his head and gave her a mock shiver. "At least the mashed potatoes, anyway."

No doubt about it. Ian Saberton had to have been a *most* difficult child.

And Abby couldn't wait to have seventeen more just like him.

## THE END

# A Note From the Author

Macon, a city resplendent in Southern charm. Though the scale of 1864 Macon was much grander, I chose to focus on a single workable quadrant. Rich in history, this city on the banks of the Ocmulgee River was a hub of activity as two major railroad lines crossed within its borders. Detailed accounts were left for us to experience the hopes, fears, outrage, and dismay of Macon's citizens as they awaited Union siege upon their beloved city.

Like most Americans, I have ancestors who fought on both sides of the war between the states. The atrocities for which the Civil War is known are horrendous and rightly challenged. As I delved into countless personal journals, memoirs, and family accounts, I discovered multi-faceted people deeply committed to God, family, and home on both sides. I would have been remiss not to display the good in Georgia's history, and her people, along with obvious injustices. Of the 1.2 million soldiers who have died defending our country, 620,000 of them died in the American Civil War at the hands of fellow countrymen. Needless to say, the Civil War left lasting scars on the heart of our nation.

Folklore has it, Georgia's women really did help save several townships from Sherman's devastation. Some are rumored to have had past love affairs with the general, therefore he spared their homes. Others say, as in the case of Savannah, wives of

Confederate Officers banded together to meet with the general and offered a peaceable surrender in exchange for their homes and livestock.

General William Tecumseh Sherman caught me by surprise. When I started research for this book, I was certain I knew who he was, and had preconceived notions about why he was (and still is in some parts) despised by the South. His unconventional show of force effectively brought demise to the Southern Confederacy. However, when I dug deeper, I found accounts of his compassion and uncharacteristic mercy that I wasn't expecting.

As a child, he was farmed out to neighbors when his father died, and his mother was unable to care for her children. Julianne Sherman McFadden was purely a figment of my imagination. Although the general had a great fondness for his sisters, blood and adopted, Abby's mother was a fictional character created solely to enhance the story.

Any dialogue I attribute to him in regard to the war, or that of any other of the actual generals making an appearance in this book, was taken from quotes from the men, themselves. Otherwise, I took storytelling liberties to develop and benefit the story as a whole. *Field of Redemption* was inspired by both historical accounts and fictitious events, artistically embellished to edify certain Biblical truths—which are unchanging and eternal.

## FOR FURTHER READING

1. Jacqueline Jones, *Saving Savannah, The City and The Civil War*, Vintage Books 2008

2. Richard W. Iobst, *Civil War Macon*. Mercer University Press 2009

3.  Eliza Frances Andrews, *The War-Time Journal of a Georgia Girl*, Cherokee Publishing Company 1908

4.  Janet E. Croon, *The War Outside My Window, The Civil War Diary of LeRoy Wiley Gresham*, Savas Beatie 2018

Books available in The Saberton Legacy Series:

*True Nobility*
*Field of Redemption*

Keep up with the latest on the release of Zachery and Aurora's Story, *Book Three of the Saberton Legacy*, coming early 2020!

www.loribateswright.com

# My Heartfelt Appreciation

As with the first book, I had assistance from many talented people along the way.

Thank you to my cherished mentor, Lena Nelson Dooley, for her trusted purple pen. You make my scattered commas behave, and keep my time period authentic. Always with an encouraging word. I love you dearly.

To Roseanna White of Roseanna White Designs for another stunning cover design. You absolutely amaze me.

To my critique group friends, Becky Wade, Lynn Gentry, Kelly Scott, Sherrinda Ketchersid, Deborah Clack, Kay Leonard, Stacy Simmons, and Shelli Littleton. You challenge, inspire, and never let me get away with "good enough," but push to make every line better. Then you give me chocolate!

Beta readers, Carol Bates, Bonnie Sanchez, Cindi Cannon, Erica Wright, Sheri Raymer, Roxanne Wright, and Betty Wimpy. I don't know what I'd do without you. You are the first ones to read my stories and your sweet comments keep me going. I love and appreciate every one of you!

Even though we don't get together much anymore, I'm so grateful for my writer friends, Laurie Westlake, Conni Cossette, Tammy Gray, and Dana Red. You were the first ones to convince me I can do this, and I love that we're still only a text message away. I treasure your friendship.

Enduring gratitude to my husband, Daryl Wright, who

spends many a solitary evening when I'm in deep writing mode. You believe in me like no other. Always encourage me to keep going, and promote my books to anyone who will listen. Love you, D.

Once again, I am so very thankful for my daughter, Ashley Espinoza. This book was challenging on so many levels, yet you helped keep the ship afloat. Whatever hat I need you to wear, you put it on and *own it*. Your knack for what works and what doesn't is instinctive. Your organizational skills keep me from rabbit trailing too far off track. Your graphics and promotional ideas make me proud. Thank you, Sis, from the bottom of my heart.

Father, to You be the all the glory. Always.

Made in the USA
Las Vegas, NV
25 October 2022

58056206R00198